A Conflict of Interests

This book is for Pauline and Brian

A Conflict of Interests

1.

Her name was Karen Whitfield. She was thirty-two years old, had shoulder-length raven black hair, a trim but well-rounded figure and was about five foot seven. She lay on her stomach in the middle of a king-size divan bed, her head turned over to the left and facing the outside wall. Her ankles, wrists and elbows were roped together and she had been gagged with a pair of tights. The green silk dress she was wearing had been raised above her hips and somebody had burned her thighs and naked buttocks with the glowing ember of a cigarette. That same somebody had then held a small-caliber revolver to her head and put two bullets into the brain.

The media were going to have a field day with this one, Coghill thought bitterly. It was the kind of juicy murder with sexual overtones they could really get their teeth into: well-to-do, attractive young housewife tortured and shot dead in her secluded, executive-style house, half a mile from the grounds of the All England Lawn Tennis Club. They'd been quick off the mark too. The 999 call had been received by the police station in Wimbledon at nine twenty-seven; by the time he'd arrived from V District headquarters in Kingston some fifteen minutes later, two local reporters and a press photographer were already loitering outside the house.

The press would want a statement from him and soon, but right now there wasn't much he could give them, apart from the victim's name and age. He'd got that information from Detective Sergeant Mace, the duty CID officer at Wimbledon, who'd arrived on the scene shortly after a Panda car had responded to the 999 call. Mace was downstairs, still interviewing the Whitfields' daily woman who'd discovered the body, and he was hopeful she would be able to tell them a great deal more about her former employer. Meantime, you didn't have to be a pathologist to see that rigor mortis had set in. The corpse was also beginning to smell, which meant death had occurred at the very least twelve hours ago. But that was something the medical examiner would have to confirm, and they were still waiting for him to put in an appearance.

"Is it okay if I make a start, Guv?"

Coghill glanced at the police photographer. "You might as well," he said. "There's no sense in hanging around for Doctor Harrison."

The photographer nodded and began shooting from the foot of the bed. Coghill moved past him to the built-in wardrobes and opened each of them in turn. The larger of the two contained a rackful of Dior, Balenciaga and Yves St. Laurent model dresses, together with a three-quarter-length mink coat, a dozen pairs of Italian and Swiss-made shoes and enough Janet Reger underwear to stock a small shop. The smaller one was less impressive; it held only three inexpensive and well-worn suits, a couple of sports jackets, a gabardine trench coat and an assortment of ties, socks, vests and underpants. There were also four pairs of men's shoes which were far from new.

As far as he could tell from a cursory inspection, none of the drawers in the dressing table had been disturbed and her jewelry was still there, packed inside little red boxes under a collection of Italian silk scarves. A half hoop of diamonds set in platinum, a sapphire and diamond ring, a large emerald and a solitaire as big as a fingernail; at a rough guess, Coghill thought they were worth all of thirty thousand pounds. Robbery could have been a motive, but if that was the reason why Karen Whitfield had been tortured, it was evident the killer hadn't been interested in her jewelry.

He opened the sliding glass door to the adjoining bathroom and gave the room a quick once-over. Bidet, pedestal washbasin and a triangular-shaped bath with gold taps like something out of *Ideal Homes*. He looked inside the linen basket and on top of a pile of discarded shirts and socks, saw a pair of lace-trimmed panties which matched the oyster satin slip the victim was wearing. The window was fitted with a Chubb lock, as was the narrow elongated one high up on the outside wall of the master bedroom, another sign that the Whitfields were very security conscious, though he didn't recall seeing a burglar alarm. Closing the door behind him, Coghill went out on to the landing.

The second bathroom and lavatory were next to the airing cupboard and beyond them was a small nine-by-nine bedroom which was used as a study. It looked out on to the back garden, which was mostly lawn, and screened from the houses in the parallel road by a row of tall poplar trees planted shoulder to shoulder. An executive desk faced the window and there was a filing cabinet in the far corner. The drawers to both pieces of furniture were locked and the keys removed.

There were two other bedrooms at the front. To the right of the staircase was a large single with a French window, which opened on to an L-shaped verandah that extended around the side of the house over the double garage. Directly opposite was a fairly large double bedroom, oblong-shaped and lengthways on to the street. At the far end, were two fitted cupboards on either side of a wide bookshelf, on which there was a partially assembled model of a B-52 bomber. Other model aircraft were suspended from the ceiling and there was a montage of posters on the dividing wall, one of which showed a basket of oranges capped by an onion with the caption, "You don't get to the top by being like everyone else."

Coghill moved to the window and looked out on to a quiet street lined with horse chestnut trees. The house was on a bend near the top of St. Mark's Hill, about thirty feet back from the road and high enough above it to guarantee that no passer-by could see into the sitting room on the ground floor. The detached properties on either side were at differing elevations and appeared a good deal older, as did those across the street, which were spaced much farther apart. He thought it likely that the Whitfield residence had been built on a small plot of land that had originally belonged to one of the neighbors, and that the local planning authority had imposed certain restrictions in the interests of privacy. It was the only explanation he could think of for the narrow, elongated windows in the master bedroom and the large single at the front.

A Ford Granada drove slowly past the ambulance and the Panda car that had responded to the 999 call, and then pulled into the curbside. Recognizing the burly figure behind the wheel, Coghill waited until Leonard Harrison had gotten out of the car and pushed his way through the gaggle of reporters on the pavement before he left the bedroom and went downstairs to let him into the house.

"I see the vultures have gathered, Tom," Harrison observed, glaring at the pressmen.

"Yes. They were already here when I arrived. Somebody must have tipped them off."

Harrison grunted, then stepped past him into the hall. "Sorry I'm late," he said, "but I was up most of the night finishing my notes on the postmortems I did on the victims of that traffic pile-up on the Kingston bypass last Sunday evening. I was sound asleep in bed when your people phoned me." His face suddenly brightened and he raised the small black bag he was carrying in his right hand. "However, now that I'm here, where's the body?"

"Upstairs in the master bedroom," said Coghill. "She's been dead some time."

"And beginning to smell a bit?"

"Yes."

"Well, she would in this heat, wouldn't she?" Harrison went on down the narrow hallway and bounded up the staircase, taking the steps two at a time as though eager to get to work.

Mace was still interviewing the Whitfields' daily woman in the lounge-diner. Opening a door off the hall to his right, Coghill signaled he wanted to have a word with him and withdrew to the kitchen.

Harry Mace was forty-eight and nearing the end of his career. Methodical and reliable were two adjectives which featured in his annual assessment with monotonous regularity, damning him with faint praise. Long ago he'd come to the inevitable conclusion that he would remain a detective sergeant until the day he retired, a fact of life which he accepted philosophically.

"What have you got so far?" Coghill asked him as he ambled into the kitchen.

"Not a lot." Mace flipped through his notebook. "Mrs. Godfrey came to work for the Whitfields shortly after they moved in four years ago. Trevor Whitfield is a director of Travelways and works at their head office in Charing Cross Road. Apparently he's away on a business trip at the moment and isn't expected back until Saturday week, nine days from now. It seems his wife was also in business and owned a dress shop in Wimbledon High Street called Karen's Boutique and another somewhere in the New King's Road over in Fulham. The Whitfields have a son aged twelve who's a boarder at Grange Preparatory School in Newbury. According to Mrs. Godfrey, the last time she saw her employer alive was yesterday when she left the house and drove off to her boutique in the High Street."

"What time was that?"

"About ten-fifteen." Mace smiled wryly. "I gather she never got out of bed much before nine-thirty. Mrs. Godfrey has a key to the house and she always makes her a cup of coffee and takes it up to her room before she gets on with the housework." He turned over a page. "I'm told the Whitfields have two cars, a brand-new Volkswagen Golf and a Saab which is about a year old. I haven't been able to check that; both up-and-over doors to the garage are locked and there's no window."

Harry was right, Coghill thought; what he'd learned so far didn't amount to very much. Nine murders out of ten were committed in the family and this one was beginning to look as though it was in the same category. The killer hadn't broken into the house; Karen Whitfield had opened the door to him and invited him inside. That meant she must have known him fairly well and had no reason to suppose she would come to any harm.

"What do we know about the Whitfields, Harry?" he asked. "Did they hit it off?"

"They never seemed to quarrel, at least not in front of Mrs. Godfrey. According to her, they were very fond of each other."

Mace shrugged his shoulders. "She could be wrong, of course, but I doubt if she can shed any further light on their relationship. From what little she did tell me, it's pretty obvious that Mrs. Whitfield was a very private sort of person, the kind of woman who kept herself to herself."

"It's possible she may know where the Whitfields were living before they moved to Wimbledon."

"I'll ask her."

"You do that," Coghill said. "And while you're at it, find out what you can about the deceased's family—parents, any brothers or sisters and so on. Meantime, I'll contact Travelways and ask them how we can get in touch with Trevor Whitfield."

He went through the hall to the alcove under the staircase, looked up their number in the directory and dialed 836–0479. The pleasant-voiced woman who answered the phone seemed a little nonplussed when he asked to speak to Mr. Whitfield's secretary and suggested he should have a word with the personnel branch. There was a momentary silence, then a brisk voice said, "Draycott—Personnel."

Coghill gave his name, informed Draycott he was a detective inspector with V District and told him that he should check his identity with Commander Franklin at New Scotland Yard before phoning the Whitfield residence in Wimbledon.

"Why should I go to all that trouble?" Draycott asked him impatiently.

"Because this is an emergency and I don't want you to think you're dealing with a practical joker."

"I get the idea."

"I'm glad you do, sir," Coghill said and put the phone down.

A door opened and closed and was followed by the sound of Harrison's footsteps on the landing above.

Coghill backed out of the alcove and looked up at him. "What can you give me, Leonard?" he asked.

"The body temperature is sixty-nine point one. As a rough yardstick, the heat loss is about one point five degrees per hour. This would mean death probably occurred some time between two and four o'clock yesterday afternoon, but don't quote me until I've done an autopsy." Harrison came down the stairs, still talking. "There are no particles of skin under the victim's fingernails and the absence of any bruises on the torso would seem to indicate that she offered no resistance. I could find no trace of semen on her slip or on the bedspread, which you'd expect if she had been sexually assaulted. However, I've taken some smears and we'll know one way or the other after I've examined the slides under a microscope." He stopped on the bottom step, eyebrows raised in a perplexed frown. "Her panties are missing, Tom."

"They're in the linen basket," said Coghill. "I'll have them delivered to you in a plastic bag."

"Fine." Harrison stepped down, ambled toward the front door and opened it. "Phone me around seven tonight and I'll give you a verbal resumé of my findings."

"That's what I call service, Leonard."

"Yes, well, I want to clear the decks; it's the Ladies' Semifinals tomorrow and I've got a ticket for the center court. Mind you, it looks as though Wimbledon's faced with a rival attraction today."

Coghill followed his gaze and saw the number of reporters had grown considerably since Harrison had arrived. They had also been joined by a couple of TV crews and there were the usual curious onlookers among the crowd. He didn't want them still hanging around when Harry Mace and the police constable from the Panda car started on their house-to-house inquiries, but they would never agree to move off unless he made it worth their while. A brief statement of the facts coupled with the promise of a more detailed briefing at a press conference that evening should do it. Where and when? The first question was easy to answer; Wimbledon Police Station might have fewer facilities than the District Headquarters at Kingston, but it was near the scene of the crime. There was little point in holding the briefing before Harrison had completed his postmortem, and there was also the next of kin to be considered. It was essential the victim not be named before Trevor Whitfield had been informed that his wife had been murdered. Seven-thirty looked like a reasonable bet; that would give the BBC and ITV reporters sufficient time to file a story for inclusion in their late evening news programs.

"The sooner you move the body, Tom, the sooner I can get on with the autopsy," Harrison reminded him brusquely.

"Right." Coghill glanced at the police constable on duty at the bottom of the drive and was about to call him over, when the telephone started to ring. "That will be Draycott," he said, voicing his thoughts aloud.

"Who's he?"

"A colleague of Whitfield's."

"You'd better answer it then," said Harrison.

Coghill reached past him, lifted the phone off the hook, told the caller to hang on a moment and cupped his hand over the mouthpiece. "Would you do me a favor, Leonard?" he said. "Ask those ambulance men to back their vehicle up to the house."

"Certainly."

"Thanks a lot." Coghill removed his hand from the mouthpiece and apologized to Draycott for the delay.

"I believe you said there was some kind of emergency, Inspector?"

"Yes. It concerns Mr. Trevor Whitfield. I'm afraid his wife has been murdered."

There was a long pause, then in a shocked voice, Draycott said, "When did this happen?"

"Her body was found by the daily help this morning. Naturally, we want to get in touch with him as soon as possible."

"That may take a little time. At the moment, I should think Mr. Whitfield's coach party is halfway between Vienna and Budapest."

"Coach party?" Coghill repeated. "I'm not with you."

"Trevor is away on one of our deluxe tours," Draycott explained patiently. "Seven European capitals in fourteen days; Paris, Vienna, Budapest, Prague..."

The ambulance backed up the steep drive, its transmission grinding loud enough to drown the rest of the itinerary. Above Draycott's monotone, Coghill heard the attendants get out and open the rear doors; then they clumped past him and went up the staircase, carrying a stretcher between them.

"Naturally, we'll find someone to relieve him," Draycott continued. "With any luck, Trevor should be able to catch a plane from Budapest late this afternoon."

Coghill said, "What's all this about a relief? I was given to understand that Mr. Whitfield was on the board of directors."

"A director?" Draycott almost choked on a derisive laugh.

"What is he then?"

"A good linguist, Inspector, fluent in French, German and Italian. He's also a pleasant and good-looking young man; that's why we hired him as a guide."

"I see. How long has he been working for your tour company?"

"Over four years," said Draycott. "He joined us in March '78 nine months after leaving Sussex University. Trevor was hoping to get a job with the EEC in Brussels, but I gather the commission had all the interpreters they needed."

Coghill frowned; it didn't add up. Unless he had been a mature student, Whitfield would have been twenty-two or twenty-three when he left Sussex University in '78, yet Mace had told him they had a son aged twelve. The apparent discrepancy suggested that Trevor Whitfield was not the natural father and it was possible his wife had been married before.

"Not that he has any reason to be dissatisfied with his present position," Draycott went on. "He's on a reasonably good salary and all expenses paid."

"What do you call reasonable?" Coghill asked him pointedly.

"I can't see why that should concern you."

"Well, it does, Mr. Draycott. You may find the question embarrassing, but I'm investigating a homicide and I'd appreciate a straight answer."

"He's on five thousand a year." Draycott cleared his throat somewhat noisily. "Look, I'm rather busy just now. If I may, I'll call you back later and let you know what flight Trevor will be on."

"I'd be grateful if you would," Coghill said and hung up.

There was a mink coat hanging in the wardrobe of the master bedroom and thirty thousand pounds' worth of jewelry in the top drawer of the dressing table. There were two expensive cars in the double garage, the house would fetch at least eighty thousand at today's inflated prices and his son was away at boarding school. Even taking into account his wife's boutiques, Coghill couldn't see how Whitfield could afford such an extravagant way of life on a salary of five thousand per annum.

2.

Coghill went down St. Mark's Hill and turned left into the High Street, keeping a sharp look out for Karen's Boutique. Most of the pressmen outside the house had departed, satisfied with a short statement of the known facts and the promise of a more detailed briefing that evening. The TV reporters were an exception and they had decided to stay on for a while. Their cameramen had the statement on video, but it seemed they still had some footage left and were intent on giving the viewing public a general impression of the neighborhood. There was no point in getting uptight about it, however; to object to their continued presence would invite adverse criticism of the police, and that was something he could do without.

So far, the press was being very cooperative. How long that happy state of affairs continued would depend on the way he handled the briefing that evening. Coghill doubted if a resumé of the postmortem would satisfy them, and on the basis of the information he'd already released, they'd probably made up their minds about the motive. The victim had been young and attractive, they had his word for that, and there were no prizes for guessing that Karen Whitfield had captured their interest. They'd want to know all about her and the successful business ventures that had enabled the Whitfields to live in such a desirable and secluded neighborhood.

At least that aspect of the investigation was no longer quite the mystery it had been an hour or so ago. Thanks to a bunch of keys Coghill had found in one of her handbags, he'd been able to open the desk and filing cabinet in the spare bedroom. The drawers in the desk were used as a depository for receipts for bills from the gas and electricity boards, various insurance policies, the title deeds to the house and a wad of bank statements relating to the Whitfields' joint account with Lloyds. From the way these household accounts were stapled together and itemized, it was obvious Karen Whitfield had been a very methodical woman, but it was the contents of the filing cabinet which had really given him an insight into her considerable business acumen.

The memorandum and articles of association which he'd found in the top drawer told him that Karen Boutiques Limited had been incorporated on February 8, 1973, and the balance sheets for the subsequent years, prepared and audited by her chartered accountants, Richard Atkinson and Company, showed that the business was in a very healthy financial state. After examining the various cash books, it was evident to Coghill just who had been the breadwinner in the family.

Karen's Boutique was on the left-hand side of the road, opposite the post office. Unable to find a parking space in the High Street, Coghill left the Volvo in Belvedere Grove and walked back to the shop.

The premises were smaller than he'd expected, but the elegant window displays on either side of the entrance gave the place a touch of class, and he thought the absence of any price tags on the clothes was a sure sign the clientele were drawn from the upper income bracket. It so happened that as of that moment, the well-heeled customers were conspicuous by their absence and, apart from two bored-looking sales assistants, Coghill found he had the place to himself. For a while, neither one seemed inclined to acknowledge his existence; then the taller of the two, a willowy blonde dressed in a smart but severely cut navy two-piece, came toward him, her mouth stretched in a welcoming smile that showed a lot of capped teeth.

"Good morning, sir," she said politely. "May I help you?" Her diction was perfect, but the accent affected and contrived.

"I hope so," Coghill said and produced his warrant card. "Is there somewhere we can talk in private?" His eyes went to the glass partition at the far end of the boutique. "The office perhaps?"

The saleswoman nodded and moved ahead of him to open the door. "I'm afraid you may find it a little cramped in here," she said with a faintly apologetic smile.

The office was no bigger than a glorified cubbyhole with barely enough room for the essential items of furniture—a desk, two upright chairs, a large Chubb safe and the inevitable filing cabinet.

"Oh, I don't know about that," Coghill said, "you should see where I work, Mrs.—?"

"Strachey, Mrs. June Strachey." Her eyes narrowed speculatively. "What is it you want to see me about?" she asked.

Coghill gave her the bald facts and provoked an expression of shocked incredulity. Her jaw dropped and the tip of her pink tongue explored the bottom lip. It took June Strachey some time to find her voice; when finally she did, it was husky and scarcely above a whisper.

"Murdered? I can't believe it, Karen didn't have an enemy in the world. Why should anybody want to kill her?"

"I don't know," Coghill said. "That's why I wanted to have a word with you."

"Me?" Her eyes widened into a puzzled stare.

"Well, you must have known Mrs. Whitfield better than most. I imagine you saw her every day of the week?"

"Oh, no." She shook her head. "No, Karen only came in every other day. She used to visit the branch in Fulham on Mondays, Wednesdays and Fridays."

"Then I assume she was here yesterday?"

"Yes, until midday."

"Anything unusual about that?" Coghill asked. "I mean, did she always lunch at home?"

"Karen didn't have a set routine. Sometimes she stayed all day and sent out for a sandwich, sometimes she left after an hour or so. It depended on how busy we were and whether or not she had another business appointment."

"Things must have been pretty slack yesterday."

"What?"

Coghill pointed to a thin batch of invoices on the desk fastened together with a bulldog clip. "It doesn't look to me as though you had many sales."

"Actually, we had a better than average day." June Strachey brushed a stray wisp of hair off her face. "Besides, you have to remember this isn't the sort of boutique that depends on a high turnover."

You can say that again, Coghill thought. It was an even bet that Karen's Boutique charged its clients eighty to ninety pounds for a simple dress they could have purchased from Marks and Spencer's for less than thirty. The labels would be different of course, and there were bound to be some fancy trimmings to go with the price tag, but even so, they were still paying over the odds.

"If business was so brisk yesterday," he said, "why did Mrs. Whitfield leave at noon?"

"Karen had a business appointment, at least that's what she told me."

"With whom?"

"Her accountant, I imagine. I know she tried to phone him while we were checking the cash sales for the previous day, but apparently he wasn't there and she left a message asking him to call her as soon as he came in. I presume he did, because about an hour later I heard the phone ring while I was busy attending to a customer."

"That would seem a logical assumption." Coghill smiled wryly. June Strachey wasn't the chatty kind and it was clear the aloof bit wasn't just an act for the customers.

"Do you happen to know who she dealt with at Richard Atkinson and Company?" he persevered.

"Who are they?"

"Her accountants."

"Oh? I've only ever heard Karen mention a Mr. Oliver Leese." The small pink tongue made another brief appearance and moistened the bottom lip. "I suppose he must be one of the partners?"

Coghill said he reckoned she was probably right, then asked June Strachey how long she had been working for Mrs. Whitfield.

"I've been the manageress here ever since the boutique opened five years ago," she told him.

"That was before the Whitfields moved to Wimbledon?"

"Yes. I saw the job advertised in the local paper and applied for it. The interview was held at the Fulham branch in New King's Road."

"I see." Coghill edged toward the desk and leafed through the sales invoices. There were eight in all, two of which had been charged to a credit card. The largest bill came to £89.95, while at the other end of the scale, somebody had bought a silk scarf for £18. Computing the various sums in his head, he arrived at a total of £340.81. "Any idea where she was living in those days?" he asked casually.

"I think Karen said she had a flat in St. John's Wood. Or was it Maida Vale?" June Strachey gave him a helpless smile. "I'm sorry to be so vague but it was a long time ago."

"It's not the sort of thing you'd remember anyway." Coghill paused, then tried a different tack. "About that phone call?" he said. "What sort of mood was Mrs. Whitfield in after she spoke to Leese? Did she appear worried or tense? Or was she just her usual self?"

"Now that you mention it, she did look rather annoyed."

The dividing line between fact and supposition was becoming more than a little blurred. June Strachey had told him everything she knew and was merely responding to suggestion. It was, Coghill decided, time to call a halt.

"Thank you for being so helpful," he said cheerily. "I'm sorry to have taken up so much of your time."

"You haven't," she assured him. "We're not busy at the moment."

Coghill could see that for himself. The boutique was still empty and the sales assistant June Strachey had been talking to when he arrived was busy filing her fingernails. He thanked the manageress again and went out into the street. The phone booth outside the post office caught his eye and, waiting for a break in the traffic, he crossed the road and entered it.

The A to D telephone directory had been vandalized, but the

page he wanted was more or less intact. Richard Atkinson and Company, Dover Street, Piccadilly, London W1; their name and address had been on the front cover of the memorandum and articles of association that had been drawn up for Karen Boutiques Limited. Coghill ran a finger down the listings until he found their number, then dialed it. Thereafter, it took him less than a minute to discover that no one by the name of Oliver Leese had ever been associated with Richard Atkinson and Company.

If Leese was now something of an enigma, Karen Whitfield's system of accounting had become an even bigger mystery. There were retailers who scrupulously accounted for every penny that went into the till and there were those who tried to defraud the Inland Revenue and kept two sets of books, but it seemed she was in a class of her own. According to June Strachey, £340.81 represented a better than average day for the Wimbledon branch, but the deposit slips he'd seen back at the house showed that Karen Whitfield had regularly banked upward of seven hundred pounds per day. Even more surprising, this artificially inflated income had been reflected in the balance sheets and in the tax returns submitted to the Inland Revenue.

There were, Coghill thought, only two possible conclusions to be drawn from that; either the New King's Road branch was a positive gold mine or else Karen Whitfield had had another source of income. Leaving the phone booth, he made his way to Belvedere Grove, got into the Volvo and drove out to Fulham.

Leese paid off the taxi, walked up the flight of steps by the garage and let himself into his mews flat off Cadogan Square. The telephone bill, a circular and a statement from Barclays Bank had arrived in his absence and were lying on the doormat. Picking them up, he went through the hall, dumped his briefcase and overnight bag in the bedroom and then went into the living room to fix himself a drink and listen to the messages on the answering machine. There was only one, and Karen Whitfield left him in no doubt that he was required to call her back as soon as possible.

Leese figured she could only have phoned him an hour or so ago; had Karen tried to reach him yesterday or the day before, there would have been several other messages from her on the tape. For a few heady moments he toyed with the idea of ignoring her instructions but, on reflection, decided it would be stupid to antagonize her, and dangerous too. If she had a mind to, Karen could ruin him; there was enough incriminating evidence locked away in a safety-deposit box at the London branch of the First National Bank of America to do just that.

Karen hadn't left a number where she could be contacted but, this being a Wednesday, Leese knew that she would have gone to Fulham. Leaving his gin and tonic on the low coffee table, he picked up the phone to call the boutique; as he did so, somebody rang the front doorbell. Grim-faced, he replaced the receiver and went out into the hall, half-expecting to find her on the doorstep.

His visitor was an amiable-looking man in a light gray suit. He was about five foot nine, had hazel-colored eyes, brown hair, a round, almost cherublike face and an infectious smile.

"Mr. Leese?" A warrant card appeared briefly in the palm of his left hand. "I'm Detective Sergeant Patterson." His eyes creased to emphasize the friendly smile. "I'm glad I caught you this time."

"Caught?" Leese swallowed nervously.

"I called on you twice yesterday, but there was no reply."

"I was away in Amsterdam," Leese said. "I've only just this minute returned."

"Then you won't have heard that two of the flats were broken into on Monday night?"

"No." He peered back over his shoulder. "My place hasn't been touched."

"I wouldn't be too sure of that, sir." Patterson moved a pace nearer. "This burglar was a real artist. He knew exactly what he wanted and didn't leave any mess behind him. He could have cleaned out your safe without you knowing it."

"Where did you get the idea that I had a safe, Sergeant?"

"I thought all these mews flats had one. Of course, I can understand why you have to be a bit cagey about it."

"You can?" Leese said in a hollow voice.

"Well, it's a simple matter of security, isn't it, sir?"

"I suppose it is, Sergeant."

"Mind if I come in?" Patterson moved into the hall and closed the door behind him. "It will save us both a lot of time if you check the contents of your safe while I'm in the neighborhood."

"I hardly think that's necessary," Leese said, then froze, his eyes riveted on the small snub-nosed revolver pointed at his stomach.

"A point twenty-two Iver Johnson," Patterson calmly informed him. "It makes a noise about as loud as a firecracker, but it's very lethal."

"Jesus."

"There's no need to be alarmed, Mr. Leese. It won't go off, provided I get a little cooperation from you." Patterson jabbed the barrel under Leese's breastbone, hard enough to wind him. "You want to lead the way?" he invited.

Leese nodded, turned slowly about and walked into the living room. His mouth had suddenly gone bone-dry and his legs felt as though they no longer belonged to him.

"I'm told the safe is behind that Shepherd print above the fireplace," Patterson said.

"It's not a print." The denial was instinctive and smacked of vanity.

"My mistake. I should have guessed you'd own an original. What did it cost you? Twenty grand?"

"Something like that."

Leese unhooked the painting and rested it carefully against the nearest armchair. For a few blank seconds he couldn't remember the combination; then it came to him, 22–5–39, the date of his birth. Hands shaking, he went through the sequence, spinning the dial to make five complete turns in a clockwise direction until the opening number was in line with the mark. There then followed four revolutions anticlockwise to 5, three forward to 39, and two back to zero. The pattern finally completed, he moved the dial forward again to withdraw the bolt bar and, yanking the handle down, opened the safe.

"You can take a rest now," Patterson told him cheerfully. "Face down on the carpet, both hands behind your back."

He stepped well clear. Leese was a good two inches taller and had a weight advantage of at least twenty pounds. Even though he could see the older man was about ready to wet himself, Patterson wasn't about to take any chances.

"Have you got a briefcase?"

"What?" Leese twisted his head around and looked up at him, mouth slack and breathing heavily.

"A briefcase."

"There's one in the bedroom."

"Good." Patterson moved to the sofa and picked up a cushion. "Better put this under your head," he said. "I don't want you to be uncomfortable."

"I'm not."

"No arguments, I know what's best, Mr. Leese."

Patterson bent over him, rammed a knee into his spine and held the cushion over his head. Leese made a faint mewling sound like that of a lost kitten; then Patterson squeezed the trigger and emptied three chambers into Leese's skull, the cushion effectively muzzling the crack of each shot. As he stood up, a slowly widening pool of urine seeped across the Indian carpet and an unpleasant smell of excreta rose in the air.

Patterson slipped the revolver into his hip holster, dug a pair of cotton gloves out of his jacket pockets and put them on. That done, he went into the bedroom, emptied the contents of the briefcase onto the divan and returned to the living room to clean out the safe.

The video cassettes were stacked one on top of the other, their numbered spines toward him. Working swiftly, he packed all fourteen of them into the briefcase, closed the safe and rehung the painting.

There remained one final chore, the magnetized electronic bug that had been fixed to the metal base of the answering machine. Tucking the briefcase under his arm, Patterson detached the listening device and slipped it into his pocket. Then, still ice-cool, he let himself out of the flat, closed the door behind him and deftly removed his gloves before going down the staircase to the cobbled mews below.

3.

Franklin picked up his clipboard and pretended to study the notes he'd made while Coghill had been briefing him. Had Detective Superintendent Bert Kingman been in charge of the Whitfield case, he would have stayed put at the Yard and left him to get on with the job, but Kingman was away on a package tour to Majorca and that made a difference. For all that Coghill was a highflyer and would probably make assistant commissioner one day, he had never led a major investigation before, and from the moment the initial flash report had come through on the teleprinter, this factor had been uppermost in Franklin's mind.

The way Franklin saw it, he could do one of two things: either recall Kingman from leave or go to the assistant commissioner in charge of C Department and request him to appoint a senior officer from the Regional Crime Squad to lead the inquiry. At the same time, he hoped Coghill would make things easier for him by indicating that he would welcome either alternative. Yet, despite some pretty broad hints, this hadn't happened so far, which in retrospect didn't altogether surprise him.

Coghill was ambitious, resourceful, highly intelligent and well-educated. He'd read law at Nottingham University, got a good second-class honors degree, then joined the Metropolitan Police Force. Within eighteen months, he'd passed the written examination to sergeant and four years ago, at the age of twenty-eight, had been promoted to inspector. His service to date had been more or less evenly divided between the uniformed branch and CID, with a slight bias in favor of the latter. As a detective constable he'd cut his teeth with the Obscene Publications Squad, and on his first promotion had done a stint with Serious Crimes.

He had a good record and was tough in every sense of the word, both physically and mentally. Every confidential report that had been written about Coghill had stressed his complete dedication to the force, and Franklin believed it was this single-mindedness that had led to the breakup of his marriage.

"Trevor Whitfield," he said, breaking a long silence. "What time is he expected to arrive at Heathrow?"

"Eighteen-fifteen hours," said Coghill. "Travelways has been in touch with him, and Draycott, their personnel manager, will meet Whitfield at the airport along with Sergeant Mace and myself. I've also contacted the Grange School and briefed the headmaster. In the event that Whitfield's flight is delayed for any reason, he'll break the news to his stepson. We don't want the boy learning about his mother's death from the media."

"Too right."

"Provided there are no snags, I'll merely introduce myself to Whitfield and leave Mace to wetnurse him while I handle the press briefing at seven-thirty. Once that's out of the way, we can get a preliminary statement from him; then, depending on what he tells us, we can give his tail a real twisting first thing tomorrow. Of course, it's possible Whitfield may be able to explain where the mysterious cash input to Karen's Boutiques Limited came from."

"But you think it unlikely?" Franklin suggested.

"He may not want to if there was any funny business involved." Coghill shrugged. "We've no proof, but every instinct tells me the company was just a front. One thing's certain; the additional income hasn't been earned through the boutique in Fulham. Their takings are about on a par with the Wimbledon branch."

"That's something the Fraud Squad can look at, Tom." Franklin placed the clipboard to one side, leaned back in the chair and clasped both hands behind his neck. "You can then concentrate on Mr. Oliver Leese. It could be he was the last person to see Karen Whitfield alive."

"If the phone call June Strachey overheard was from him and if we can prove he was in Wimbledon yesterday." They were two big ifs and it did no harm to remind Franklin that it was only an assumption. "Up to now, we're not having much luck in that direction," Coghill went on. "None of the neighbors remember seeing Karen Whitfield again after she left for work. I'm hoping somebody will come forward when her photograph appears on TV and in tomorrow's newspapers."

"How far are you going to take the press into your confidence?"

"All the way. I intend to give them the facts as we know them."

"You'll be faced with a barrage of questions."

"It would be a turn-up for the book if I wasn't," Coghill said laconically. "The victim was a very attractive woman and they'll want to give their readers all the usual trivia. That's another reason why I'm planning to meet Trevor Whitfield at the airport."

"They may also ask if we've any ideas about a possible motive," Franklin warned.

"If they do, I'll say it's early days yet and we're keeping an open mind."

"And have you?"

"What? An open mind?" Coghill faced the older man. "I like to think so," he said.

It was a long way from the truth and they both knew it. The circumstances were such that anybody directly involved in the investigation was bound, even at this stage, to have his own pet theory about a motive.

"Sex and sadism seem to go hand in hand for some couples, Tom."

"Yes."

"And sometimes they go a little too far and one of them ends up dead. In some cases, you may even find peripheral evidence which suggests the murder has been carefully premeditated, but more often than not, it's usually misleading." Franklin smiled briefly. "I suppose what I'm really saying is, keep it simple and don't go looking for complicated explanations. They invariably cloud the issue."

"Yes, sir."

In Coghill's view, there was nothing simple about this particular murder, but it was politic to agree with the area commander, especially as time was running on.

"I'm glad we see eye to eye, Tom." Franklin unclasped his hands and glanced at his wristwatch. "Bert would give you the same advice if he were here."

"Are you going to recall Superintendent Kingman from leave?"

"I won't have to," Franklin lied. "You know Bert, he'll be on the first plane out of Majorca the minute he sees the headlines in the overseas edition of *The Times*."

"Yes, I suppose that will be his immediate reaction," Coghill said wryly.

"Too right." Franklin bared his teeth in a gleaming smile. "Do you have any other questions?" he asked.

"Not at the moment."

"Good. Let me know what you make of Whitfield."

Coghill agreed to do that, then left the office and went downstairs to the security compound behind V District Headquarters where Mace was waiting for him in the Volvo.

Patterson turned off the Victoria Embankment into Northumberland Avenue and parked the rented Datsun on the left-hand side of the road, just short of the Metropole Building. Seven forty-eight: by now, Raschid al Jalud should be at Waterloo Station, hurrying through the concourse toward the bank of pay phones a few yards beyond the ticket office. He'd had the Libyan criss-crossing the town for close to an hour and he wasn't finished with him yet. Smiling to himself, Patterson got out of the Datsun and walked over to the railway arch and the cluster of phone booths near the Embankment Underground station. Entering the first one he came to, Patterson consulted the list of numbers he'd noted in his pocket diary, then lifted the receiver and dialed 834–1399. At Regent's Park and Tottenham Court Road, Jalud had been obliged to wait until the preselected booth became vacant, but this time contact was established at the first attempt.

Patterson said, "Your next rendezvous is the Playhouse Theatre. Take a Bakerloo or Northern Line train to the Embankment and turn left when you leave the station. The Playhouse is a semi-derelict building on the corner of Craven Street and Northumberland Avenue. Have you got that?"

There was a sudden eruption which sounded like a camel belching, then the Arabic phrases came thick and fast. None of them were polite, all of them were physically impossible.

"Speak English," Patterson told him curtly.

"Go to hell," Jalud hissed. "I'm tired of this foolishness."

"Colonel Qadhafi would say the same and more. One glimpse of your starring role in this particular home movie and you'd be out of a job."

A long sigh came over the line and he pictured the Libyan, his sallow, weasel-like face glistening with perspiration. "You want to repeat my instructions?" he invited.

"The Playhouse Theatre on the corner of Craven Street, turn left outside the tube station."

"Right. See you ten minutes from now."

Patterson hung up on him, left the phone booth and strolled into the gardens by the Embankment. The security check he was running on Jalud was largely bluff, but the little creep had no way of knowing this. As far as he was concerned, a legman was watching his every move. It wasn't difficult to achieve that kind of conditioned response in somebody who was scared shitless and incapable of thinking straight. The ironic thing was that he had Karen Whitfield to thank for that, the unwitting ally who'd reduced Jalud to a blancmange long before he'd gotten into the act.

Patterson lit a cigarette, chose a park bench near the gates where he could see anyone leaving the Underground station and sat down. For all her alleged shrewdness, the Whitfield bitch had been like any other hooker; strip away the sophisticated veneer and she was just a greedy, blackmailing call girl who didn't have enough sense to know when the leeching had gone too far. She'd looked on Jalud as a sure-fire touch, an asset to be milked dry in furtherance of her unique, long-term pension fund. Had she been more politically aware, it might have dawned on her she was playing with fire.

A dozen or so passengers emerged from the tube station, among them the instantly recognizable figure of Raschid al Jalud, a slim, black-haired little man in an expensive gabardine suit. Waiting until he'd disappeared around the corner into Northumberland Avenue, Patterson double-checked to make sure the Libyan wasn't being shadowed by one of the Embassy security men before he went after him.

Under the railway arches, several tramps were bedding down on the pavement for the night; behind them, a couple strolled hand in hand toward the river. The man, Patterson observed, had wispy blond hair and towered above the girl, a diminutive redhead whose enticing pelvic action was emphasized by a faded pair of skin-tight blue jeans. Allowing them to draw well ahead, he turned into Northumberland Avenue and casually approached Jalud.

"Hello there." Patterson smiled, clapped the Libyan on the shoulder, then gripped his left arm above the elbow. "How long have you been waiting for me?"

Jalud glared at him. "Too long," he snapped, "far too long."

"Yeah? Well, I'm sorry about that. I guess I didn't allow enough time."

Still smiling, he steered the Libyan across the road to where the Datsun was parked. The courting couple were on the far side of the Victoria Embankment now and were leaning against the parapet, seemingly enthralled by the Shell Building on the south bank. Keeping an eye on them, Patterson opened the offside door and told Jalud to get in.

"What?"

"You're driving." He shoved the Libyan inside, closed the door and then walked around the car and slipped into the passenger seat. Glancing into the side mirror, he saw that the couple had turned about and were gazing in their direction. "Don't look now, but I think we've got company." Patterson dug the door and ignition keys out of his pocket and handed them to Jalud. "A tall, gangling blond Englishman and a redhead. He's wearing a windcheater over a thin rollneck sweater; she's in jeans and a sleeveless T-shirt. You seen them before?"

"I don't think so."

"You'd have noticed the girl, Raschid, she has the kind of tight little butt you admire so much."

"You do me an injustice."

Patterson laughed. "My mistake, I was forgetting your taste runs to the more seductive—right?" He prodded the Libyan in the ribs. "What are we waiting for?" he said. "Let's go."

"Where to?"

"Straight up the avenue to Trafalgar Square. I'll direct you from there; meantime, stick to the inside lane."

Jalud nodded, found the right key for the ignition and started the engine. Shifting into gear, he checked that the road was clear behind and pulled out from the curb.

"Did you . . . ?" He swallowed nervously. "Did you see Karen Whitfield?"

"Sure, we had a very agreeable talk." Patterson reached inside his jacket and took out a video cassette. "Your problems are over, Raschid."

"How can I be certain of that?"

"You want me to describe the movie, how she used her dildo on you?"

"That won't be necessary," Jalud said, tight-lipped.

"No, I don't suppose it is. You're not likely to forget a kinky scene like that in a hurry." Patterson opened the glove compartment, stowed the cassette away and closed the lid. "We want to head into The Mall," he said. "Soon as you move into Trafalgar Square, filter off to the left and go through Admiralty Arch."

"Save your breath." Jalud noticed the lights were against them at the top of Northumberland Avenue and braked to a halt. "I know my way around London."

"Damn right," Patterson told him. "That's been your trouble, the reason why you got yourself into such a jam."

"So what? You took care of the problem, didn't you?"

"I put a couple of bullets into her head. She wasn't breathing too well when I left the house."

"There's been no mention of her death in the newspapers." Jalud saw the lights go from amber to green and let the clutch out. "Or on the radio," he added.

"They haven't found Oliver Leese yet, but they will."

"Who?"

"Oliver Leese, the guy who filmed your sexual exploits from the adjoining room." Patterson smiled. "I did you proud, two for the price of one."

"You were paid twenty-five thousand dollars cash in advance."

The inference was clear: as far as Jalud was concerned, payment had already been made in full and he could go fly a kite. "What about the rest of the deal, Raschid?" he asked. "You're not thinking of welshing on our agreement, are you?"

"I assume you mean the franchise to provide the logistical support essential to our operations in Chad?"

"What else?" Patterson grunted.

"The matter is in hand," Jalud assured him, "but you must be patient. Although Colonel Qadhafi expressed interest in your proposal when I spoke to him the day after our meeting in Tripoli seven weeks ago, I got the impression he was well satisfied with the existing arrangements organized by your former colleagues in the CIA. However, I'm sure I can talk him around in time."

They were well into The Mall now, approaching Marlborough House on the right, and time was running out in more senses than one. For all his smooth talk, Patterson knew the Libyan meant to double-cross him. The way he'd clenched the steering wheel and temporized before answering his question was proof of that. There was also every chance Jalud would arrange to have him eliminated when he eventually returned to Tripoli.

"You want to get into the outside lane," Patterson said tersely. "We're turning right at the traffic lights ahead."

"As you wish."

Jalud tripped the offside indicator, drifted toward the center, then made the turn and drove past St. James's Palace into Pall Mall, where the one-way circuit obliged him to turn left and head up to Piccadilly. Twenty yards beyond the alleyway leading to the back entrance of the Stafford Hotel, Patterson told him to pull into the curb and stop.

"This is where I leave you," he said.

"You leave me?" Jalud blinked. "Shouldn't it be the other way round?"

"The Datsun belongs to Rent-a-Car Limited, but it's yours until

Saturday." Patterson opened the door and got out onto the pavement. "About the cassette," he added, "you'll recognize the room but not the man."

"I don't understand."

"It's really very simple, Raschid. I'm holding on to your particular home movie, it's the only life insurance policy I've got."

"Bastard."

"It takes one to know one," Patterson said and slammed the door.

There was a moment of stunned silence before Jalud found his voice and began mouthing a string of obscenities. Unperturbed, Patterson walked away and left him to it. At four-thirty that afternoon, he had parked his BMW in St. James's Square and fed the meter with sufficient loose change to insure it would run into the free evening period. Dawdling along until the Libyan had calmed down and moved off, he eventually crossed the road and turned into King Street. Five minutes later, he collected his car from outside the London Reference Library and drove out to his flat in Highgate.

Some detectives get all the lucky breaks, some get none; Harry Mace was one of the unfortunates. He did everything by the book and never cut any corners, but somehow he always ended up with egg on his face. The moment Coghill walked out of the press conference at Wimbledon Police Station and saw Mace's lugubrious expression, he knew it had happened again.

"Hello, Harry," he said. "I thought you were supposed to be keeping an eye on Trevor Whitfield."

"I was." Mace gave him a sheepish grin and opened a door off the hall. "Mind if we talk in here, Guv? It's more private."

"Right." Coghill followed him into the interview room and closed the door. "So what happened?" he asked.

"Remember that Stanley Quainton he tried to phone from the airport?"

"Yes."

"Well, he called him again from the hotel soon after you'd left for the press conference, and this time Trevor got lucky. Quainton showed up at the Merton Hotel about half an hour ago and carted Whitfield off to his house in Putney. He said that if there were any further questions we wanted to ask Trevor, he would run him out to St. Mark's Hill at ten o'clock tomorrow morning."

"How very decent of him," Coghill said drily.

"Yeah, wasn't it. Of course, I could be wrong, but I got the impression that this Quainton is a lawyer, one of the sneaky kind."

It never rained but it poured, Coghill thought, and just when everything was going nicely. Although Draycott had invited Trevor to spend the night at his house, Whitfield had politely declined and Mace had booked him a room at the Merton. Now, just when he was ready to make him jump through the hoop, Whitfield had slipped through their fingers and they were stuck with a dodgy lawyer.

"You got any more bad news, Harry?" he asked.

"Not at the moment," said Mace.

"Thank Christ for that." Coghill rubbed his eyes. "I assume you took Quainton up on his offer?"

"Yeah. I told him we'd like to see Whitfield at nine-thirty." Mace smiled. "I didn't see why we should make life easy for him."

"Good. Let's you and me call it a day." Coghill opened the door. "See you at nine-thirty, Harry," he said.

"I'll be there on the dot, Guv."

Coghill smiled, nodded to the desk sergeant and walked out into the station yard. Harry Mace might have reached his ceiling careerwise, but he knew the detective sergeant had something he lacked—a wife to go home to. Feeling deflated and empty, he got into the Volvo and headed out toward Acton and the lonely flat he'd bought after he and Janice had split up.

Patterson removed the cassette from the video machine and replaced it with another of the deck of home movies he'd stolen from Leese. Depressing the play button, he picked up the half-empty beer can and returned to his armchair. As usual, a series of frame numbers appeared on the small screen, then the room came sharply into focus and the camera zoomed in on Karen Whitfield. This time, in addition to a pair of ultra high-heeled shoes, black nylon stockings and a red lace garter belt, she was also wearing a gown and mortarboard. Her expression was stern, a pose that was emphasized by the cane she was flexing with both hands. A naked man knelt in front of her, his head almost touching the floor and enveloped in a pillowcase. As a further humiliation, the victim's wrists were handcuffed behind him and his ankles were chained together.

After two hours of watching Karen Whitfield in action, Patterson was beginning to think he was wasting his time. It had occurred to him that if Raschid al Jalud was a typical client, it was reasonable to assume her other customers were equally important and influential, but so far none of their faces had struck a chord. Bored to distraction by the sound of her strident voice and the muffled grunts coming from the man, he glanced at his wristwatch and saw that it was five minutes to twelve. At this rate, it was going to be a very long night; there were eight cassettes he hadn't seen yet and each of them lasted approximately half an hour. He should have asked Karen Whitfield who else had a star part in her porno movies, while he was at it. By the time he had finished with her, she had been in a very talkative mood, but all he'd wanted to know then was the spine number of the video tape that featured Raschid al Jalud.

Patterson raised the beer can to his mouth, then froze as Karen Whitfield unmasked her victim and helped him to his feet. Jeremy Ashforth: novelist, roving reporter, political commentator and TV personality. He recognized the face, recalled the name even before she announced it for the benefit of the hidden camera. Shit, the guy even had a reputation in the States—the epitome of liberal opinion, supposedly.

Ashforth was money in the bank if he played it carefully. The direct approach was too dangerous, because it would link him to the murder, but there were other possibilities. With his prestige and influence, a hostile intelligence service would certainly be interested in controlling a man like Ashforth. And there was a Soviet operative in Paris he'd done business with in the past who'd always given him a fair price. Viktor Orlov was no fool, though; he'd want to see what was on offer before they agreed to terms.

Patterson licked his lips. He would arrange a private viewing for Orlov and whet his appetite with Raschid al Jalud. That was the perfect sweetener and it might also buy him a little extra insurance. But first things first. Tomorrow he would change his identity and find an alternative safe house in London before Raschid decided to put a Libyan hit team onto him. Meantime, there were still the eight video cassettes he hadn't looked at yet and there was no telling what they might yield.

4.

Caroline Brooke was twenty-six, articulate, highly intelligent and blissfully unaware that she was in danger of becoming institutionalized. An army brat, she had been packed off to boarding school at the age of eleven, progressed to Lady Margaret Hall, Oxford, seven years later and, on the recommendation of her tutor, had been offered an appointment with DI5 one month after she had graduated with a first in mathematics. At Leconfield House, she was known as the Miss World of K Desk, an accurate if somewhat misleading description. Apart from the occasional theater or dinner date when she had nothing better to do, men did not figure prominently in her life. Terrorist groups and subversives were Caroline Brooke's all-consuming interest; first into the office, the last to leave, she rarely stopped thinking about them even when at home.

Every weekday, Caroline Brooke left her flat in Dolphin Square at seven forty-five and walked to Pimlico Underground station. Every morning she bought a copy of the *Daily Telegraph* from the newsagent in the entrance hall and read the main items during the short train journey to Green Park. Although Karen Whitfield was not listed in the DI5 card index, she recognized her face the moment she saw the picture on the front page and immediately knew where to find the connecting link. A phone call the previous evening from the surveillance team assigned to Raschid al Jalud triggered her photographic memory and minutes after arriving at the office, she obtained the relevant file from the central registry.

Raschid al Jalud was a kinsman by marriage of Colonel Qadhafi. Posted to London in July 1980 as a cultural attaché, he had come to the notice of DI5 four months later as a result of a tip-off from the SIS, whose overseas sources suggested the Libyan government had appointed him to liaise with and support the provisional IRA and other terrorist groups operating in Western Europe. Until his wife and children had joined him in May of the following year, Jalud had led a bachelor existence. During that time, he had visited an apartment on the fifth floor of Abercorn House in Maida Vale on a number of occasions. Unable to pinpoint exactly which flat he frequented, Surveillance had clandestinely photographed everybody entering or leaving the block of flats when he was known to be there. Among the collection retained in an envelope at the back of Jalud's file were three snapshots of Karen Whitfield.

Gratified that her memory for faces hadn't let her down, Caroline Brooke sent for the duty officer's log and read the verbatim report submitted by the surveillance team assigned to Jalud. They had shadowed the Libyan from his terraced house in Regent's Park to Tottenham Court Road and Waterloo Station, before losing him near the Metropole Building in Northumberland Avenue. The subject who'd met Jalud outside the Playhouse Theatre and driven off with him in a Datsun was described as male Caucasian, five foot nine, weight approximately 165 pounds, light brown hair, round face. There was one other piece of information; the linguists who'd analyzed the recording of a telephone conversation Jalud had had earlier that evening were convinced the caller either had a slight East Coast American accent or was a Canadian from Vancouver. Put together, it didn't amount to much, but she knew there was an equally vague description of a CIA dissident on the card index. A quick check persuaded her the unknown man could be Orville Patterson, sometimes known as Oswald Pemberton.

There remained the registration number of the Datsun—CVA 231Y. Locking the door of her office, she went down the corridor to room 28 and tapped out a request for information on the IBM computer. Twenty seconds later, the central vehicle licensing authority at Swansea came back with the information that the Datsun was owned by Rent-a-Car Limited of 285 Kilburn High Road.

Armed with this information, Caroline Brooke returned to her office and wrote a minute to her superior. It read:

> I have reason to believe that Raschid al Jalud was acquainted with Karen Whitfield and may even have had relations with her before his wife joined him in London. If this assumption is correct, then the message Jalud received yesterday evening saying that the caller had resolved the matter satisfactorily, becomes much more sinister. I also believe that the man who subsequently met him outside the Playhouse Theatre could be Orville Patterson who left the CIA in November 1973 to go freelance, but this identification is very tentative. According to the *Daily Telegraph*, the officer in charge of the Whitfield investigation is Detective Inspector Coghill. There is no way of knowing whether he is yet aware that the deceased was acquainted with Jalud, but it would be a disaster from our viewpoint were he to pursue this possible line of inquiry. If Detective Inspector Coghill should ask to interview him, Jalud would undoubtedly be recalled and he is much more valuable to us here in London than cooling his heels in Tripoli. I therefore strongly recommend that we take such preventive action as is necessary to safeguard our interests.

Coghill removed his jacket, draped it over the back of the chair, then sat down next to Mace. Quainton and Whitfield faced him across the dining room table, an ill-matched pair and the most unlikely of friends. Quainton was overweight and overbearing; he looked old enough to be Whitfield's father and had acted as though he were from the moment they'd arrived at the house half an hour later than had been stipulated. There had been no apologies, no explanations, just a throwaway disclosure that apart from being a close friend of the family, he also happened to be Whitfield's solicitor. Behind his back, Mace had winked knowingly, as if to say I told you so.

"I realize this may be very distressing for you," Coghill began quietly, "but we need your help, Mr. Whitfield."

"My help?" Whitfield repeated and glanced sideways at Quainton.

"To establish a possible motive," Coghill informed him. "Of course, it's conceivable your wife could have been murdered by a pervert who gets his kicks from bondage and sadism, but the postmortem seems to have ruled that out. Doctor Harrison, the pathologist, is satisfied your wife was not sexually assaulted, and for my money, there's too much premeditation about the whole business. The killer was in possession of a small-caliber revolver and the clothesline he used to tie her up was brand new."

"We have a tumble-dryer," Whitfield said in a hollow voice.

"So we noticed." Coghill took out a pack of Silk Cut and lit a cigarette. "Did your wife have any enemies? Her first husband, for instance?"

"What?" Whitfield looked up, mouth agape.

"The headmaster of Grange School told me Darren was your stepson, so I naturally assumed your wife had been married before."

"Yes." Whitfield nodded several times. "His name was Cairns, Michael Cairns. They were divorced in 1972, eighteen months after Darren was born. I understand Cairns emigrated to New Zealand the following year."

It was all a little too pat for Coghill's liking. Yesterday evening, Whitfield had told him Karen was an only child and had no living relatives. Now, the one person who could have filled in some of the blank spaces in her life had conveniently disappeared to the other side of the world. He wondered how long Quainton had known her, but the solicitor wasn't volunteering any information.

"When did you first meet your wife, Mr. Whitfield?" he asked, taking a different tack.

"Sometime in July 1977. I'd just come down from university and had started work with a small travel agency near Marble Arch. I rented a room in Maida Vale in those days and Karen used to catch the same bus from the same bus stop. One day we said more than good morning to each other and things sort of took off from there." A hesitant smile flickered across Whitfield's face. "I proposed to her ten weeks later. Karen was five years older than me and at first she was a little bothered about the difference in our ages, but I finally talked her around."

Coghill could understand why she had hesitated. Trevor Whitfield was twenty-seven now, but still appeared immature and, although he was very good-looking, there was something rather effeminate about the long sweeping eyelashes and the way his curly brown hair was styled. He was, however, the sort of man who would appeal to the mothering instinct in some women.

"We were married at the registry office in Kilburn on Saturday, the tenth of September, and I moved into her flat at Abercorn House."

"Can we have the exact address?" Coghill asked.

"Yes, certainly. It was flat 52, Abercorn House, Abercorn Close, Maida Vale."

Mace repeated the address and wrote it down in his notebook.

"Then, four years ago you moved to Wimbledon?"

"That's right. Karen already owned a boutique in Fulham and was thinking of leasing another premises here, so the flat in Maida Vale was no longer convenient."

"Who did the conveyancing on this house?"

"I did," said Quainton. "I've represented Mrs. Whitfield since 1975, when she asked me to vet the terms of the contract for the shop in the New King's Road she proposed to rent. I later advised Karen to buy the property on a mortgage when the landlord offered to sell her the leasehold."

"How did she raise the deposit?"

"No problem," said Quainton. "Karen had five thousand pounds in her current account and a further twenty thousand invested with the Abbey National and Halifax Building Societies. I understand she inherited a large house in Tonbridge from her parents and sold the property at a considerable profit after it was converted into two self-contained flats."

"That was pretty smart of her," Coghill said.

Quainton stared at him, eyes cold as a fish. "Karen had a good head for business, Inspector. That's why she formed herself into a Limited Company."

"With how many directors?"

"Just two," Whitfield said, chipping in. "There are a hundred ordinary shares split eighty-twenty in Karen's favor." His expression became wistful. "Perhaps I should say there *were* a hundred ordinary shares."

"Oliver Leese?" Coghill said. "Where does he fit into the picture?"

"He's a freelance photographer. Karen always used him whenever she arranged a fashion show for her customers."

The explanation was a shade too glib, as though Whitfield had had forewarning of the question and had been told exactly what to say.

"That wasn't what I heard from June Strachey. She was under the impression that Leese was your wife's accountant."

"Really?" Whitfield glanced at his companion and frowned. "I can't think where she got that idea, can you, Stanley?"

"No," said Quainton. "I can only assume she must have got hold of the wrong end of the stick." A supercilious smile appeared on his full lips. "There hasn't been a fashion show for the Wimbledon boutique yet, Inspector, but I know Karen was thinking of holding one."

"I see." Coghill leaned forward and stubbed out his cigarette in the ashtray. "Do you know where we can reach Leese?" he asked.

"Oliver has a flat in Brompton Mews off Cadogan Square," said Whitfield. "I'm afraid I don't know his phone number offhand, but I could look it up for you. It's bound to be on one of his invoices upstairs."

"No need to go to all that trouble, Mr. Whitfield," Coghill told him. "My sergeant can get it from Directory Inquiries if you don't mind him using your phone."

"No, not at all."

Mace nodded, left the table and went out into the hall.

Quainton waited until he heard him lift the receiver off the hook, then said, "May one ask why you're so anxious to get in touch with Mr. Leese?"

"We've reason to believe he could be the last person to have seen Mrs. Whitfield alive. We know she tried to phone Leese on

Tuesday morning and left a message with somebody asking him to call her back. According to Mrs. Strachey, the phone rang just before noon and Karen left the boutique a few minutes later."

"And?"

"We think she may have picked him up from the station and brought him back to the house." Coghill shrugged. "Of course, it's all supposition, but we have to start somewhere and you never know, somebody may remember seeing her at the station."

"Which one?" Whitfield asked.

"Both," said Coghill.

Karen's photograph was on display in the entrance to Wimbledon Park and Wimbledon, mounted on billboards with an arresting caption in block capitals which read: HAVE YOU SEEN THIS WOMAN? Two detectives were also in attendance to draw the attention of passengers arriving and departing from either station to the notice boards. And four uniformed officers were making door-to-door inquiries, covering all the shops and private houses in the immediate neighborhood.

"It seems to me you're looking for a needle in a haystack," Quainton observed. "I realize thousands of people are flocking to Wimbledon for the tennis championships, but I would have thought you had a different crowd of spectators every day."

"You'd be surprised how many attend the whole fortnight. And another thing," Coghill reminded him, "you're overlooking the coverage we've had from the media. Millions of viewers will have seen Karen's photograph on TV last night and heard our appeal for information. She also made the front page of most newspapers this morning."

"I trust you've had an encouraging response?"

"Very encouraging."

In anticipation of the inflow, Coghill had had the GPO install a couple of emergency lines. By the time he and Mace had left Wimbledon Police Station, Detective Sergeant Ingleson, the officer in charge of the crime index, had already received twenty-eight phone calls, some of them from obvious hoaxers.

"The public can be very cooperative at times," Quainton said vaguely and lapsed into silence.

A bell pinged out in the hall and Whitfield jerked his head around to look at the door. Lips pursed and whistling tunelessly to himself, Mace ambled into the room and returned to his chair.

"No answer," he said laconically. "All I got was an answering machine advising me to try another number." He consulted his notebook. "Zero one, eight one three, two six nine three. There was a long ringing tone but no Mr. Leese."

"I think it would be helpful if Mr. Whitfield gave us a description of him, Harry," Coghill said.

"Seems a good idea." Mace turned to a clean page, took out a ballpoint pen and waited expectantly.

"Oliver's thirty-eight," Whitfield said. "He's a little taller than me—about five-eleven—and much heavier. I would think he weighs all of fourteen stone. He has fair hair going thin on top and parted up on the left side. His eyes are gray and he has a longish face. Oh, and there's a two-inch scar on his forehead."

"Do you know how he got that?" Coghill asked.

"The result of an accident. Oliver slipped on the polished floor in his kitchen and struck his head against the steel drainboard. At least, that's what he told me."

"Thank you, Mr. Whitfield, you've been very helpful." Coghill stood up and slipped his jacket on. "I think that's about it for now, but we may want to talk to you again."

"Yes, of course."

"Will you be staying here or with Mr. Quainton?"

"Here, I think." Whitfield fingered the knot in his tie. "There are things I must arrange—the funeral and so on. I can go ahead with that, can I?"

"Any time."

Coghill shook his hand, said goodbye to Quainton and walked out into the hall with Mace. Whitfield followed them to the door and let them out of the house. Somewhat inconsequentially, he said it looked as though they were going to have another scorching hot day.

"Well?" Mace said when they were halfway down the short drive. "What do you make of him, Guv?"

"I think he's hiding something." Coghill walked around the

Volvo, got in behind the wheel and waited for Mace to join him. "Yesterday evening I thought the news of his wife's death had completely shattered him, but now I've changed my mind. I don't think he gives a damn about Karen or his stepson. He's just worried that we may uncover a few unpleasant facts he can't explain away."

"My feelings exactly." Mace tugged the lobe of his left ear. "Question is, where do we go from here?"

"Maida Vale," said Coghill. "I think we ought to give Abercorn House the once-over."

"I'd better let Control know where we're going."

"You do that, Harry. And while you're at it, give them Leese's description." He turned the ignition key, started the engine and shifted into gear. "Tell them we want it circulated to all districts."

Coghill glanced into the side mirror, saw there was nothing behind them and pulled away from the curbside.

Patterson turned right outside Kennington Underground station and went on down Clapham Road, following the route he'd memorized from *Nicholson's Street Finder.* The flat he was hoping to rent was in Linsdale Gardens, but the owner lived in Richouse Terrace. A quarter of a mile beyond the Underground station, he turned right again into a street of terraced houses, each one fronted by a privet hedge behind wrought-iron railings set in a low brick wall. Late Victorian or early Edwardian, he thought, low-cost housing built for the working class. When you'd spent as much time in London as he had, you got to know something about its architecture. He walked on, counting off the numbers until he reached 48 Richouse Terrace.

The front door was wide open. A small boy about four years old was sitting on the step, performing aerobatics with a toy Spitfire that looked decidedly battered. Lying supine on the tiled path was a large black Alsatian.

"Is he friendly?" Patterson asked.

The boy held the Spitfire at the top of a barrel roll and nodded solemnly. Contrary to his assurance, the Alsatian was anything but friendly. As Patterson raised the latch and pushed the gate open, the dog leapt to its feet and advanced toward him, hair up, top lip drawn back, teeth bared and snarling.

Above the furious barking, a shrill voice yelled, "For Christ's sake, Rosie, shut that bloody noise."

The woman was thin, sallow-faced and had her dark hair pinned up in a bun. She was wearing an apron over a brown silk dress, and a pair of carpet slippers that had seen better days.

"Mrs. Drobnowski?" Patterson inquired when the Alsatian finally stopped barking. "My name's Pearce. I believe the City Bureau phoned you?"

"Oh, yes, the Canadian salesman. You've come about the flat in Linsdale Gardens." Telling the dog to stay, she opened the gate and joined him on the pavement. "It's only a short walk from here."

Linsdale Gardens was a carbon copy of Richouse Terrace, except that the house Mrs. Drobnowski owned looked a little more dilapidated than most. The usual privet hedge was missing and the tiny strip of lawn had been concreted over. The window frames needed a lick of paint but the front door was a glossy yellow.

"My husband's still doing the place up," Mrs. Drobnowski informed him and produced a bunch of keys from the pocket of her apron. "But your flat's been completely renovated."

From what? Patterson wondered. The hallway didn't look too good; the staircase wasn't carpeted and the linoleum on the floor was a mosaic of hairline cracks. The flat was on the first floor to the right of the landing and consisted of two rooms knocked into one. There was also a small kitchen and an even smaller bathroom. Most of the furniture was plywood with a thin veneer that was supposed to be walnut, and the curtains were skimpy and almost diaphanous.

"What was the rent again?" Patterson asked.

"Forty pounds a week."

It would still have been daylight robbery at half the price, but it suited his purpose. "Okay, I'll take it," he said.

The BMW would stick out like a sore thumb in the neighborhood; so would the brand new Ford Fiesta he'd planned on buying. A five-year-old Mini was, he decided, about par for the course.

"Can I move in this afternoon?"

"You'd have to sign the lease and I'd want a month's rent in advance," Mrs. Drobnowski told him.

"Will you take a check?"

"I prefer cash."

"Who doesn't?" Patterson took out his billfold and peeled off a wad of ten-pound notes that made her eyes light up.

5.

Abercorn House presented a streamlined appearance, its aerodynamic curves owing a lot to the Hollywood influence of the mid-thirties. It was fronted by a small forecourt, with sufficient parking space for twelve cars on either side of a rock garden and ornamental fountain. Double swing doors in the entrance opened into a carpeted foyer, where there was a reception desk manned by an elderly hall porter who was reading a copy of *The Sun* when Coghill and Mace walked into the apartment house. A warrant card thrust under his nose blanked out the topless blonde on page three and claimed his reluctant attention.

"I'm Detective Inspector Coghill, this is Detective Sergeant Mace," Coghill informed him.

"And my name's Nolan, sir, Kevin Nolan. What can I do for you?" He was an Irishman from the southwest and had a soft brogue.

"We're investigating the murder of Mrs. Karen Whitfield."

"Ach, yes." Nolan inclined his head and looked sage as though about to impart some vital piece of information. "She's on the front page and I saw her picture on TV last night."

"Lots of people did," Mace said.

"Is that a fact now?" The grizzled head dipped again. "Funny thing is, I thought she was Mrs. Cairns."

"That used to be her name," Coghill said. "Until she married again five years ago."

"Really?"

"I'm told she lived here at one time."

"She still does." Nolan pointed to the letter rack inside the entrance. "That's her, flat 52, Mrs. S. K. Cairns. She was a real nice woman, always had a cheery word for me."

I bet she did, Coghill thought. "You mind telling me when you saw her last?" he asked.

Nolan frowned, looked up at the ceiling and started counting off the days on his fingertips. "It must have been a week ago last Monday. Mind you, I didn't see as much of her as I used to in the old days."

He recalled that Karen Whitfield had moved into Abercorn House some time during the late spring of 1973. From little snippets she'd dropped, Nolan had gathered she was a buyer for one of the big department stores in the West End. Dickins and Jones, or was it D. H. Evans? He wasn't sure which now, but she had obviously been well paid. She had had to be when apartments in Abercorn House were changing hands at £37,500 in '73 and there was a ground rent of £198 per annum on top of that.

"You could tell that woman had class just by looking at her," Nolan went on. "So I wasn't surprised when she became a fashion editor for one of them glossy magazines."

"When was this?" Coghill said.

"About six years ago. I remember Mrs. Cairns once showing me an article she'd written. Of course, it wasn't under her own name."

"That doesn't surprise me," Coghill said drily.

"She used to do a fair amount of work at home. Had quite a few visitors too; other writers and the like. Contributors, she called them. I recognized one of them: Jeremy Ashforth, him that's on TV."

"You actually saw Ashforth with Mrs. Whitfield?"

"Not exactly. But he was here several times and he always took the lift up to the fifth floor."

"Recently?" Mace inquired.

Nolan shook his head. "No, this was before he became really famous. I can't recall when he was here last, but it must have been a couple of years ago, perhaps longer. Truth is, I'm getting on a bit and my memory's not what it was."

"It happens to us all sooner or later." Coghill took out a pack of Silk Cut, offered Nolan a cigarette and lit up. "Was anyone with Mrs. Whitfield the last time you saw her?" he asked.

"No, she arrived alone, but an Arab-looking gentleman showed up a few minutes later and he's no stranger to this place. Mind, I'm not saying he did call on her; there are that many people coming and going, it's hard to keep track of them. Anyway, it's not my job to inquire what they're doing here."

Nolan took messages, ran errands, opened doors and got the repair men in whenever anything went wrong. To hear him talk, the central heating system had a mind of its own and only functioned spasmodically in the winter, much to everybody's annoyance. And the lifts were the bane of his life; not a month went by without one of the residents being marooned between floors.

"Any chance we'll get stuck?" Coghill asked him.

"Why?"

"Because the sergeant and I are going up to have a word with her former neighbors."

"You'll be wasting your time," Nolan said. "She was never one for popping in and out of other people's apartments. Kept herself to herself she did, a real fine lady."

"So you said before."

"And meant every word," Nolan called after them. "I was very sorry when she changed jobs and went to work for that American advertising agency. Never saw so much of her from then on."

"That's the way it goes."

Coghill dropped his cigarette into the wastebasket, joined Mace inside the lift and closed the gate behind him. There was a significant delay between the time he pressed the button for the fifth floor and the moment when the lift finally responded to the signal.

"No two ways about it," Mace observed. "Nolan was definitely her number-one fan."

Coghill grunted. "She certainly pulled the wool over his eyes."

"And Trevor Whitfield? Do you think he knew she still owned this flat?"

"I think so, Harry. But you can bet he'll pretend he didn't when we confront him with it."

Coghill waited for the lift to stop shuddering, then opened the gate and glanced up and down the corridor. There were ten apartments on the fifth floor, six on the right of the lateral passageway, two on either side of the twin lifts. Number 52 was almost directly opposite.

"What do I take?" Mace asked. "Odds or evens?"

"Odds," said Coghill. "After we've given Karen's apartment the once-over."

"Do we have a key?"

"No. I'm relying on your knowhow."

"Oh, shit." Mace went over to the apartment, examined the door and reached into his hip pocket for a slim black wallet containing a bunch of master keys. "I hope you realize this is strictly illegal," he muttered.

"Let me worry about that."

"I was just sounding a warning note." Mace examined the lock again, tried three different Yale keys and finally managed to open the door.

There were four bedrooms, two bathrooms, a kitchenette, a dining room and a lounge off the hall. Of the three single bedrooms, the one adjoining the master suite was no bigger than a dressing room. It contained only two items of furniture, a built-in cupboard housing a tripod and a Bolex 16mm movie camera, and a low table with steel legs which was positioned under a large two-way mirror. In the adjoining master bedroom, this two-way mirror was incorporated in a dressing table and double wardrobe unit which took up the entire dividing wall. Hanging from the rail in the right-hand unit were a collection of gym suits, hot pants and rubberized jump suits. On the rack below were a dozen pairs of ultrahigh-heeled shoes and thigh-length leather boots. A pair of handcuffs, several padlocks, an assortment of chains, a riding crop and a number of canes were jumbled together on the top shelf of the other wardrobe.

"Seems our Karen had some very interesting and unusual hobbies," Mace observed.

"And she made a bundle out of them." Coghill lifted a lamp from one of the bedside tables and showed him the mike in the base. "This whole room is wired for sound."

"We've got a motive then?"

"Yes. Looks like Karen bled one of her clients white and he turned nasty when she couldn't or wouldn't hand over the film."

They had two possible suspects: Jeremy Ashforth and a man of Arabic extraction who had visited one of the fifth-floor apartments on a number of occasions. Coghill thought there was a chance some of the neighbors might come up with a few other candidates.

As it happened, they failed to get an answer from two apartments, and of the remaining seven residents they interviewed, not one had seen Karen Whitfield the last time she was known to have been in residence at Abercorn House. All of them, however, could recall having noticed at least one of her visitors in the past, although none were able to put a name to the faces they attempted to describe. The one positive lead was the fact that no less than four residents had observed the same overweight, blond-haired man on different occasions, a description that bore a passing resemblance to Oliver Leese.

Their inquiries completed, Coghill and Mace left Abercorn House shortly after two o'clock and began the journey back to Wimbledon. Approaching Marble Arch, they received a radio message from Control, instructing them to proceed to 17 Brompton Mews off Cadogan Square where Oliver Leese had been found dead.

Brompton Mews was a narrow cobbled street between Cadogan Square and Pavilion Road. An ambulance, two patrol cars, a Rover 2000 and a Ford Capri were parked in the vicinity of number 17, where two obvious plainclothesmen were talking to a police constable who looked as though he wasn't old enough yet to put a razor over his face. Inside the flat, a police surgeon, a forensic expert, a photographer and two more plainclothesmen from S District were gathered around Leese, who lay face down on the bloodstained carpet in the living room. The officer in charge was Detective Superintendent Rowntree, a burly Yorkshireman who greeted Coghill with a perfunctory handshake and gave him an equally laconic rundown.

"Your request for information started the ball rolling. Desk sergeant at Lucan Place decided to put one of his probationary constables onto it and sends him around here. The constable rings the bell, doesn't get any response and goes calling on the neighbors. The lady next door tells him Leese was expected to return yesterday from a business trip on the Continent, so he goes back, looks through the window and sees a body lying on the floor. Being a bright lad, he whips out his truncheon, busts a windowpane and climbs into the flat. The killer found it a lot easier; he just rang the bell and was invited inside."

"There were no signs of a forcible entry?" Coghill said.

"Not a bloody one." Rowntree wrinkled his nose in disgust. "This fucking room still pongs to high heaven," he said.

"Excreta?" Coghill said and sniffed.

"Yeah. Leese shat himself when he realized his visitor was about to shoot him." Rowntree took Coghill by the arm and steered him into the kitchen. "Two bullets in the head from a small-caliber revolver," he continued. "Same as Karen Whitfield."

"There's another connection; they knew one another."

"Aw, for Christ sake, Inspector, that's a glimpse of the blinding obvious. Why else would you have circulated his description?" He smiled derisively, then said, "Apart from that, I happen to know she phoned him, because there's a message from her on the answering machine."

"Karen Whitfield was a call girl," Coghill said evenly. "Leese put her act on film whenever she was entertaining an influential client. Then, later on, they would lean on their victim."

"Can you prove that?" Rowntree growled.

"Karen might have lived in Wimbledon, but she also had an apartment at Abercorn House over in Maida Vale. The master bedroom is wired for sound, there's a large two-way mirror above the dressing table and I found a movie camera in the adjoining room. The rest is supposition."

Rowntree delved into his pockets, took out a pack of Wrigley's chewing gum, unwrapped a stick and popped it into his mouth. "I'd still like to hear it," he said.

Coghill nodded, kept it brief and to the point. The killer had wanted a particular film and had burned Karen Whitfield with the glowing ember of a cigarette until she had told him where it was.

"You're saying Leese had it?"

"And maybe a few more besides. Of course, it doesn't necessarily follow he kept them here in the flat."

"I think he did." Rowntree moved his jaws like a cow contentedly chewing the cud. "There's a combination safe behind the oil painting in the living room. We've sent for a locksmith, but I've a hunch we'll find it's been cleaned out. Judging by the untidy heap of papers on Leese's bed, it looks as though the killer emptied his briefcase and took them away in that."

Somebody with a personal axe to grind would have taken only the one cassette; a professional hit man might have seen the other video tapes as a way of making a little extra on the side.

"Leese had a visitor yesterday," Rowntree went on. "A woman across the street saw him leave the flat—about five foot nine, medium build, brown hair, round face. I bet you've had any number of sightings to match that description."

"Give me a minute and you'll have the latest head count."

Coghill returned to the living room. Leese was still lying on the floor, head facing toward the grate. The police surgeon had finished his preliminary examination and the forensic expert was busy taking his fingerprints before running a comparative check with the Criminal Record Office to see if the deceased had any form. Lifting the phone, he dialed 218–5999, one of the two emergency numbers the GPO had installed at Wimbledon Police Station, and got Detective Sergeant Ingleson on the line.

A ticket collector, the newsagent in the entrance hall and a cabdriver waiting in the rank outside Wimbledon Park had all observed Karen Whitfield leave the station with a man dressed in a casual but expensive-looking gray suit. None of these witnesses, however, could agree on his physical characteristics, which had made life difficult for the officer who'd attempted to make up a composite Identikit likeness. Smiling wryly, Coghill put the phone down and returned to the kitchenette.

"Well?" Rowntree stopped chewing and gazed at him expectantly. "Am I right?"

"Only partially," Coghill told him. "We've got one round-faced man, but his hair is mousy, graying or fairly blond. He could also be either five-seven or five-eleven and his weight seems to fluctuate between ten and twelve stone."

"Shit." Rowntree scowled. "Wouldn't you just know it."

"One of the witnesses thought he had a Canadian accent."

"Big deal."

"It's a start."

"Well, don't get too excited; the odds are it won't do you any good." Rowntree removed the chewing gum from his mouth and dropped it into the wastebasket. "Who's your guvnor?" he asked abruptly.

"Bert Kingman." Coghill thought he knew what the superintendent was getting at and added, "He's holidaying in Majorca, but he'll be back soon enough."

"Bert will be wasting his time if he hops a plane. Take a tip from me and warn him off."

"Why?"

"Because your area commander is going to talk to my area commander and when they've finished jawing, they'll decide to hand both murders over to the Regional Crime Squad. Naturally, those sods will pick our brains and we'll end up doing most of the legwork, but there'll be no glory in it for you and me."

It was a long speech for the Yorkshireman. Coghill suspected it was also a highly accurate prognosis.

The loose minute Caroline Brooke had written first thing that morning had acquired a pristine folder, a file number and one typewritten sheet of foolscap by the time it was returned to her desk toward midafternoon. Patterson's name, initials and known aliases appeared on the front cover in block capitals, and her superior had evidently thought the contents sufficiently hypersensitive for the file to be classified top secret.

The former CIA man, she learned, was forty-six years old. Born in Moorefield, West Virginia, on March 21, 1936, and the youngest of seven children, Patterson had left high school without any educational qualifications at the age of sixteen to work in a coal mine. One year later, he'd enlisted in the United States Army, who'd sent him first to Fort Benning, Georgia, then to Stuttgart in West Germany. Other tours overseas had followed on his way up the promotion ladder from private first class to master sergeant—Japan, Okinawa and an eighteen-month spell in Korea with the 24th Infantry Division.

Until 1964, Patterson had never heard a shot fired in anger, but from then on, it had been a vastly different story. To join the Green Berets, he'd reverted to sergeant, but had got his former rank back six months after becoming an adviser to the 16th ARVN Regiment operating in the Thua Thien province of South Vietnam. The Mekong Delta, the Ho Chi Minh trail, Laos, Cambodia, wherever the action was, Patterson had been there, winning himself a chestful of medals and a battlefield commission in the process. Along the way, a talent spotter for the CIA had decided he was the sort of operative their counterinsurgency department needed. A lack of formal education had been more than offset by experience gained in the field and the fact that he had a natural ear for languages and was fluent in German and French, the latter tongue acquired from a part-Vietnamese mistress he kept in Saigon. Mustered out of the army with an honorable discharge in June 1969, Patterson had exchanged his jungle fatigues for a gray flannel suit and a desk at Langley.

The brief was noticeably reticent about his career with the CIA, but it appeared that Patterson had had some sort of roving commission in the Middle East. Eighteen months after he'd left the agency, the FBI had issued a warrant for his arrest in connection with drug trafficking and the suspected homicide of two law enforcement officers in Galveston, Texas, sometime between May 24 and 28, 1975. The CIA was also anxious to question him about three thousand M16 rifles and one million rounds of 5.56mm ammunition which had allegedly been shipped to Chile.

Without going into too many details, the head of K Desk had indicated there were several good reasons why DI5 should do everything in their power to apprehend Patterson on behalf of these two agencies. To this end, the director general himself had said he was prepared to sacrifice Raschid al Jalud if or when the necessity arose. In the meantime, however, Caroline Brooke was to take whatever action was thought necessary to shield the Libyan diplomat from any police inquiries connected with the Whitfield case.

Caroline Brooke placed the file on one side, opened her copy of the *Daily Telegraph* at page 3 and studied the photograph taken of Coghill as he arrived at Wimbledon Police Station for the press briefing. A tallish man with an angular face that suggested a strong character, she thought, and good-looking too. She would need to keep an eye on him if Raschid al Jalud was to be safeguarded, and there was only one way to do that. Lifting the phone, she called the DI5 contact at New Scotland Yard.

Eight miles away at Linsdale Gardens over the river in Kennington, Patterson finished unpacking everything he intended to leave behind and got to work on the floorboards in the bathroom. The blade of a penknife served to raise the linoleum around the pedestal washbasin; then, using a nail extractor, he loosened and removed a plank two foot long by six inches wide. That done, he carefully laid the .22 caliber Iver Johnson revolver in the cavity between the joists, together with all the video cassettes, except the one featuring Raschid al Jalud. The floorboard and linoleum replaced, he collected a suitcase of clothes from the bedroom and drove out to Heathrow, where he left the Mini he'd purchased that morning with the Ace Airways garage. Half an hour later, he boarded the 4:00 P.M. Air France flight to Paris.

6.

The offices of Quainton, Phipps and Slingsby were located in Putney High Street above a florist's shop and a ladies' hairdressing salon. A brass plate on the wall to the right of the narrow passageway between the two shops informed Coghill that the partners were also Public Notaries and Commissioners for Oaths. There was no sign of either Phipps or Slingsby, but he and Mace did come across an earnest-looking man in his mid-forties who claimed he was the managing clerk and asked if he could be of any assistance. Coghill said he hoped so, told him they were police officers and briefly explained why they wanted to see Mr. Quainton. The clerk buzzed the solicitor on the intercom, repeated the message, got a monosyllabic grunt from Quainton and then showed them into his office.

The room was at the back of the building, overlooking the courtyard behind the ladies' hairdressing salon. It also afforded a depressing view of row upon row of terraced houses, which Coghill thought must be the reason why Quainton had arranged the furniture so that he had his back to the window. There were four trays on the desk in front of him, In, Out and two Pending, all of them overflowing with bulky files done up with narrow red tape. The ashtray to his right was brimming with cigar stubs and a pall of blue-gray smoke eddied below the ceiling. Not surprisingly, the white paintwork on the window frame was now a brownish-yellow.

"Well now, Inspector," Quainton said, "what can I do for you?" His offhand manner and limp handshake suggested he was not pleased to see them again.

"It concerns your client, Mr. Trevor Whitfield."

"He's not my client."

"You were present when we questioned him this morning," Coghill pointed out.

"But not in an official capacity. I represented the late Mrs. Whitfield."

"When she purchased the boutiques in Fulham and Wimbledon and the house in St. Mark's Hill."

"You have a good memory, Inspector," Quainton said acidly.

"Did you know she was a prostitute?"

Quainton blinked several times, then said, "A prostitute?" in a voice that didn't sound convincingly incredulous.

"She had a wider variety of contraceptives in her flat at Abercorn House than most chemists have on their shelves." Mace looked up from his notes with a cheerful smile. "We also found three canes, a whip and various items associated with bondage."

"Prostitution wasn't the only thing she was into. We've reason to believe Mrs. Whitfield blackmailed a number of her clients." Coghill eyed the solicitor thoughtfully. "I have a feeling that's where most of the income to Karen Boutiques Limited came from."

"You're overlooking the fact that her accounts were regularly audited by Richard Atkinson and Company. They're a very reputable firm."

"Sales receipts can be fudged," Coghill told him. "So can purchases."

"I wouldn't know about that. The company accounts were no concern of mine. I merely did the conveyancing on the various properties."

"Whitfield must have known what his wife was up to when they were living at Abercorn House."

"I imagine he couldn't help but know she was engaged in prostitution." Quainton opened a drawer in the desk, took out a pack of Panatella cigars and lit one. "However, you may find it considerably more difficult to prove he was aware of her other activities. Still, I can see it would be in his interest to be cooperative."

"Maybe you should be present when we question him?" Coghill suggested.

"When's that?"

"Now," said Coghill.

Quainton gazed at the files lying in the various trays on his desk and pursed his lips. "I'm a little busy at the moment," he said.

"It shouldn't take long, an hour to an hour and a half at the most. You can spare him that much of your time, can't you?"

"It seems I'll have to." Quainton mashed his cigar into the ashtray, stumped over to the door, removed his jacket from the hanger and slipped it on. "My car's parked in Rushmore Avenue, a good five minutes' walk from here."

"We'll meet you at the house then."

"I think that would be best," Quainton said.

Coghill nodded, beckoned Mace to follow him and left the office. When they came out onto the street, he crossed the road, entered a snack bar that was almost directly opposite and ordered two coffees. Ten minutes later, Quainton emerged from the passageway and turned left.

"He's a regular streak of greased lightning," Mace observed. "A fiver says he's been on the blower to Whitfield."

"Damn right," said Coghill. "Quainton wants to save his skin. He's probably advised Whitfield to do the same."

Air France flight 1600 was supposed to arrive at Charles de Gaulle, but a sudden strike by the baggage handlers resulted in the plane being diverted to Orly, where it finally landed ten minutes behind schedule. Once through Customs and Immigration, Patterson caught the airport bus to Les Invalides where he flagged down a cab and told the driver to take him to the Hôtel Jules César in the Avenue Ledru-Rollin. From the Jules César, he picked up another cab and headed across town to check into the Fondary, a modest pension in the 15th Arrondissement.

Patterson unpacked, left the pension and from a pay phone on the corner of the Rue de L'Avre and Letellier, dialed the code for Trinité followed by 001764. The number rang for some considerable time before anyone answered, then a soft, effeminate voice said, "Société de Bibliothèque."

"My name's Kingfisher," Patterson said, "Henry Kingfisher. Would you please inform Monsieur Viktor that I'm in town for a couple of days and would like to do business with him again. You can also tell him that I have some interesting material on offer which I know he'd want to see."

"Very good. What did you say your name was, Monsieur?"

"Kingfisher," said Patterson. "I'm staying at the usual place."

He hung up, backed out of the telephone kiosk and walked on down the Rue de L'Avre to the nearest café. Previous experience had taught him it would take the cutout about an hour to contact Viktor Orlov and organize the standard security check, and he passed the time over coffee and a large cognac.

Leaving the café, Patterson walked to the Métro station at La Motte Picquet, rode a Line 8 train to Concorde, then detoured to Louvre before going on to Abbesses via Marcadet Poissonniers and the first checkpoint at the southeast corner of Sacré Coeur. When he arrived at the appointed place, he removed his jacket, draped it over his left arm and sat down on a wooden bench. Knowing that somewhere among the milling crowd of tourists somebody was watching his every move, he loosened his tie, undid the top button of the shirt and crossed his feet at the ankles to complete the recognition signal. Exactly ten minutes later, he got up, put his jacket on again, walked back to the funicular and stood there for some moments, watching the cars shuttle backward and forward, before making his way into the Place du Tertre.

He strolled around the square, pausing every now and then to gaze at the canvases on display, his eyes constantly sliding to the telephone kiosks over by the Rue Norving. No less than four budding artists tried to persuade him to have his portrait done in pen and ink, but he politely declined their offers and moved on.

Up to that point, the security check had gone smoothly, but it started to fall apart when he entered the predesignated telephone kiosk and found it had been vandalized. He tried the backup in the Rue Gabrielle and discovered it too was out of order. There remained only the drop in the Place Pigalle, but Patterson figured it would be some time before Orlov's people cottoned onto the fact that the communication network had broken down. Uncertain what to do, he returned to the Place du Tertre, wandered into a snack bar and ordered coffee and a couple of hotdogs.

The coffee arrived in a cup not much bigger than an eggcup and the hotdogs had a rubbery texture that even the tomato relish couldn't disguise. Patterson ate them without enthusiasm, asked for another coffee to wash the taste from his mouth and then started chain-smoking one cigarette after another. Presently, the girl sitting next to him left the snack bar and a thickset, middle-aged man in a baggy suit took her place at the counter. The stranger turned sideways, reached across Patterson for the ashtray he was using and deftly transferred a folded slip of paper into his jacket pocket.

It was a development Patterson had not expected and it made him feel uneasy. The way Orlov's people had made contact didn't bother him, it was the fact that he'd no idea they were tailing him which was disturbing. There was no ignoring it, he was slipping, making the kind of error only a greenhorn would. Angry with himself, he walked out of the snack bar and started back to the Métro station. Halfway there, he took the slip of paper out of his pocket and saw the meet had been set for 2210 hours at Laval's bakery, twenty-five meters from the junction of the Rue Nic-Fortin and the Avenue de Choisy in the 13th Arrondissement.

Away in the distance he could hear the rumble of an approaching thunderstorm. In his present despondent mood, he considered it a bad omen.

It didn't take much to get Whitfield thoroughly rattled. A brief description of what they'd found at Abercorn House, a few pointed innuendos concerning his role in the setup and the color had gone from his face and his voice was reduced to a hoarse whisper. "I had no idea"—he murmured it over and over and kept glancing to Quainton for moral support, but nothing was forthcoming from that quarter.

"Don't kid yourself," Coghill said. "We could have you for

living on the immoral earnings of a common prostitute."

"I have a job."

"Oh, come on, you couldn't afford a house like this on five thousand a year."

"We bought it on a joint mortgage," Whitfield said with as much dignity as he could muster. "Of course, I admit the monthly repayments to the building society were debited to Karen's personal account, but I always gave her my director's fee from the company."

"And that's your story, is it?"

"Yes. It happens to be true."

"Really?" Coghill shook his head and looked doubtful. "Well, I think I should tell you the Fraud Squad will go through the books with a fine-tooth comb. Among other things, they will contact every supplier your wife dealt with, and if any of the invoices are forgeries, you're going to find yourself in very serious trouble."

"Karen had eighty percent of the voting shares. I merely did as I was told."

Whitfield appeared to think that nobody could touch him on that score. Turning to Quainton, Coghill suggested he put him wise, then sat back while the lawyer detailed his responsibilities under the Companies Acts. By the time he'd finished, the younger man knew exactly where he stood and was looking even more apprehensive. For good measure, Coghill told him there was a distinct possibility he would also be charged with several offenses under Section 21 of the Theft Act of 1968.

"I've never stolen a damned thing in my life." Whitfield pulled a handkerchief from his jacket pocket and dried his sweaty palms. "Never," he repeated.

"The inspector is referring to blackmail," Quainton told him curtly. "In legal parlance, this means unwarranted demands with menaces. Of course, as I've already pointed out, the police might not find that quite so easy to substantiate unless they can persuade one of the victims to give evidence. But I wouldn't be too confident about that, if I were you. There's always a chance somebody will give them an anonymous tip-off."

"Thanks," Whitfield said, "thanks a lot, Stanley. You're a big help."

Coghill could see the reason for his bitterness: Stanley was dumping him, washing his hands of the entire affair like some latter-day Pontius Pilate. The process had started when he and Mace had stopped off at his office in Putney, and now Quainton was merely putting the finishing touches to it.

"I'm afraid you've been used, Trevor," he said quietly.

"Used?"

"By Karen." Although Coghill was throwing him a lifeline, there was a good deal of truth in the assertion. Whitfield was essentially a weak character, immature, easily led and something of a drifter. He'd come down from university with no clear idea of what he was going to do with his life and had happened to bump into Karen at exactly the wrong moment for him. She had been looking for a front, someone who would give her a cloak of respectability, and he had apparently filled the bill. It was even possible he'd fulfilled some kind of need. "You were her camouflage, Trevor," he went on, "part of the trappings of a middle-class and respectable married woman. With that kind of image, who would ever suspect she was a prostitute and a blackmailer?"

"I suppose that's one way of looking at it," Whitfield said in a dull voice.

"Trouble is, she pushed one of her clients too far and he turned nasty and hired himself a professional killer. At least, that's the theory we're working on."

"I see."

"We think she had a list of potential victims, people who'd gone with her and were vulnerable for one reason or another. It's likely she assessed how much they had to lose, how much they could afford to pay, and made some notes to that effect in a pocket book or a diary. Perhaps you've seen one around the house?"

"No. No, I can't say I have." Whitfield raised a hand to his mouth and nibbled at the thumb like a baby with a teething ring. "Karen never kept a diary."

Coghill was pretty sure there was a diary or some sort of sucker list, but Whitfield wasn't prepared to admit it for fear of incriminating himself. "Husbands and wives are not always completely open with one another," he said, trying a different tack. "I mean, take Karen Boutiques Limited—I don't suppose your wife gave you a blow-by-blow account of the business, did she? As far as you were concerned, the cash came rolling in and she banked it. You weren't to know if she was simply transferring the money from a personal account, were you?"

"No."

"And maybe she had some sort of deed box, too?"

"It's possible."

There was a long silence, then Quainton decided to give Whitfield the benefit of his advice, and told him he had nothing to lose and everything to gain by being completely frank about his wife's affairs. The inference was both clear and accurate: if he was cooperative, the police wouldn't press charges under either Section 30 of the Sexual Offenses Act of 1956 or the Theft Act of '68. It was, however, some little time before the penny dropped; when finally it did, Whitfield was slightly more forthcoming.

"I seem to remember Karen mentioning she had a safety-deposit box at the First National Bank of America in Park Lane."

Coghill could have wished for more precise details, but he sensed Whitfield could be pushed just so far and no farther. In any case, the fact that he would be unable to quote a box number to First National was unlikely to be a problem; a search warrant would satisfy the bank and forestall any objections from the branch manager.

"Tomorrow morning," he said, "sharp at eight forty-five, I want you spruced up and waiting when we arrive to pick you up."

"Where are we going?"

"To the bank," Coghill told him. "You may have some explaining to do when we open the safety-deposit box."

Quainton said he assumed his presence was not required and looked very put out when he learned otherwise. He didn't say a word thereafter, merely vented his anger on the Vauxhall Chevette, taking off like a Grand Prix driver with the tires screeching a protest.

In a more leisurely fashion, Coghill and Mace returned to

Wimbledon Police Station. In the eight and a half hours they'd been away, the number of calls received on the two hot lines had jumped to 187, an average of one every 2.7 minutes throughout the day. Of this total, Detective Sergeant Ingleson, the officer in charge of the crime index, figured 11 were definite hoaxes, 163 were from people who thought they recognized Karen Whitfield and had seen her at various times in various places, while another 4 were from obvious nut cases who wanted to confess to her murder. The remaining 9 were from witnesses whose information tallied with the known movements of the deceased on the day in question.

A further Identikit likeness of the suspect had been put together with the help of additional witnesses who thought they'd seen him in the area of Wimbledon Park Station. The main differences between it and previous versions were the eyes, which were narrower and farther apart, and the mouth, which was almost a straight gash. Although there was still nothing very remarkable about the face, Coghill had it photocopied and issued to the investigating officers. The initial inquiries in St. Mark's Hall had drawn a blank, but he decided to cover the neighborhood again. The homicide had been carefully planned and it was possible the killer had reconnoitered the area beforehand. With this in mind, Coghill wanted to know if any of the residents had noticed a man resembling the unidentified suspect at any time during the past ten days or so.

He was five minutes into briefing the officers detailed for the job when Franklin rang up to inform him that Kingman was on a Dan Airways flight from Majorca arriving at Gatwick at 2100 hours.

Franklin said, "It might be an idea if you met him at the airport, Tom. You see, it's been decided that 6 Regional Crime Squad will coordinate the investigation of the Leese and Whitfield murders, and Bert will need bringing up to date before the conference tomorrow at ten-thirty. Naturally, you'll be there to hold his hand."

"Ten-thirty could be a little awkward for me," Coghill said, and told him why.

"You think the contents of this safety-deposit box may provide us with a definite lead?"

"I'm hoping they will."

"In that case, we'll put the conference back half an hour," Franklin said and put the phone down.

Lean, dark and sardonic were three adjectives that described Detective Superintendent Bert Kingman to a T. The half-smile on his mouth was deceptive because it was always there, whether he was angry, bored or quietly amused. Observing him from a distance as he waited for his baggage to appear on the revolving conveyor belt, even Coghill, who knew him better than most, had no idea what sort of mood he was in. Alice Kingman, on the other hand, a plump woman with dyed blond hair, was an open book. Her mutinous expression was an obvious sign she was not pleased that their holiday had been cut short. It was also apparent by the way her lips never stopped moving that she was giving her husband an earful. Not that it had any effect on Kingman; face still impassive, he grabbed their luggage from the conveyor, loaded the suitcases onto a trolley and wheeled them through Customs. The one time his face registered a flicker was when he noticed Coghill among the crowd of onlookers, and then only an eyebrow lifted briefly.

"Hello, Tom," he grunted. "What are you doing here?"

"Meeting you." Coghill turned to Alice Kingman, politely expressed a hope that she'd had a comfortable flight and got a sulky smile in return.

"Whose idea was it?" Kingman demanded. "Charlie Franklin's?"

"Yes, but I would have come anyway."

"You shouldn't have bothered, Tom. I left our car at the airport garage."

"I know, you told me you were planning to do that." Coghill moved ahead, held the door open for the Kingmans, then joined them on the pavement outside the terminal building. "Still, now that I am here, I'll run you out to the garage. If nothing else, it'll save you a ten-minute wait for the bus."

"I'm not used to this four-star treatment." Kingman glanced at him suspiciously. "So what's behind it?"

It was, Coghill decided, hardly the right moment to tell Bert he might just as well have stayed on in Majorca, and he waited until he'd gotten the Kingmans settled in the Volvo before attempting to answer the question. Even so, he found it hard going, especially with Alice breathing down his neck and grinding her teeth in anger. Unlike his wife, however, Kingman was not the least put out by the knowledge that the Whitfield case had been taken over by the Regional Crime Squad.

"You seem to think we've had a raw deal, Tom," he said finally.

"Don't you?"

"I'm not so sure." Kingman pointed to the road junction up ahead and told him to turn right into a narrow country lane that led to the airport garage. "Have you talked to this Jeremy Ashforth?"

"Not yet," Coghill said. "I thought it best to wait until we had something more definite on him."

"It's just as well you did. You've got a bad number on your hands when the likes of Jeremy Ashforth gets involved with a high-class prostitute. You can find yourself under all kinds of pressure."

"I don't believe that," said Coghill. "Nobody's above the law."

"Then you've got a lot to learn," Kingman growled.

Patterson moved farther back into the shop doorway of Laval's bakery, seeking what shelter he could from the driving rain. The thunderstorm that had started earlier in the evening was still around, rumbling intermittently, and now the heavens had opened again, the sudden torrential downpour flooding the gutters. He wondered how much longer Orlov's people would keep him waiting, wondered too if any of the residents living above the shops across the street had noticed him and, if so, whether they'd considered his presence suspicious enough to phone the police. On a night like this, there was every reason to assume they would be glued to their TV screens, but after that initial cock-up in the Place du Tertre, he wasn't prepared to bet on it.

A car turned into the Rue Nic-Fortin from the direction of the Avenue de Choisy and cruised slowly down the street to stop opposite the bakery. Somebody opened the rear nearside door and, braving the rain, Patterson crossed the pavement and scrambled into the Peugeot. The man sitting next to the driver got out, followed him into the back and slammed the door. As Patterson settled himself between them, the man to his left produced a strip of black velvet from his pocket and proceeded to blindfold him.

"It is necessary, you understand?"

"Oh sure," said Patterson. "I'm used to Viktor's little foibles."

The Peugeot shot forward, tires drumming on the cobblestones, the driver making a right turn at the top of the street. Other turns followed in rapid succession, so that within a short space of time, Patterson had lost all sense of direction. After a while, the drumming noise from the tires changed to a high-pitched whine and he guessed they were traveling on the Boulevard Périphérique, their speed fluctuating between fifty and seventy miles an hour. About fifteen minutes later, the driver turned off on to a slip road, and shortly after that, the drumming noise started up again. At one stage, Patterson was convinced they were going round and round in circles; then suddenly the Peugeot shot through some kind of archway and skidded to a halt.

Both doors opened and he heard his escorts get out. Presently, a hand gripped his left elbow and, responding to a none-too-gentle tug, Patterson wriggled across the seat, ducked his head below the sill and placed a tentative foot on the cobblestones. As he straightened up, another hand seized his right arm and a gruff voice said, "There's a staircase six paces ahead. Just rely on us and you'll be all right."

Wooden steps, a cool atmosphere and a faint musty smell that reminded him of mushrooms. It came as no surprise to Patterson when the blindfold was removed and he found himself in a wine cellar.

Orlov said, "It's good to see you again, my old friend."

"And you, Viktor."

The Russian was sitting on a trestle table at the far end of the cellar, his feet clear of the floor and swinging rhythmically back and forth like a pendulum. He had the broad shoulders, deep chest and narrow waist of a prizefighter, an impression that was reinforced by a misshapen nose and the scar tissue above both eyebrows. In fact, Orlov had never been in a boxing ring in his life and the facial injuries were the result of a traffic accident in Beirut some years back when he'd rammed into a truck that had shot out of a side street.

"Let's see now," Orlov mused, "when was the last time we met?"

"It must have been all of eighteen months ago." Patterson reached into the pocket of his plastic raincoat and brought out the video cassette. "Got a present for you," he said. "A blue movie."

"Blue?"

"Pornographic. The star of the show is Raschid al Jalud, a kinsman of Colonel Qadhafi."

"Do we know him?"

"Your people in London do."

"Then we already have him under our thumb."

"How about Jeremy Ashforth, novelist, international TV personality and opinion former?" Patterson moved closer, kept his voice low. "What would you give to have him under your thumb?"

"I should think we might run to twenty-five thousand dollars."

"Make it a cool half million and I'll throw in a couple of British politicians and a candidate for the presidency of the EEC."

"My people would want to see what they're buying first."

Patterson nodded. "No problem," he said. "I can arrange a preview in London, but it's strictly cash on delivery and you have to be there when the switch is made." He smiled and offered his right hand. "Do we have a deal, Viktor?"

"I think we do," Orlov said and shook his outstretched hand.

7.

First National had just opened for business when Coghill walked into the bank with Mace, Whitfield and Quainton in tow. The teller he approached had never seen either a warrant card or a search warrant before and insisted on checking their authenticity with the security guard on duty in the main hall before he agreed to inform the branch manager that a police officer wished to see him. It was also the first time the branch manager had been presented with a search warrant, but he could recognize a legal document when he saw one. Access to the customers' vault, however, was restricted and he was a little unhappy that Coghill wanted the others to be present when Whitfield opened his wife's safety-deposit box. That, plus the fact that Whitfield professed not to have a key and would require the duplicate held by the bank, gave him the excuse he needed to ring the head office and seek advice. Once he'd obtained their permission, there were no further problems; Whitfield signed for the duplicate key and the chief cashier, accompanied by a beefy security guard, escorted them down to the customers' vault.

The vault was protected by a reinforced steel door and a time lock that had been opened at nine-thirty. Subdivided by vertical steel bars set close together, the nearer of the two cages was adequately furnished with chromium-plated, tubular steel chairs and tables for the benefit of the customers. Beyond the second gate, the safety-deposit boxes were stacked from floor to ceiling on three sides of the room, each one locked into the frame like a miniature drawer in a giant-sized filing cabinet. The chief cashier handed the authorization slip to the security man in charge of the inner strong room, waited until he had delivered the correct box to Whitfield, then left them to it.

The steel box was two foot six inches long by six inches wide and was a treasure trove of five-, ten-, twenty- and fifty-pound notes bundled neatly together with elastic bands. Beneath the currency was a small address book indexed from A to Z.

"There must be all of ten grand there," Mace said, eyeing the money piled on the table.

"Better count it, Harry," Coghill said. "And while you're at it, check the serial numbers to see if any of them run in sequence. List those that do and we'll see if we can't trace the notes right down to the cashier who paid them over."

Coghill pulled out a chair and sat down to examine the address book. There were no names inside, only code words, like *Rabbit*, *Weasel*, *Stoat* and *Boar*. Each entry resembled a bank statement, with regular payments deducted from a debit figure at the top right-hand side of the page. In some cases, the client had obviously paid off the "overdraft" and a diagonal line had been drawn through the column of figures to show the account had been rendered in full. Under the code words, a series of letters indicated the sexual foibles of the clients. Having served with the Obscene Publications Squad earlier in his career, Coghill knew what the letters *D*, *CP*, *B*, *O*, *GS* and *AC/DC* stood for.

"AC/DC," he said abruptly; "is that where you come into the picture, Trevor?"

Whitfield turned a delicate shade of pink and reared back as though he'd just touched a live wire and received a nasty shock in the process. "What the hell are you implying? That I'm gay?"

"Are you?"

"For Christ's sake, I married Karen, didn't I?"

The indignation was there, but it lacked conviction. First impressions were often misleading, and because a man looked effeminate, it didn't necessarily follow that he had homosexual tendencies, but in Whitfield's case, Coghill believed he was the exception who proved the rule. It could be that this latent streak was the reason why Karen had taken up with him in the first place. Perhaps in the young ex-university graduate she had sensed that here was somebody who, for monetary gain, would be prepared to accommodate the bisexual tastes peculiar to certain of her clients.

"There's such a thing as libel by inference, Inspector," Quainton observed snidely.

"And you think your client should sue me?"

"Good heavens, no. What on earth gave you that idea?"

"I thought you just did," Coghill said.

He flipped through the address book again, noting that a dozen or so entries had a phone number listed under the code word. They were obviously the small fry; the bigger fish were not in the directory and had started out with large "overdrafts." Various hieroglyphics suggested that Karen Whitfield had taken a leaf out of the *Michelin Guide* and invented symbols to compile a potted history on each client, but their significance was not readily apparent. He went through the five pages allocated to the first letter of the alphabet, looked for a symbol that would describe Jeremy Ashforth and found a quill and a small box. He also saw that Ashforth's tastes for bondage, corporal punishment and oral sex had landed him with a debit balance of twelve thousand pounds, a little under half of which had been repaid before Karen Whitfield was murdered.

"I wasn't far off," Mace said. "The exact total is nine thousand eight hundred and seventy-five."

Coghill looked up. "How about the serial numbers?"

"I made a note of them as I went along. Roughly fifteen percent of the total cash is in sequence."

"Good. That should give us something to work on."

"Not so good," Mace said. "A fair number of the fivers are brand new and, in many cases, the withdrawal was less than a hundred pounds. Chances are those sums were drawn from a cash point, and tracing them back to a particular customer could be a mite difficult for the bank."

"So how many series do you think were actually passed across the counter?"

"Eight at the most."

"Well, that's better than nothing. Do you feel like doing some more addition?"

"Do I have any choice, Guv?"

"Not a lot," said Coghill. "Make a note of these figures—850, 2300, 12,000, 1750, 5000..."

He called out the opening debit balance at the top of each page, reached the *J*'s, then paused, his eyes drawn to the symbols below the code word *Miranda:* a palm tree, an oil derrick, two stars and a crown. The desert, oil and a full colonel? Libya? Colonel Qadhafi? No, that couldn't be right; Qadhafi hadn't set foot in London and, according to the letter code, this character was a transvestite who enjoyed corporal punishment and being sodomized by a woman equipped with a dildo. He stared at the hyphen between the oil derrick and the badges of rank and wondered if this was meant to show the client was related to Qadhafi.

A discreet cough from Mace ended the speculation and he continued to read out the debit figures right through to the end page. Then he told Mace to start adding and browsed through the address book again, recording Ashforth's details and such telephone numbers as were listed on a separate sheet of notepaper, while he waited for the grand total.

"I make it a hundred and eighty-five thousand," Mace finally announced.

"Well, well." Coghill leaned back in the chair and smiled bleakly at Quainton. "That's some inheritance."

"What?"

"You told me Karen was able to find the deposit on the shop in Fulham because her parents had left her a large house in Tonbridge which she'd sold at a considerable profit."

"Yes, that's what I was led to believe." Quainton cleared his throat noisily. "I'd no reason to think she was lying. One has to take a certain amount of information on trust."

"I doubt if the Fraud Squad will have much difficulty linking this blackmail racket to Karen Boutiques Limited."

"I'm sure you're right, but I can't see how that should concern me. I've never had anything to do with the company."

Coghill raised a quizzical eyebrow and turned to Whitfield. "I guess that leaves you holding the dirty end of the stick, Trevor."

"Me?"

"You're the sole surviving director."

"I thought . . ." Whitfield swallowed nervously and tried again. "I thought it had been agreed you wouldn't press charges."

"We were talking about blackmail and living on the immoral earnings of a prostitute," Coghill reminded him. "Nobody said anything about offenses under the Companies Acts."

"That's not what you gave me to understand, is it, Stanley?"

"You couldn't have been listening properly," Quainton said.

"You told me I had nothing to lose and everything to gain if I was completely frank about Karen's affairs." Whitfield shook his head. "That's some advice I'm paying for," he said bitterly.

"Well, obviously you weren't frank enough," Quainton observed coldly.

"It's not too late to get out from under, Trevor." Coghill passed the address book across the table. "There are half a dozen clients listed in there who are AC/DC. You put a name to them and we'll forget about any funny business with the company."

"I've told you before, I'm not gay."

"Maybe you didn't have much choice." Coghill lowered his voice so that the security guard in the adjoining strong room shouldn't overhear. "You were a graduate just down from university, but the business world didn't want to know and the only job you could get at the time was with some potty, little backstreet travel agency. They didn't pay you enough to keep body and soul together, but one day you happened to meet this girl, Karen, and she seemed to like you. I think she could see you were having a hard time and she slipped you some pocket money. Then, later on, when you got to know her better and things were still as difficult as ever, she told you how you could make a little extra on the side and you sort of went along with the idea as a favor to her. Isn't that how it was, Trevor?"

There was a long pause. As usual when he was under stress, Whitfield raised a hand to his mouth and nibbled at the thumb for comfort. Finally, like a man closeted with a priest in a confessional, he felt compelled to tell the whole sorry story and somehow justify himself in the process. Much of what he said was pure hocus-pocus, but Coghill waited patiently for the inevitable crunch point and allowed him to ramble on in a breathless voice.

"Gervase, Dudley, Joshua, Lawrence," Whitfield said. "I only know their first names, except for Harold Egremont."

"What does he do for a living?"

"Egremont's retired now, but he used to be a bigwig in the Ministry of Ag and Fish, or so he told Karen. I think he lives in Guildford."

"Can't you be more specific?"

Whitfield frowned and made a great show of racking his brains. "I'd like to be more helpful, really I would, but it all happened such a long time ago."

One name, one very incomplete address; Coghill could have wished for more, but he guessed it was all he was going to get. Turning to Mace, he said, "I think that about wraps it up, Harry. You'd better take the Volvo and run our friend back to Wimbledon. I'll cadge a lift from Kingman after the conference."

"Right."

"When you've done that, go and see the exchange supervisor and ask her to check these numbers out." He leaned forward, passed the sheet of notepaper to Mace. "I want the names and addresses of the subscribers."

"A question," Quainton said. "When can my client expect to take possession of the safety-deposit box?"

"I'm impounding the address book. The cash stays where it is until the Fraud Squad has examined the accounts."

"That's what I thought you'd say." Quainton pushed his chair back and stood up. "I assume I'm no longer required?"

Coghill nodded, said he was free to go and thanked him for his help. Quainton said it had been a pleasure, but made no effort to sound as though he meant it.

Patterson left the Métro at St. Michel and headed toward the Quai de Montebello and the bookstalls on the Left Bank. Although, on Orlov's instructions, he had phoned Trinité 001764 earlier that morning, he hadn't expected anything to come of it. Nothing was ever straightforward when the KGB was involved, and he'd figured they would spend several days figuring out all the angles before giving him a definite yes or no. But instead of the usual stall, Moscow had evidently given Orlov the green light, and he found their prompt response vaguely disquieting.

Some Russians you could trust, but not the faceless men in Dzerzhinsky Square; they would send their own mothers to the Gulag Archipelago if it suited their purpose. Maybe they were planning to double-cross him? After all, why should anybody pay good money for the video tapes when, with a little forethought, they could get them for nothing? The cassettes weren't the only negotiable items either; both the CIA and the FBI would like to lay their hands on him. Patterson supposed he could walk away, forget the whole deal and be safe, but there was a cool half million at stake and nobody ever got rich without taking a few chances along the way.

Patterson stopped at the first bookstall, scanned the crowded shelves as though looking for a specific title among the second-hand books and old magazines on display, then moved on to the next kiosk. In no apparent hurry, he drifted from vending stall to vending stall, checking every now and again to make sure no one was following him. Approaching E. J. Vannier et Fils as casually as he had the other curbside traders, he searched the shelves for the book he'd been told to buy. Spotting it between old copies of *Paris Match*, Patterson asked the elderly woman behind the counter for the only copy she had of Jean Moulin's *Premier Combat*. The purchase made, he then crossed the Pont de l'Arche Vêché, turned into the Esplanade Notre Dame and sat down on a park bench.

The paperback, published by Les Éditions de Minute, was a factual account of the Resistance Movement in Chartres during World War II, with a preface by Charles de Gaulle. According to the inscription on the flyleaf, the book at one time had belonged to a Denise Rousell of 116 Avenue de la Libération in Nice. The telephone number of the contact in London was disguised in the postal code.

Patterson thought there could only be two reasons why the contact number had been passed to him in such a complicated fashion. Either the KGB had wanted Denise Rousell to have a good look at him before they eventually met in London, or else one of their photographers had been quietly taking his picture from among the crowd of tourists aiming their cameras at Notre Dame. The latter possibility was certainly ominous, but he doubted if Moscow would sell him out before the video tapes were in their possession. Nevertheless, it was better to be safe than sorry. He had traveled to Paris on a Canadian passport under the name of Pearce, and the hotel registration slip he'd completed on arrival would now have been collected by the local police and lodged in the Panthéon. To cover his tracks, he would catch the first available flight to Munich, collect one of the duplicates from the deed box he'd deposited with the Dresdener Bank and return to England as Herr Otto Prole, sales representative for I. G. Farben.

The conference was held in Franklin's office on the eighth floor. It was chaired by the deputy assistant commissioner (crime), but apart from introducing Detective Chief Superintendent Tucker from the Regional Crime Squad, he left it to Charlie Franklin to go through the agenda.

Rowntree, the burly Yorkshireman from S District, led off and gave a lucid account of the Leese investigation to date which, it transpired, had made some progress. The postmortem had placed the time of death between eleven A.M. and five P.M. on Wednesday, the thirtieth of June, approximately twenty-four hours after Karen Whitfield had been murdered. The pathologist had found two entry wounds but only one exit, which accounted for the fact that only the fragments of one soft-nose bullet impacted on the floor had been recovered from the scene of the crime. The second bullet had been deflected into the lower jaw and was lodged behind the left incisor. Although its shape had been distorted, Ballistics had identified it as a .22 caliber rimfire. Finally, British Airways had confirmed that Leese had been a passenger on Flight 228 from Amsterdam arriving Heathrow at nine A.M. on the day in question, and one of the neighbors in Brompton Mews had supplied a vague description of a man who'd been seen leaving the mews flat at approximately eleven-thirty.

"It would take Leese the best part of an hour to get to his flat from Heathrow." Tucker sucked his teeth, then said, "This visitor was pretty quick off the mark, wasn't he?"

Rowntree shrugged. "It could just be he was lucky to find him at home."

"I don't believe chance has anything to do with it. This murder has all the hallmarks of a professional hit and it's reasonable to assume the killer arranged to have the flat kept under surveillance."

"We've questioned all the residents and they don't remember seeing anybody loitering in the neighborhood." The Yorkshireman glared at Tucker, his jaw set and bristling like a bulldog. "Furthermore, on-street parking is not allowed in Brompton Mews and the surrounding area is regularly patrolled by traffic wardens."

"I was referring to electronic surveillance, Superintendent."

Tucker was cool and disdainful. No two men could have been less alike: Rowntree the epitome of the gruff, hard-nosed detective, the other slim, distinguished-looking and easily mistaken for a Foreign Office diplomat in a well-cut suit that fitted him perfectly. It was obvious to Coghill that there was no love lost between them, and he wondered if they had crossed swords at some time in the past or whether they had simply taken an instant dislike to one another.

"You mean the place was bugged," Rowntree said in a flat voice.

"I think so."

"There was no sign of forcible entry."

"So what? The device was probably outside the flat, attached to the wall under the window ledge."

"We went through the flat with a fine-tooth comb, inside and out. And you know something, Chief Superintendent? We didn't find a bloody thing that bore the slightest resemblance to a bug."

The atmosphere was explosive. Franklin clucked his tongue, then glanced pointedly at the deputy assistant commissioner. Oblivious to what was going on around him, Kingman continued to doodle away in the notebook he was balancing on his knee. Out of the corner of his eye, Coghill watched him draw a large mushroom-shaped cloud.

"I suppose there's no harm in going over the place again," Franklin murmured.

"Provided it's done with a fresh eye."

The deputy assistant commissioner smiled at the girl from the typing pool who was recording the minutes of the meeting, and told her he was of course referring to the Regional Crime Squad. Having settled that point, he then asked who was going to bring them up to date on the Whitfield case.

"I think Tom should," Kingman said. "You'd only get it secondhand from me."

"Where would you like me to begin?" Coghill asked.

"With the safety-deposit box," Tucker said curtly.

"We found it contained nine thousand eight hundred and seventy-five pounds in cash." Coghill reached into his jacket pocket and brought out the address book. "In here are the code names of thirty-seven clients from whom Karen Whitfield was planning to collect close to two hundred thousand. Eleven of these can be eliminated, because they paid her off and presumably recovered the incriminating material she was holding on them. Moneywise, at least twelve among the remaining twenty-six are considerably better off now that she's dead, but this could be misleading. It's possible the man we're looking for had an entirely different motive."

"Like what?"

"Well, he could be a VIP who would be thrown out of office or compelled to resign if the seamy side of his life-style got into the newspapers."

"It's an interesting theory, Inspector, but can you prove it?"

"I think so. There are various symbols below each entry which suggest Karen Whitfield used a form of shorthand to describe her clients. It's not the easiest of ciphers to crack, but the hall porter at Abercorn House gave me a name and it checked out."

"Oh yes? What was the name?"

"Ashforth," Coghill said, "Jeremy Ashforth. He's represented by a quill and a box which I took to be a TV screen."

Tucker raised a sceptical eyebrow, asked to see the address book and spent some minutes browsing through it.

"We could waste a lot of time trying to unravel this code." He looked up, a bleak smile creasing his mouth. "What does Whitfield have to say about it?"

"Nothing," said Coghill. "He'd never seen the address book until this morning."

"That's his story, but we know different, don't we?"

"I'm inclined to believe him. I'm not saying he didn't have a shrewd idea what his wife was up to, but he's the sort of weak character who'd prefer to let sleeping dogs lie."

"Then we'll just have to lean on him a bit harder."

"I made a deal with him," Coghill said quietly.

"You'd no right to do that, Inspector."

"If I hadn't, he would never have told me about the deposit box."

"Really? Well, if Mr. Whitfield thinks he's in the clear, he's in for a nasty surprise."

"I gave him my word there would be no comeback."

"Your word is no longer relevant," Tucker informed him curtly and then went into a huddle with Franklin and the deputy assistant commissioner.

Coghill felt his face flush with anger; he tried counting up to ten but it had no effect. The rage was still there, expanding like a balloon about to burst. Slowly and very deliberately, Kingman uncrossed his legs and brought a heavy foot to bear on his toes, warning him to cool it. Moments later, the huddle at the top table broke up.

The outcome was exactly on the lines Rowntree had predicted the day before. Tucker was free to pick their brains and they would end up doing most of the work while all the credit went to the Regional Crime Squad. Listening to Franklin as he outlined the division of responsibilities that were to be observed from now on, Coghill also got the impression that somebody high up had decided the investigation should be contained within strictly defined parameters.

8.

Although he was regarded as cold and ruthless by his colleagues, it was generally conceded that Nicholas Vaudrey would be a hard man to replace as head of K Desk, when he retired at the age of sixty in a year's time. A former paratrooper who had taken part in the D-day landings and the Rhine crossing, he had ended the war as a GSO3 (Intelligence) at brigade headquarters and had then deferred his release from the army in order to serve with the 6th Airborne Division in Palestine, where he had worked hand in glove with Special Branch. Demobbed in May 1947, Vaudrey had applied for emergency teacher training at a college in Weymouth, from where he had subsequently obtained a post at St. Edward's English High School at Kuala Lumpur. Barely three months later, following a declaration of a state of emergency by his excellency the governor, he had been back in uniform again, having tendered his resignation to join the Malay Regiment.

One of the first to volunteer for the SAS when the regiment had been reformed in the Far East, he had gained experience in counterinsurgency operations against the Chinese Communists that had led to a permanent regular commission in the Intelligence Corps and a series of similar undercover appointments in Kenya, Cyprus and Aden. Seconded to the Home Office in the wake of the Bogside riots and the reemergence of the IRA, Vaudrey had been an obvious candidate for recruitment when, in 1970, DI5 had been told to establish a special bureau to deal with this new threat.

At the time, nobody had envisaged that he would become the head of K Desk, but it so happened that the officer selected to organize the whole setup had suffered a fatal heart attack only days before the section was due to become operational, and Vaudrey had stepped into his shoes. He brought to the job a wealth of practical experience that few people in DI5 could begin to match, and a shrewd if devious mind. Despite these qualities, however, Vaudrey suffered from an inferiority complex; as the only member of the desk who was not a university graduate, he felt he had to prove his intellectual superiority at every opportunity. Usually, this took the form of a hostile cross-examination whenever one of his subordinates was required to brief him.

Adept at writing comprehensive minutes, Caroline Brooke tried to avoid these face-to-face confrontations whenever possible, but this was one occasion when she couldn't escape. The way the Whitfield case was going, there simply wasn't time to analyze the latest developments in a carefully worded brief. As concisely as she knew how, Caroline told Vaudrey exactly what had transpired at the conference held by the deputy assistant commissioner of police, then sat back to await the inevitable grilling.

"You believe this prostitute was blackmailing Raschid al Jalud," Vaudrey began in a deceptively mild voice.

"Along with Jeremy Ashforth and thirty-five others of a similar ilk."

"Of a similar ilk?" Four deep furrows appeared in his lined forehead. "What precisely do you mean by that, Caroline?"

"Influential people who are vulnerable to pressure and can't afford a public scandal."

"But so far the police only have the one name?"

"I think we have to assume they'll have a lot more by now. There were fourteen telephone numbers listed in the address book and it wouldn't take them more than an hour to get the names and addresses of those subscribers from British Telecommunications."

"Quite."

"And I understand Detective Inspector Coghill virtually told them how to break the cipher."

"Ah yes—Coghill." Vaudrey picked up a long, slim paperknife and toyed with it, slowly tapping the blade on the desk as though setting the measure for a funeral march. "A highflyer, ambitious and intelligent—and a potential source of trouble?"

"That was my assessment," Caroline said cautiously.

"Was?"

"He's no longer in charge of the investigation."

The deepening furrows told her it wasn't the positive assurance Vaudrey was looking for. He wanted to be absolutely certain the police were aware they should refrain from questioning Raschid, but there was no guaranteeing this unless he was prepared to disclose their interest. And even then, it was doubtful if they would agree to leave the Libyan diplomat out of it.

"You also said Coghill was very independent-minded, the sort of man who likes to do things his way?"

"I've never met him, Nicholas, but that's what I was told."

"How do you suppose he would react if he got the impression his superiors were deliberately ignoring certain information?"

"I imagine he would be very angry."

"And?"

Caroline shrugged. "He might be inclined to do something about it."

"How about Tucker? What sort of attitude would he take?"

The cross-examination had started in earnest now, the questions following one on top of the other, his tone of voice much sharper. She also noticed the slow drumbeat had increased in tempo, a sure sign that Vaudrey wouldn't stand for any middle-of-the-road opinion which left him none the wiser. Unfortunately, what the DI5 contact had told her about Tucker could be summed up in a couple of sentences. A good detective with an impressive record who was a long way yet from reaching his ceiling. A bit of a hard taskmaster but smooth as silk with superiors.

"Tucker has an eye for the main chance," she said. "I doubt he'd rock the boat if told to leave Jalud alone."

"Colonel Qadhafi's kinsman is not the only one I'm worried about," Vaudrey said testily. "Excluding Ashforth, there are thirty-five others in that damned address book, any number of whom could be security risks. I'd like to know who they are and what they do before I see their names in the newspapers."

Caroline was about to assure him their contact at the Yard would keep them fully informed, but then remembered Vaudrey already knew that and realized he was after the address book itself.

"We don't want another public scandal."

"Is there any danger of that?" she asked.

"Women like Karen Whitfield appear to exercise a fatal attraction for the rich and famous. I don't know why it is, Caroline, but power and success often seem to foster an urge toward self-destruction."

Vaudrey in a philosophical vein was an alien experience, so out of character that she had no difficulty in recognizing the ulterior motive behind it. Wanting no part of it, she ventured to suggest there was no reason to believe Karen Whitfield had been in contact with a hostile intelligence service.

"Don't act coy with me," Vaudrey snapped. "You're intelligent enough to realize there would be hell to pay if the press discovered she had been a call girl."

"It's no business of ours to protect these men from the consequences of their own stupidity."

"That's where you're wrong. People need to respect their leaders. Show them that their feet are made of clay and pretty soon nobody believes in anybody anymore. Patriotism is replaced by cynicism and apathy and then the rot sets in and there's a lowering of standards all around."

The hypothesis had more holes in it than a colander, but there was no doubting Vaudrey's sincerity. He really believed the nation would be in a far better state if only the media would curb their habit of knocking every pillar of society.

"I want that address book, Caroline. Tell our friend we'll break the code and supply all the details they need."

His intentions were obvious. The information channeled to the Regional Crime Squad would be disseminated on a need-to-know basis and any names that might prove embarrassing would be withheld. Equally disturbing was the fact that Vaudrey expected her to obtain the address book and there was therefore a distinct possibility that her head would be on the chopping block if anything went wrong.

"They'll be reluctant to part with it unless we offer them something in return, Nicholas."

"Like what?" Vaudrey asked.

"We could put them on to Patterson." She watched Vaudrey lay the paperknife aside and then stare at her through narrowed eyes. "We don't have to be specific," she added hastily. "We could say we've had a vague tip-off from a source who has to be protected."

"It won't do, Caroline." Vaudrey shook his head. "Won't do at all. Even if there were strong grounds for thinking Patterson was involved, we can't have the police frightening him off with 'Wanted' posters all over the place. You'll just have to quote the Official Secrets Acts to our friend."

"I don't think that would carry much weight, coming from me." Caroline gave him a disarming smile. "I'm just a senior executive officer. It would be much more impressive if the Official Secrets Acts were quoted by an assistant principal."

"I see. And what do you suggest we do about Coghill? I mean, we don't want any inspired leaks to the press from that quarter, do we?"

"I suppose not," she agreed reluctantly.

"What we need is an early warning system."

"Around Jeremy Ashforth?"

"How right you are," Vaudrey said cheerfully. "Have a word with Surveillance and let me know how soon they can put it into effect."

Caroline nodded dumbly. Somehow Vaudrey had contrived to leave her holding the baby and she had a feeling the infant was about to do something nasty in its nappy.

Mace had his jacket draped over the back of the chair and was sitting next to Ingleson. There was a wad of statements in front of him that had been taken from the residents of St. Mark's Hill and he was going through them, dictating the more significant points to Ingleson, who was entering and cross-referencing the details in the Crime Index. Engrossed in the task, neither man heard Coghill enter the room.

"Anything I should know, Harry?" he asked.

Mace looked up, hurriedly removed the cigarette clinging to his bottom lip and mashed it in the ashtray. "I've got the names and addresses of those subscribers you wanted, Guv." He twisted around, delved into the breast pocket of his jacket and produced a slip of paper. "All of them seem to be nobodies, but obviously they aren't short of a bob or two. I also got the exchange supervisor to run a check on Harold Egremont, the bigwig from the Ministry of Ag and Fish that Whitfield told us about. There's a G.W.H. Egremont listed in the Surrey Directory who lives in Alexandra Avenue on the outskirts of Guildford. He could be the one we're looking for, although I'd have expected him to be unlisted."

"There can't be too many Egremonts in this world, Harry." Coghill took the slip of paper from him, walked over to the open window and perched himself on the ledge. "Not that it's our problem any more."

"The Regional Crime Squad," Mace said in a flat voice.

"Right. It's their province now."

Coghill explored the roof of his mouth with a furry tongue and found that it too was tacky. Kingman had insisted they stop off at the Grape Vine for a quick one on the way back from the conference, but it hadn't stopped there. Safe in the knowledge that he had an official car complete with driver, Bert had put away four large gin and tonics and had plied him with almost as many, ostensibly to drown his sorrows. The lunchtime session hadn't affected Kingman, but it had left Coghill with a muzzy head and a strong inclination to find a quiet corner where he could curl up and sleep it off.

"What are we left with then?" Mace asked him.

"The prime suspect, our moon-faced man." Coghill stifled a yawn. "We made any progress in that area?"

"Maybe. We have a statement from a Mrs. Underwood who thought she saw somebody like our suspect driving a BMW. The car came down the hill past the Whitfield house, then came back up again a few minutes later and had to swerve and make an emergency stop to avoid her Pekinese when it ran out into the road. The driver gave Mrs. Underwood a right mouthful, called her a goddamned stupid bitch."

"He had an American accent?"

"Or a Canadian one," Mace said.

"I don't suppose she took the registration number?"

"No, but somebody else did. Right, Fred?"

Ingleson nodded and pulled a card from the Crime Index. "A young lad by the name of Christopher Youens at Number 26. He's educationally subnormal, lives at home and spends a large part of the day upstairs in his room looking out of the window. Cars are an obsession with him and he's quite an expert on them. Anyway, he has this notebook in which he records the license number, make and type of every vehicle he sees. According to him, the vehicle in question is a 1978 BMW 300, license number NVY 241R."

"Is he a reliable witness?" Coghill asked.

"Well, like I said, he's something of a car buff. For instance, he told the constable who interviewed him that the BMW was first registered in York, which, of course, is plumb right. Then too, Mrs. Underwood couldn't remember exactly when this incident with her dog had occurred, but young Christopher is positive it happened on Monday, the twenty-first of June, and there's an entry in his notebook to prove it. He also claims he saw the BMW again two days later, around eleven-thirty in the morning, but I wouldn't rely on that being a hundred percent correct. According to his mother, Christopher is apt to embroider the facts when he's the center of attention. What he doesn't know, he makes up."

"The twenty-first of June, a week ago last Monday." Mace scratched his chin. "You know something, Guv? That was the last time Nolan remembered seeing Karen Whitfield at Abercorn House. Maybe this guy followed her back to Wimbledon?"

"Maybe's the operative word, Harry. Have we requested a trace from the Central Licensing Authority yet?"

Ingleson started to tell him he was expecting a call from Swansea, then one of the two emergency phones on the table rang out and he broke off to answer it. Grabbing a pencil, he made a few notes on a scratch pad, thanked the caller for being so helpful and hung up.

"It seems the vehicle had one previous owner," Ingleson said, interpreting his own original form of shorthand. "He traded it in for a new model with S. V. Motors toward the end of April this year. S. V. Motors is the main BMW agent in the UK and six weeks later, its branch in Hampstead sold the car to a Mr. Oscar Pittis of 192 Southwood Road, Highgate."

"That's where we start, then." Coghill pushed himself off the ledge and stood up. "Grab your coat, Harry, and bring one of the Identikit pictures with you."

"Who's driving?"

"You are," said Coghill. "You've still got the keys to the Volvo."

192 Southwood Road was near the top of Highgate Hill and within easy walking distance of the village green. A large, three-story detached house, it had been converted into six self-contained flats, two on each floor. Beyond a tall privet hedge, a tiled path led to an old-fashioned door with a stained-glass window in the transom which depicted the sun rising into a cloudless blue sky. Glancing at the wooden panel fixed to the wall on the left side of the door, Coghill saw that a Mr. O. Pittis occupied flat number 3 and pressed the appropriate button. The bell produced no response other than a regular tapping noise somewhere behind him and, half turning in that direction, he saw the net curtain in one of the downstairs bay windows had been drawn aside and a white-haired old lady was smiling at him. Quickly eyeing the list of names on the panel again, he returned her smile.

"Mrs. Hayden?" he said in a voice loud enough for her to hear, and got an answering nod. "We're police officers."

The smile became even wider and was followed by several more nods; then the net curtain fell back into place and she moved away from the window. A few moments later, a sharp buzz told him the lock had been tripped and, pushing the door open, he stepped into the hall.

Mrs. Hayden was there to greet them, a plump woman with apple-red cheeks who Coghill thought was altogether far too trusting, especially since she scarcely glanced at their warrant cards before inviting them in for a cup of tea. Nothing he said appeared to register with her, either; still beaming, she showed them into the living room and left them alone while she bustled off to the kitchen to put a kettle on the gas.

The living room was chockablock with heavy Victorian furniture, potted plants and old photographs in silver frames along the mantelpiece and on top of the upright piano abutting the dividing wall. A large black cat was stretched out in the middle of the sofa and an equally fat tabby occupied the seat of one of the two armchairs on either side of the fireplace.

"Jesus," Mace said in an awed voice, "you'd have to go some before you found another room like this."

"It is cozy, isn't it?" Mrs. Hayden said behind him. "Do please sit down and make yourselves comfortable."

With only a limited amount of space available on the sofa, they weren't exactly spoiled for choice. Somewhat apprehensively, Mace sat down on one side of the supine cat, Coghill the other.

"You mustn't be nervous of old Hector," Mrs. Hayden told him. "He's ever so friendly."

"I like cats," Mace said, a touch defiant. To prove it, he put out a hand to stroke the tomcat; just to show his appreciation, good old friendly Hector gave a low yowl and bit his thumb.

"Oh dear," Mrs. Hayden said. "I can't think what's come over Hector; usually he's very passive."

"About Mr. Pittis?" Coghill reminded her gently.

"Yes, indeed, the nice gentleman in number three. I was ever so sorry to see him leave, he always had a kind word for me."

"You mean Mr. Pittis is no longer living here?"

"He moved out yesterday morning, packed his suitcase and went—just like that. Apparently, his head office recalled him to Vancouver. Perhaps that's why he didn't bother to leave a forwarding address."

"Do I gather Mr. Pittis is a Canadian?" Mace asked, chipping in.

"Yes. How silly of me, I should have mentioned it before. Mind you, his accent was hardly noticeable, and he was very surprised when I asked him where he came from. Said I was the only person he'd met who'd guessed he wasn't British, but you see I've got a very sharp ear for dialects. I used to give elocution lessons, you know."

"Really?"

"Correct me if I'm wrong, Sergeant, but I believe you were born in Fulham."

"You're absolutely right," said Mace.

"You see, I'm never wrong." She clapped her hands and rocked backward and forward in the chair, thoroughly pleased with herself.

Coghill said he was very impressed, invited her to say where she thought he came from, then, after she'd informed him that he'd been born in Nottingham but had been living in the London area for some years now, steered the conversation back to Pittis.

"We understand he owns a BMW, license number NVY 241R?"

"That explains it."

"What?"

"Why you want to see Mr. Pittis. He was involved in a traffic accident, wasn't he?"

"You must be psychic, too," Coghill said smiling.

"I knew there was something fishy," she said gleefully. "No one in his right mind would sell a beautiful car like that to buy an old white Mini. And the way he parked it down the hill made me even more suspicious. Carrying those heavy suitcases all that distance when he could have left the car right outside the house just didn't make sense."

"If the Mini was down the hill, how could you see it from this room?" Mace asked.

"I waited until he'd gone, then went out to the front gate. That's how, young man."

"I don't suppose you happened to see the license number?" Coghill smiled. "Not that we'd expect you to remember it."

There was a momentary hesitation and he recalled what Ingleson had said of Christopher Youens and wondered if she too would be tempted to embroider the facts, but in the end, she shook her head.

"I'm afraid my eyesight is not as good as it used to be."

"There's nothing wrong with your memory though, is there?" Coghill said gently. "I mean you'd remember a face and describe it more accurately than most people."

Mace reached inside his jacket, unfolded a photocopy of the Identikit likeness and passed it to her. "This is only one of the descriptions we've been given," he said.

"Goodness me." She held the picture at arm's length and studied it thoughtfully. "I suppose there is a slight resemblance, but Mr. Pittis was much better-looking."

"According to various witnesses, his height is between five foot seven and five eleven."

"Ridiculous. He was five foot nine, the same as my late husband."

Pittis also had hazel-colored eyes, brown hair parted on the left, a round, almost cherublike face and an infectious smile. Amiable was a word Mrs. Hayden used time and again to describe his character.

"I wish everyone was like you," Coghill said. "It would make our job so much easier."

"People aren't as observant as they were when I was a young woman. I suppose it has something to do with the pace of life these days." A shrill whistle from the kitchen interrupted her philosophizing. "That's the kettle boiling," she said and glanced at Coghill, a pleading look in her eyes. "You will stay and have some tea, won't you?"

They had better things to do with their time, but she was a lonely old woman with only two overfed cats for company, and they owed her something.

"I could use a cup of tea," Coghill said and smiled.

Six-thirty: Kingman figured it was time he called it a day and went home to Alice. Truth was he could have left the office at four had he been prepared to run the risk of provoking yet another bitter row. Alice was still angry that their fortnight's holiday in Majorca had been ruined, so it was only politic to give her the impression he was snowed under. He stood up, slipped on the jacket he'd draped over the chair, then swore as the phone chose that very moment to start trilling. Answering the call, he found he had Franklin on the line.

"I've not caught you at an inopportune moment, have I, Bert?" he asked.

"Of course you haven't." He had, but it wasn't advisable to say so. Even though they had known one another for years, Franklin was the area commander and a certain amount of diplomacy was called for.

"If there's somebody with you, Bert, I can always call back later."

"I'm on my own," Kingman told him.

"Good. As it happens, I wanted to have a word with you about Tom Coghill and it would have been a little embarrassing for both of us if he'd been there."

"What's on your mind, Charlie?" Kingman said, cutting him short.

"Well, as you know, I'm not one to interfere, but the Whitfield investigation is drawing a lot of flak from various quarters and everybody up here is walking around on eggshells."

"And Tom is not the most tactful of men?"

"Right. There are a number of people in the Home Office who would like to see him taken off the case. I said that might be a little difficult to arrange without arousing his suspicion."

"I don't see any problem, Charlie."

"You don't?"

"Hell no. The crime rate in Wimbledon is one of the highest in London. Every burglar knows there are rich pickings to be had in that area."

"Yes, but can you sell it to Coghill? He's never been on a murder case before and, in his shoes, I'd raise all kinds of hell."

"Don't you worry, Charlie, I'll handle him with kid gloves."

"Splendid. I knew I could rely on you." Franklin sounded vastly relieved. "Believe me, Bert, I shan't forget this favor in a hurry," he added, and then put the phone down.

"You can bet your sweet life you won't," Kingman said aloud. "Not as long as I'm around to remind you."

9.

Coghill left the Volvo in the security compound behind V District headquarters, walked around to the front entrance of the building and took the lift up to Kingman's office on the second floor. It was Kingman's habit on a Saturday morning to go through the unsolved case load with his deputy and review what progress had been made during the week. Usually this took place around nine-thirty, but late the previous evening, he'd phoned Coghill at home to inform him they'd be meeting on the dot of eight because he was hoping to whisk Alice off to Bournemouth for the weekend. Despite the formidable number of files piled on his desk, the gabardine slacks and tan-colored shirt he was wearing were two obvious signs he intended to do just that.

"Doesn't look too good, does it, Tom?" Kingman waved a hand at the crowded filing trays. "We're about top of the league for unsolved crimes and the top brass are making unfavorable comparisons. I've got Charlie Franklin on my back and I want him off. Now, as I see it, robbing Peter to pay Paul is about the only way we'll make any impression on this backlog."

"So?"

"So I've been looking at the number of officers committed to the Whitfield investigation and wondering if we can't shed a few?"

"I'd be reluctant to lose anyone just now," Coghill said.

"Because of this man Oscar Pittis?"

"Well, there are a couple of fairly good reasons for thinking he might have been involved. His BMW was observed in St. Mark's Hill on one, possibly two occasions. Then there's the fact that he sold the car and cleared out of the flat in Southwood

Road the day after Leese was murdered."

"He didn't leave a forwarding address either," Kingman mused.

"Not according to Mrs. Hayden. We tried to contact the estate agent yesterday evening to see if he could shed any light on him, but the office was closed. Mace is going there this morning to have a look at the lease Pittis signed and ascertain exactly when he did move into the flat. I've also arranged for an artist to call on Mrs. Hayden; with her help, I think we can produce a better likeness than the present Identikit picture. We'll photocopy the finished effort and show it to the residents of St. Mark's Hill. I thought we'd ask S District to do the same with Brompton Mews."

"You'd better channel it through the Regional Crime Squad," Kingman said. "They're running the show now."

"Does that mean we literally have to refer every worthwhile piece of information to Tucker before we can follow it up?"

Kingman studied him thoughtfully for some moments, then said, "What's behind that question, Tom? Are you on to something?"

"Not yet, but we will be when the new owner of the BMW contacts the Central Licensing Authority."

The abrupt departure suggested that Pittis wouldn't have had time to advertise the car and had therefore probably sold it at a loss to some garage, rather than a private motorist. In either case, the new address would indicate roughly where the transaction had taken place, and from that starting point, there was a chance they would be able to trace his subsequent movements, perhaps even to the dealer from whom he'd bought the secondhand Mini. It would take a lot of time and effort, and from the sour expression on Kingman's face, Coghill knew he'd already calculated what the task would involve in terms of manpower.

"The same rule applies, Tom. As soon as you hear anything from Swansea, pass the details straight to the Regional Crime Squad."

"Well, if that's the way it's going to be, I suppose we could afford to release some officers from the investigation."

"Good," said Kingman, "I'm glad we see eye to eye. Mace,

Ingleson and a DC can handle it from now on. Naturally, you and I will keep a finger on the pulse in between dealing with this little lot."

Kingman picked up a bundle of files and in a few clipped sentences summarized each case in turn. Nothing he said was new, but no salesman could have put it across better. Most of the burglaries he referred to had been committed in broad daylight on the spur of the moment by tearaways who'd noticed a house was unoccupied and had taken anything to hand. More often than not, the haul had not come up to their expectations and the burglars had then vented their frustration on anything to hand, vandalizing furniture and fittings. At the other end of the scale was a gang of thieves who did their homework well in advance, knew who were the most affluent residents in Wimbledon and had visited a large number of them. The amateurs were probably local unemployed teenagers who would go to the well once too often and get caught in the process; the professionals came from another patch and were likely to be in business for a long time unless somebody shopped them out of spite.

"It's the villains who work the upper end of the market that I want to see behind bars," Kingman said, winding up.

"Right."

"You know what to do then."

Coghill nodded. "We lean on our snouts and give the fences a hard time."

"That's the style." Kingman pushed his chair back and stood up. "It's all yours, Tom," he said, indicating the files with the wave of a hand.

There was, Coghill thought, enough there to keep him fully occupied for the best part of a month and maybe, just maybe, that was the whole idea.

The address book had been forwarded in a double envelope, the outer one addressed to The Secretary, P.O. Box 650, the inner marked "For attention Head of K Desk" and franked "Discreet handling, officer to officer." It had reached Vaudrey late on Friday afternoon and he had passed it on to Caroline Brooke with a brief note instructing her to take appropriate action soonest. The word *soonest* had been underlined twice and he had added a postscript to the effect that, if possible, the task should be completed by 11:00 A.M. the following day.

Interpreting the symbols had been child's play, but it had been a time-consuming and often irritating business to discover the identity of the person referred to by a code name. *Who's Who, Kelly's Trade Directory, Whitaker's Almanack*, the Bar List and other official registers had proved valuable aids when the subject's occupation and interests had been adequately described, but at the end of the day, there had remained a hard core of six who were still without a name.

A painstaking review early that morning had led nowhere and she had been left with several possible names for the recalcitrant half-dozen. However, none of these men were public figures of any account, a factor that had persuaded Caroline that further research would be a waste of time. As it was, the final list that she presented to Vaudrey would never have gotten past the supervisor had one of the girls in the typing pool produced it, but, as she was quick to point out, it was the content that mattered, not the appearance.

"I see you were right about Raschid al Jalud." Vaudrey looked up scowling. "The question is, does Coghill know he's on the list?"

"He may have guessed the entry referred to a Libyan from the various symbols, but it's unlikely he could identify him without access to the *Diplomatic Blue Book* and that's not issued to police districts."

Vaudrey nodded, bent over the typewritten list again and studied it carefully, the lines on his forehead becoming more pronounced with every passing minute. "Two life peers, three members of Parliament, including a former junior minister in the last Labour government, a senior civil servant from the Ministry of Agriculture and Fisheries, the secretary of the Havelock Committee appointed to review the organization of the security services, a merchant banker . . . My God, how did she get to meet these people?"

"Who knows? Perhaps one man put her in touch with the next?"

"Members of the same club, are they?"

"Club?" she repeated in a small voice.

"Brooks's, White's, The Athenaeum, the Reform or whatever."

"I haven't the faintest idea. You merely told me to break the code."

"You're an intelligent young woman," Vaudrey said. "It should have occurred to you that there had to be some common denominator between these top people." A wintry smile made a brief appearance. "Excluding Karen Whitfield, of course."

"You want me to find a connecting link?"

"I'm surprised you should ask."

There was, Caroline thought, no answer to that. A stupid question had drawn the kind of acid retort it deserved and Nicholas had been unable to resist a golden opportunity to deflate her. She waited guardedly for the next barb, but Vaudrey merely uncapped his fountain pen and went through the list yet again, making the odd tick in the margin as he hummed tunelessly to himself. The only other sound in the room came from the Westminster chiming clock on top of the bookcase.

"When do you want this brief, Nicholas?"

"The sooner the better," he said without looking up.

"Then hadn't I better get on with it?"

"Just hold on a minute." Vaudrey turned a page over and added a few more ticks before handing her the list. "I'd like you to type out the names I've indicated and send them on to Scotland Yard with a short covering letter. You can say that, as yet, we haven't succeeded in identifying the remainder, but they will follow in due course. Keep it vague and make some excuse about how difficult it is to find a logical pattern in a one-time personal code. They'll understand."

"I'm sure they will." Caroline stood up. "Meantime, I presume we'll hang on to the address book?"

"Naturally." Vaudrey waited until she was halfway to the door, then said, "Incidentally, what are your plans for tomorrow? Are you free around lunchtime?"

"More or less. There are one or two personal chores I should attend to, but nothing vital."

"Good. Shall we say my flat, twelve noon? There's a rather nice American I'd like you to meet."

Caroline nodded and, resisting the temptation to slam the door behind her, returned to her own office down the corridor. Still seething at the way Vaudrey had involved her in a conspiracy to withhold information, she sat down at the typewriter and began to peck out the list of names, venting her anger on the keys as she did so.

Mace had met all kinds of landlords during the course of his work, but he especially despised those like the owners of 192 Southwood Road whose property company was registered in the Bahamas for tax purposes. Within minutes of meeting Mr. Alec Gordonston, he had also developed a strong aversion toward their local agent. A dapper, black-haired little man in his early thirties, with a military mustache and an overinflated opinion of himself, Gordonston had been extremely reticent about the business affairs of his clients and equally reluctant to produce a copy of the lease Pittis had signed, until Mace intimated that, if necessary, he could always return that afternoon armed with a search warrant. The implied threat to his leisure time had had a marked effect on Gordonston, who thereafter had bent over backward to be helpful, furnishing not only the agreement but also a key to the flat before Mace got round to asking for it.

The flat was ultramodern, from the fitted kitchen with breakfast bar, built-in refrigerator, dishwasher and eye-level grill to the fully tiled bathroom with its shower stall, bidet, pedestal wash-basin and sunken bath. The lounge was a contrast in black and white: white carpet, white walls, white velvet drapes, black vinyl three-piece suite and an occasional table with what appeared at first sight to be a black marble top, but on closer inspection turned out to be a plastic imitation. It was the same with the dining room, where the pieces of furniture were plainly cheap copies.

"A bit different from the flat below," Mace observed.

"You mean the one Mrs. Hayden is occupying?" Gordonston wrinkled his nose. "Well, of course, she was a sitting tenant when the present owners acquired the property."

"What about the other tenants? Weren't they protected by the Rent Act?"

"They were much younger than Mrs. Hayden and we made them a generous offer."

I bet you did, Mace thought. You probably dangled just enough for them to find the deposit on a flat of their own and offered to arrange a mortgage to cover the rest of the purchase price if the building societies turned them down.

"What did you say the rent was on these flats?"

"One hundred and ten pounds a week in the winter, but they rise to a hundred and seventy-five from June through to September."

"I'd be surprised if they didn't," Mace said wryly.

The rents were bound to go up during those months; it was the peak holiday period and the property company would be anxious to cream their share of the foreign tourists visiting London. It explained why no lease ran for more than six months and he could see why, with so many people coming and going, a man who wanted to remain anonymous would find that advantageous. Except Pittis had reckoned without Mrs. Hayden, who must have been the bane of his life as well as that of the estate agents who'd done their level best to get her out of the flat she was occupying.

"And Pittis paid you three months' rent in advance effective from Saturday the fifteenth of May, the date he moved in?"

"Yes."

"Cash or check?"

"Deutschemark traveler's checks from American Express." Gordonston ran a hand over his sleek black hair. "He had a thick wad of them in various denominations from a thousand down to fifties. I think the exchange rate was then about four marks seventeen to the pound. I know I had to give him just over three pounds' change out of the petty cash."

"I'm not a mathematician. How many marks did he give you?"

"Eight thousand seven hundred and fifty. My secretary will have listed the check serial numbers on the deposit slip to the bank." Gordonston followed Mace into the bedroom and looked a trifle pained when he started to go through the wardrobe and chest of drawers. "Is that really necessary?" he asked plaintively.

"Pittis told you he'd only be away for about a month. Right?"

"Yes. He said he had some business to attend to in Dublin and was then going on to Vancouver."

"Doesn't look as though he's coming back, does it?" Mace said. "The wardrobe's empty, so is the chest of drawers. You'd have thought he would have left something behind. Socks, shoes, sweaters, stuff like that."

"I'm sure there's a simple explanation."

"He's done a bunk. What could be simpler than that?"

Mace left the bedroom as it was, drawers open, cupboard doors ajar, and ambled out into the hall and gazed thoughtfully at the pay phone which had been installed in the alcove to the right of the front door. It seemed that Gordonston's employers were not the kind of people who left anything to chance and they had taken steps to insure that none of their erstwhile tenants landed them with an unpaid phone bill.

"Was Pittis required to supply a referee before he signed the lease?" Mace asked, his face innocent.

"A referee?" Gordonston's voice rose a full octave in sheer disbelief. "Jesus Christ, Sergeant, nobody in his right mind would ask a highly respectable insurance broker for a character reference. At least, I don't know of any estate agent who would."

"No, I guess you wouldn't," Mace said. "Silly of me to ask."

Any man who could afford to pay over two thousand pounds' cash in advance was bound to be all right as far as Gordonston was concerned. One look at the fat wad of traveler's checks and he'd have believed almost anything Pittis cared to tell him.

"Have you seen everything you want to, Sergeant?"

"You don't mind if I take another look at the lounge, do you?" Mace unlatched a door off the hall to his left and stuck his head inside before Gordonston had time to open his mouth. "That video machine," he said abruptly. "Does it go with the flat?"

Gordonston shook his head. "No, I imagine he must have hired it, possibly from Radio Rentals in the High Street."

"Then he probably had to pay them nine months' rent in advance," Mace said, thinking aloud.

"I wouldn't know. You'll have to ask them about that." Gordonston shifted his weight from one foot to the other in mounting impatience. "Will that be all, Sergeant?" he finally asked.

"Except for the list of check numbers you mentioned. If you leave word with your secretary, I'll collect them when I drop by the office again."

"When's that likely to be?"

"After I've seen how our artist is doing. Say about half an hour from now."

Mace let himself out of the flat, went downstairs and called on Mrs. Hayden, who promptly invited him in for a cup of coffee and steered him into the living room before he could have second thoughts.

The artist was doing very nicely, thank you. He was sprawled in one of the easy chairs eating a large slice of Dundee cake while playing nursemaid to good old friendly Hector curled up on his lap. The finished impression of Pittis was lying on the occasional table. It portrayed him as an amiable, round-faced man with a half-smile on his lips which suggested he was rather pleased with himself. Glancing at each of them in turn, Mace wasn't sure who looked the most smug, the artist, Pittis or good old Hector purring like a motor bike with a hole in its silencer.

"Herr Otto Prole?"

Patterson nodded, removed his narrow-brimmed trilby hat and smiled at the Immigration officer, as he looked up from the passport to gaze at him thoughtfully while the Special Branch officer, seated at a desk in rear, went through his list to see if they had anything on a Herr Otto Prole. Familiar with the routine, Patterson didn't allow the careful scrutiny to rattle him. Neither man had been on duty in the Terminal Building on Thursday when he'd left for Paris by Air France, but even if they had, they would never have recognized him now. His appearance had undergone a radical change: contact lenses that changed the color of his eyes to blue, hair dyed a pepperish tone, thicker eyebrows, a facial blemish in the form of a reddish-brown birthmark and heavy clear-glass spectacles which made him look slightly myopic.

"I see from the landing card that you're staying with friends in London, sir?"

"Business acquaintances," Patterson said, correcting him. "I am also booked into the Piccadilly Hotel from Tuesday and at the Motorway Inn in Birmingham next Friday." He fingered the locks on his executive-style briefcase. "I can show you the reservation slips if you wish?"

"That isn't necessary, sir." The Immigration officer had had a long and tiring day, and it wasn't over yet. The flight schedules were all snarled up, thanks to a strike by the air traffic controllers in France, and three hundred passengers from an Alitalia Jumbo were following hard on the heels of the Munich-Frankfurt-London shuttle. "I hope you have a pleasant stay in England," he said and returned the passport.

Patterson half-bowed, replaced his trilby and moved on into the luggage hall. He collected his suitcase, passed through Customs without any trouble, changed eight hundred Deutschemarks into sterling at Lloyds Bank, then adjourned to the men's washroom to revert to his former appearance. Locking himself into a cubicle, he removed the contact lenses, peeled away the extra hair stuck onto his eyebrows and ripped off the adhesive facial blemish. That done, he tucked the spectacles into his jacket pocket, flushed the toilet and left the cubicle, satisfied that nobody was likely to pay attention to the color of his hair. From a phone booth in the concourse he rang Ace Airways and told the receptionist at the garage that he had returned from his business trip earlier than expected and would they please collect him from the airport and have the Mini ready.

At 4:25 P.M., one hour after touchdown, he was on his way, driving into town on the M4 motorway as far as the South Circular. Approaching Kennington, he pulled into a shopping arcade and rang the contact number he'd been given in Paris from a phone booth. A woman with a faintly masculine voice answered the phone and said, "Cherry Tree Kennels."

"Denise Rousell?"

"Yes. Who is this?"

"My name's Kingfisher, Henry Kingfisher," Patterson said. "We've never met, but I ran into Viktor the other day and he asked me to look you up next time I was in London."

"Oh yes? How is Viktor?"

"He's okay, but it seems the book trade is suffering as a result of the depression. And talking of business, he said to tell you he'd managed to find a copy of the paperback you wanted."

"Which paperback?"

"Jean Moulin's *Premier Combat*. I thought I'd deliver it in person."

"What a good idea." Her voice tailed away, and in the brief silence that followed, he could faintly hear several dogs barking somewhere in the background. "When were you thinking of calling on me?" she asked presently.

"Whenever it's convenient."

There was another pause while Denise mulled it over, probably calculating how long her friends at the Soviet Embassy would need to set up the meet.

"The weekend is always a busy time for me, Mr. Kingfisher, especially during the holiday season. And my only kennel maid has taken the day off."

"I can see you have problems," Patterson said drily.

"Are you free on Monday evening?"

"At the moment I am."

"Good. Why don't you come to dinner?"

"Dinner?" he repeated incredulously.

"Seven-thirty for eight. My address is one five four Cherry Tree Road, which is only a five-minute walk from the Underground station at Roding Valley. Just turn right at the T-junction at the top of the station approach road and you can't miss it."

"Yeah?"

"Would you like me to repeat the instructions, Mr. Kingfisher?"

"One five four Cherry Tree Road," Patterson said dully. "Turn right at the T-junction."

"That's right. Till Monday evening then," she said, and hung up.

Patterson replaced the phone and backed out of the phone booth, confused and uncertain. For an intelligence service which was arguably the most secretive in the world, the KGB was behaving completely out of character in arranging an open meet, and he wondered if they were planning to set him up. In the paranoic field of espionage, today's ally was tomorrow's enemy, and he didn't believe in taking chances. Within the next thirty-six hours, it was essential he discover which side of the street Denise Rousell was working. Still mulling it over, Patterson got into the Mini and drove on to his flat in Linsdale Gardens.

10.

Coghill moved like an automaton from the bedroom to the hall, collected the *Sunday Times* from the doormat, then headed toward the kitchen. Still not fully awake, he left the newspaper on the table, plugged in the electric kettle he'd filled the night before and switched on the transistor radio. Breakfast normally consisted of two slices of toast, a glass of orange juice and a cup of instant coffee, but there were only a few dregs left in the carton of Sunfresh and the cellophane package of sliced bread yielded just one crust beginning to curl at the edges. The first to admit that his housekeeping left a lot to be desired, he was gratified to find there was half a pint of milk and a sizable lump of butter in the fridge, and that the jar of Nescafé in the larder was three parts full. Trimming the crust with a bread knife, he popped the slice into the toaster, then browsed through the newspaper while waiting for the kettle to boil.

The Whitfield case was no longer front-page news, but there was an article on the disturbing increase in the number of sex murders in the last year and Karen's photograph appeared with five other victims. Though living in different parts of the country, they had several things in common; all of them were married, had been in their late twenties or early thirties when they had been killed and had belonged to the top socioeconomic group. For some reason not entirely clear to Coghill, the feature writer appeared to think there was a definite correlation between the severe economic recession gripping the country and the homicides. About to read the feature again, he was interrupted by a cloud of steam escaping from the kettle, a warning buzz from the toaster and the doorbell. Rescuing the slice of bread before it became too charred to be edible, he switched off the kettle and went out into the hall to see who was calling on him.

Janice was the very last person he expected to find on the doorstep. He had neither seen nor heard from his ex-wife since the final decree had been granted twenty-one months ago, but there she was, large as life and smiling at him as though nothing untoward had happened between them. Her figure seemed a little plumper and he noticed that her auburn hair was not as well groomed as it used to be.

"Hello, Tom. Surprised to see me?"

"A little," he admitted. "It's been a long time."

"Aren't you going to invite me in?" The smile was beginning to look a mite strained and her voice sounded brittle.

"Yes, of course." He stood to one side. "The living room's the first door on your left."

"I haven't dragged you out of bed, have I, Tom?" Janice had grounds for thinking she had; he was still in his pajamas and dressing gown, unshaven, hair tousled.

"No," he said. "No, I was just about to have breakfast. Want to join me for a cup of coffee?"

"Yes, please."

"Let's go into the kitchen then," Coghill said. "It's at the far end of the hall."

Janice nodded and moved ahead of him, surreptitiously eyeing his choice of wallpaper, which he suspected didn't meet with her approval. "How many rooms have you got here, Tom?" she asked.

"Four, including the bathroom. It's a much smaller flat than the one we had in South Kensington."

"Well, it looks very cozy."

Cozy was Jan's way of saying she thought it was a poky little place, and while he was inclined to agree with her, it was all he'd been able to afford after they'd split up. His share from the sale of their flat had amounted to less than four thousand and anything larger would have entailed a crippling mortgage.

"You're becoming quite famous, Tom." Janice picked up the

Sunday Times which he'd dropped on the floor in his haste to rescue the slice of toast. "Picture in all the newspapers, interviews on TV."

"One interview," he said, correcting her. "And to be really accurate, it was only a five-minute spot outside the Whitfield house, and most of that was lost in the cutting room."

"All the same, you'll gain a lot of kudos from this case, Tom."

"I doubt it." Coghill switched on the kettle, unhooked a couple of mugs from the dresser and measured a large spoonful of coffee into each one.

"You always were a pessimist."

It was obvious Janice hadn't read yesterday's newspapers, otherwise she would have known that Tucker was coordinating the investigation. Coordinating was a gray word deliberately chosen by the press relations officer at New Scotland Yard, because the deputy assistant commissioner (crime) had wanted to keep the setup nice and ambiguous so that the media wouldn't get the idea the Leese and Whitfield murders were linked together.

"Right now, you can't see the wood for the trees," she went on, "but you will, Tom."

Janice had always been a great one for clichés and for once there was a certain amount of truth in what she'd just said. The police artist had sketched a face that had been identified by Mrs. Underwood as the man she'd had words with in St. Mark's Hill after he'd swerved to avoid her Pekinese. The same man was known to Mrs. Hayden, Gordonston and the Central Licensing Authority as Oscar Pittis and, according to American Express, their computer printout showed that the list of serial numbers Mace had obtained from the estate agents were part of 12,000 Deutschemarks' worth of traveler's checks purchased from their office in Frankfurt on May 11, four days before Pittis had moved into 192 Southwood Road. Then, on June 8, he'd bought a secondhand BMW priced at £3,750 from the Hampstead branch of S. V. Motors, for which he'd paid cash. Twelve thousand marks amounted to less than £4,000 and more than half of that had been swallowed up by the cost of renting a flat in Highgate. The facts, therefore, raised more questions than they answered because it was obvious somebody must have been financing Pittis before he'd conveniently disappeared.

"Do I get a cup of coffee or not?" Janice demanded.

"Oh, sorry, I was deep in thought."

"So I noticed." She wrinkled her nose, striving for a wry expression. "I always did come a poor second to the police force."

"You're wrong," Coghill lied. "I was thinking about you."

"I bet."

"No, really, I was wondering how things are between you and Eric."

Eric Leadbetter was a self-employed builder's supplier whom Janice had met when answering an advertisement in the old *Evening News* for a typist with some experience of bookkeeping. That had been back in the days when Coghill had been a detective constable with the Obscene Publications Squad, and there was no getting away from the fact that the extra money had come in handy at the time. Without her salary, they could never have afforded the mortgage payments on the flat in South Kensington.

"Eric went bankrupt nine months ago."

"I'm sorry to hear that; it must make things pretty difficult for you both." Coghill sipped his coffee and wondered what else he could say without sounding trite. "How are you managing? I mean, has he found himself another job, or what?"

"I wouldn't know, Tom. We separated in March, though to be absolutely honest, he walked out on me. Eric started drinking heavily after his firm went bust and I got tired of being the breadwinner so that he could drown his sorrows. We had a series of blazing rows; then one night I came home from work to find he'd packed his things and gone." She shrugged her shoulders. "End of story."

"You're better off without him, Jan."

"That's what I keep telling myself."

"Well, you'd better believe it. Leadbetter was a complete phoney."

"Maybe that was the attraction, the knowledge we were two of a kind."

It was meant for effect, inviting contradiction, but there was a lot in what Janice had said. He remembered her joining the Law School at Nottingham University when he'd been a second-year student, a very poised redhead who'd exuded an air of supreme confidence and had managed to look well groomed even in a pair of faded jeans and a floppy sweater. She had owned a Triumph TR4 sports car in those days, a status symbol which had fostered the illusion of a wealthy middle-class background. She had also affected to despise the elitist atmosphere of Oxford, and had casually let it be known that she had never considered applying for a place there because she preferred to be among real people. Later, much later, he'd met her parents and realized it was all a pretense. Her father was a foreman at the MG works in Abingdon and her mother worked in the staff canteen, but Janice was their only child and they had indulged her every whim.

"I should have been satisfied with what I already had, Tom. But you know me, I always had this craving for instant success."

"Don't think I didn't want it too," Coghill said.

Janice had begun to show an interest in him at the beginning of his final year, which had been very flattering to his ego because she had been undoubtedly the most attractive woman undergraduate on the campus. A cynical friend had observed that she had obviously marked him down as a potential highflyer, but if so, she'd suffered an early disappointment. The expected first hadn't materialized and he'd ended up with a good second-class honors, but by that time, Janice had been sleeping with him and, with the benefit of hindsight, Coghill supposed she'd decided it was too late to look elsewhere. At any rate, she'd dropped out of university and had joined him in London when he was still pounding a beat. A year later, they'd been married, but promotion hadn't come fast enough for her liking and eventually she'd cast around, looking for somebody with better prospects. That was when Leadbetter had entered the picture, and in due course she'd asked Coghill for a divorce not long after he'd been made detective sergeant.

"Do you know of any openings for a civilian typist in the police force, Tom?"

"What?"

"I've been made redundant, one of the three million unemployed."

"When did this happen?" he asked.

"Ten weeks ago. Casual work is all I can get now. I'm a month behind with the rent and I'm feeling pretty low."

"I'm not surprised." He owed Janice nothing, but for some reason he couldn't even begin to explain, his every instinct was to help her. "Tell you what," Coghill said impulsively, "we'll have lunch somewhere, talk things over and see if we can't come up with something."

"Are you sure, Tom? I don't want to monopolize your time."

"You won't be. This is my rest day and I haven't got anything planned. Give me twenty minutes to make myself presentable, then we'll drive out to The Angler's Inn at Marlow on Thames. What do you say?"

"Sounds marvelous." Another smile appeared, bright and eager this time. "I'll do the washing up and tidy the kitchen while you get changed. How's that for a bargain?"

"You're on."

Coghill left her to it, went into the bathroom and ran the electric shaver over his beard. That done, he stripped, stepped into the bath, drew the plastic curtain and turned on the shower attachment. He was still soaping himself down when she joined him in the shower. Her arms went round his neck, her mouth fastened on his and she moved against him.

Vaudrey's flat in Cheney Walk lacked a woman's touch and was just as impersonal as his office in Leconfield House. Although the sitting room was tastefully furnished, all the family photographs, curios, mementos and porcelain ornaments that reminded him of his wife had been removed and put into storage within a fortnight of her death from cancer in 1970. His needs were now allegedly seen to by an elderly live-in housekeeper, but the demands he made on her were hardly taxing since Vaudrey ate at his club every night of the week except Sundays, when the dining room was closed. A canny Scot, his housekeeper nevertheless insisted on observing the sabbath and, after preparing a light lunch for him, it was her accepted practice to take the rest of the day off. As far as Caroline Brooke could see, her only contribution toward organizing the party were the salted nuts she'd put out before leaving.

It was, however, a very intimate party; the only other guest was Walter J. Zellick III, a tall, very lean, very distinguished-looking American whose age was difficult to assess; although his dark hair was flecked with gray around the temples, his face was unlined and there was no sign of any flabbiness about the waist. Sizing him up, Caroline figured he was somewhere between thirty-eight and forty-two. She also thought Zellick held on to her hand longer than was strictly necessary while they were being introduced. A smile that was intended to show he found her attractive faded a little when a large gin and tonic was pressed into his free hand, and disappeared altogether when Vaudrey promptly got down to business.

"No need to tell you what all this is in aid of, Walt," he said cheerfully. "You want Orville Patterson and we think we're on to him."

"Right." Zellick frowned at his glass and decided he'd better down the gin and tonic before the single ice cube melted away.

"What Caroline needs," Vaudrey continued, "is some background information."

"Sure." Zellick grinned at her. "I'm forty-two and unattached. I haven't seen my ex since we were divorced in Los Angeles five years ago."

"I was referring to Orville Patterson," Vaudrey said frostily.

"Yeah? Well, he's a real bad number; if the money's right, there isn't anything he wouldn't do. I doubt Patterson was always like that, but Vietnam corrupted a lot of our soldiers and it seems he was no exception. Anyway, some of the CIA people in Saigon must have known exactly what kind of man they were getting when they recruited him into the Company. I tell you those guys damn nearly put the Mafia out of business the way they cornered the market in heroin."

"Am I right in assuming Patterson ran the distribution network from Langley?" Caroline asked.

"You catch on fast," Zellick said, in a voice which suggested he was suitably impressed.

"Not really. We already have that information on file."

"Quite so." Vaudrey removed the American's empty glass and fixed him another gin and tonic. "What Caroline would like is a detailed briefing about the man. You know the kind of thing—what makes him tick? Does he have any close associates? What are his habits, strengths and weaknesses?"

"Weaknesses?" Zellick shook his head. "I don't know of any, apart from the fact that he's totally corrupt. As for what makes him tick, I guess you could say the acquisition of money is his prime objective in life. We can't prove it, but we hear Patterson has acquired a tract of land in a fashionable part of Rio de Janeiro and is building himself a mansion that will make Buckingham Palace seem modest. Once it's completed, he'll retire and live like a king, the poor boy from Moorfield, West Virginia, who made good. He'd certainly enjoy giving the finger to the rest of us, knowing we couldn't touch him. No extradition treaty; that's the beauty of Brazil. And you can bet your bottom dollar Patterson has been cute enough to arrange a little double indemnity on the side."

"What sort of double indemnity?"

"The best there is, Caroline. He'll have married some local girl and made her pregnant."

"A careful man," Vaudrey observed acidly.

It transpired Patterson was all of that. The heroin connection had made him comparatively wealthy, and long before he'd left the CIA and ducked out of the States, he'd established several bank accounts in Switzerland and West Germany under various aliases. Along the way, he'd also acquired a collection of passports.

"He's very thorough," Zellick continued. "Doesn't make a move without preparing a fallback position. You may think you're on to him, but the chances are he's already two jumps ahead of you people."

"You're forgetting Raschid al Jalud," Vaudrey reminded him.

"Yeah, he could be the ace up your sleeve." Zellick carried his drink over to the window and stood there gazing out at the

Albert Bridge and the Battersea Park and Festival Pleasure Gardens across the river. "Patterson would like to be Qadhafi's top adviser on clandestine operations and only Jalud can make it happen. Somehow you've got to drive a wedge between those two, Nicholas."

"We're working on it," Vaudrey assured him. "It's just a question of finding the right man for the job."

"You got anybody in mind?"

"I think so. The question is, can you deliver your side of the bargain?"

"Let's see if I've got it right." Zellick slowly turned about. "You want Noraid. The boys in that outfit are one big pain in the ass as far as you British are concerned. They keep the Irish question alive in the States and thanks to their fund-raising activities, the IRA can buy all the weapons they need?"

Vaudrey nodded. "That is our assessment," he said.

"Well then, you give us Patterson and I guarantee to put Noraid out of business."

"May one ask how?" Caroline inquired.

"That's our little secret, honey." Zellick finished his drink and left the empty glass on the mantelpiece. "I'll tell you one thing, though. We sure as hell won't be taking them to court."

Patterson got off the Central Line train at Roding Valley station and started walking. Denise Rousell had told him to turn right at the end of the approach road, but as he neared the T-junction, he spotted a narrow lane behind the row of bungalows backing onto the railway and decided to follow it. The alley was crescent-shaped, conforming to the sweep of Cherry Tree Road, with a head-high wooden fence on one side marking the boundary line of the private residences and a wire-mesh fence on the other which had obviously been erected by London Transport.

There were the usual sounds of a Sunday morning in suburbia—a car radio tuned to London Broadcasting Company while the owner put a hose over the family car, two lawn mowers were at work, one electric, the other gas-driven. Through a broken slat in the wooden fence, Patterson caught a brief glimpse of a girl in a bikini sunbathing, and next door but one, an elderly man in a deck chair engrossed in the *News of the World*. Beyond the bend, the alley sloped downhill, the gradient sufficient to afford him an unobstructed view of the bungalows.

There was no mistaking Cherry Tree Kennels where Denise Rousell lived; the entire back lawn had been concreted over and subdivided into a dozen pens, the maximum number that could be crammed into a plot measuring sixty feet by forty. In the rear of the garage adjoining the bungalow, there was a large garden shed which, according to the signboard on the roof, was supposed to be a cattery. As far as Patterson could see, every pen appeared to be occupied, but the inmates seemed very docile and he assumed they'd recently been fed; then a poodle heard him coming and started to yap and was rapidly joined by every other dog in kennels. Quickening his stride, he reached the end of the lane and turned right on Cherry Tree Road to make a wide detour through the adjacent streets before returning to the Underground station.

The kennels had a lot going for it: the local residents were used to people coming and going and nobody was likely to pay much attention to a stranger. It was the sort of place the KGB would use as a safe house and, considering what was at stake, Patterson thought they might well be prepared to jeopardize the cover Denise Rousell had established for herself. Assuming they intended to play it rough, Orlov's associates would undoubtedly prolong the negotiations until nightfall before they made their move. The neighbors were a problem, but provided they backed a transit van up to the garage, there was a good chance nobody would see them as they bundled him into the vehicle. If he was lucky, they would dump him somewhere on the outskirts of London, minus the cassette and still unconscious from a shot of Pentothal. If they were feeling really mean, he might wake up to find himself in a prison cell.

He would need to be one jump ahead of them to stay in the game, and that brought him back to Denise Rousell. In his own mind, Patterson was convinced that she was the key figure, the adjudicator whom the KGB was counting on to assess the value of the material on offer. Knowing this was one thing; proving it was quite a different proposition. However, there were ways and means of discovering her real identity and background, and first thing tomorrow morning, he would drive over to Woodford and check the electoral roll.

11.

Coghill felt a hand brush against his chest and slowly opened both eyes. The sun was well down on the horizon and the fading light in the bedroom suggested the night was rapidly drawing in. He couldn't see the alarm clock on the bedside table without disturbing Janice, but all the signs indicated the time had to be somewhere between nine-thirty and ten.

It had been one hell of a rest day, he thought; lunch at the Angler's Inn, a lazy afternoon punting on the river, then back to the flat to fall into bed. From first to last, Janice had avoided the subject of her future plans, and whenever he'd tried to discuss them with her, she had promptly steered the conversation in a totally different direction. Long before they'd left Marlow on the return journey, he'd realized Janice simply regarded him as a rock to which she was determined to cling while the storm raged. On reflection, it was obvious he should have kept her at arm's length, but that was easier said than done; Janice had always known just how to arouse him and he lacked the self-denying ordinance of a monk.

"It's a shame to waste it," Janice had said, looking at the single bed, and it wasn't only sex she'd had in mind. That was only the means to an end, a none-too-subtle reminder of what he'd been missing since they'd split up. Unless he did something about it, she would gradually worm her way into his life again and he'd be back where he started, with all the heartache to come. The diagnosis was clear, the cure wasn't, and he wondered if his reluctance to hurt her was a sign of weakness.

You're not a moral coward, he reasoned with himself; tell her gently but firmly that there can be no going back, and do it now.

Acting on his own advice, Coghill placed a hand on Jan's shoulder to wake her; then the phone trilled and did it for him.

"Let it ring," Janice told him. "Pretend you're not at home."

Her voice was drowsy, but she hadn't flinched at the sudden noise and he knew she had just been lying there on her stomach, feigning sleep.

"You know I can't do that," he said.

"Why not? It's your rest day, isn't it?" She raised herself up and tried to lie across him, her mouth seeking his.

"For God's sake, Jan," he said angrily, "it could be important."

"So's this," she murmured huskily.

"Like hell it is."

Easing Janice aside, Coghill scrambled out of the divan, padded around to the bedside table and snatched the receiver off the cradle to find he had Trevor Whitfield on the line. He sounded distant and withdrawn, his voice a dull monotone as though he were in a state of traumatic shock.

"Are you all right?" Coghill asked him quietly.

"All right?" Whitfield mumbled something under his breath, laughed inanely, then said, "Why are you so determined to get me? I've never done you any harm."

"I don't know what you're talking about, Trevor."

"That chief superintendent, the one they call Fucker Tucker behind his back. He kept asking me about Lisa, said it was beginning to look as if I might have hired somebody to murder Karen because I wanted her money."

"Lisa?" Coghill said, frowning. "Who's she?"

"A girl I know in Vienna. Two days and nights nonstop."

"What?"

"Questions, nothing but questions. Stanley was there part of the time but he was no help."

Coghill reached for the pack of cigarettes on the bedside table, shook one loose and lit it. Quainton had obviously run true to form, his client's interests coming a poor second to his own when the chips were down.

"Tucker said he knew I was sleeping with Lisa and showering her with gifts."

Whitfield rambled on, becoming more and more incoherent, so that it was impossible to follow his train of thought. The girl in Vienna, the arrangements for Karen's funeral on Monday and Tucker; he switched from one subject to the next with all the agility of a grasshopper and nothing he said made any sense to Coghill.

"I've been drinking," Whitfield informed him gravely.

"I guessed as much."

"Dutch courage. That's what I needed and now I've got it."

There was a note of finality in his voice, one that was given an added and special emphasis by a loud clunk and the purring noise which followed shortly after he hung up. For some moments Coghill sat there on the edge of the bed uncertain what to do, then, coming to a decision, he stubbed out his cigarette, broke the connection and started dialing.

"What's the matter?" Janice asked softly.

"Whitfield. I have a nasty feeling he's at the end of his tether and is about to do something stupid."

"You should sign up with the Samaritans."

"It seems I already have, the way you've been using me."

He held on to the phone, the receiver pressed against his ear, his temper fraying at the edges the longer the number rang. Finally, a bored voice said, "CID. Detective Sergeant Ingleson, night duty officer."

"Congratulations, sergeant," Coghill rasped. "What kept you?"

"I'm sorry, Guv," Ingleson said contritely, "I was out of the office. Call of nature..."

"I've just had a phone call from Whitfield," Coghill said, cutting the explanation short.

"That doesn't surprise me. He rang the station earlier and asked for your home number. I said you'd probably be out, but he wouldn't tell me why he wanted to get in touch with you." Ingleson paused, then said, "Was it important?"

"I'm not sure. How did Whitfield strike you? Did he seem hysterical, depressed or what?"

"He sounded a little agitated," Ingleson admitted, "but I didn't think anything of it. In my experience, most queers are inclined to be excitable in times of stress."

"Did he sound as though he'd been drinking?"

"No. No, he was as sober as a judge when I spoke to him."

"He isn't now," Coghill said. "You'd better put your skates on and get down there fast. I'll join you there in twenty minutes, but don't wait for me. If you can't get an answer, don't hesitate to break into the house."

"It's like that, is it?"

"I hope not," Coghill said and put the phone down. Racing against time, he grabbed his clothes from the chair, put his socks on inside out, then stepped into his slacks and zipped them up while shoving his feet into a pair of slip-on shoes. "I don't know how long I'll be gone," he grunted.

"So what's new?" Janice said.

"Not a damned thing. You'd better phone for a minicab to take you home."

"You're throwing me out?" Surprise and indignation vied with each other in her voice.

"You could put it like that." Coghill pulled a thin turtleneck sweater on over his head, slipped both arms into a sports jacket and checked the pockets to make sure he had his car keys and wallet. "I don't know how much minicab drivers charge these days," he said, "but don't stand for any old buck."

"Don't worry; I'll tell him my ex is a hard-nosed copper if there's any nonsense about the fare."

"I bet you will." Coghill took out his wallet, saw that apart from two one-pound notes he had nothing smaller than a tenner, and decided he could hardly leave her just a couple of quid. "Here," he said awkwardly, "this should cover your fare."

Her eyes went to the ten-pound note on the bedside table and narrowed spitefully. "You've forgotten the silver."

"What?"

"I believe it's customary to leave a tip for the maid."

"That's a pretty cheap remark, Jan."

"Well, I'm feeling pretty cheap," she called after him, then burst into tears as he slammed the front door and went on down to the street below.

Although the traffic was fairly light, the eight-mile journey across town to Wimbledon took longer than Coghill had anticipated. Two incidents delayed him, a burst gas main in Uxbridge Road and a prowl car that stopped him near the Putney bridge for illegal use of the Volvo's warning lights and for exceeding the speed limit in a restricted-speed zone. As a result, it was past eleven o'clock by the time he reached St. Mark's Hill.

A Ford Escort was parked in the Whitfields' driveway, but the house was in darkness and there was no sign of Ingleson. As he walked up the drive, Coghill noticed that the drapes had been drawn in the living room and, through the rippled glass to the left of the front door, he could see a shadowy figure in the recess under the staircase. Then the door opened at the sound of his footsteps and a grim-faced Ingleson was there to greet him.

"Whitfield's dead," Ingleson said bluntly. "I didn't waste any time getting here, but I was too late."

"It's not your fault; these things happen and there's nothing you can do about it." Coghill went through his pockets, found a pack of Silk Cut, lit two cigarettes and gave one to the detective sergeant.

"Thanks." Ingleson drew on the cigarette and slowly exhaled. "I've already contacted everybody I can think of—Superintendent Kingman, Doctor Harrison, the pathologist, the Regional Crime Squad and Commander Franklin. I didn't see any point in sending for an ambulance, thought it best to wait until our forensic people had had a good look around."

Coghill nodded. "Where did you find Whitfield?" he asked.

"In the dining alcove off the living room." Ingleson turned about, picked up the flashlight he'd left on the hall table by the wall phone and switched it on. "I'd better lead the way, Guv," he said. "One of the fuses has blown and none of the lights are working downstairs."

Coghill followed him down the narrow hall and into the living room on the right, the flashlight beam piercing the darkness to zero in on a pair of stockinged feet dangling in space above the overturned dining chair on the floor. Then it traveled slowly upward. Although Whitfield wasn't the first suicide victim Coghill had seen, the manner of his death was easily the most bizarre. As a preliminary step, he had apparently pushed the dining table toward the French windows and placed an upright chair on the dropleaf. Next, he had made a noose out of a length of electric cord and, after kicking off his shoes, had climbed up on to the makeshift scaffold to tie the loose end to the chandelier in the ceiling. Then he had slipped the noose around his neck and removed the electric light bulb.

"The switch is on and there's a burn on the index finger of his right hand," Ingleson said, as though reading his thoughts. "I figure he stuck it in the socket and the resultant shock knocked him off the chair."

"You're probably right; that's how it must have been."

The dining table was covered with bits of plaster and the chandelier was hanging askew, its glass pendants resting on Whitfield's chest like some monstrous diamond necklace.

"The curtains were already drawn when I arrived," Ingleson continued. "When I walked around to the back of the house, I could hear a transistor radio playing in the kitchen. Had to smash the utility room window to get in; fortunately, the key was still in the Chubb lock."

A car drew up outside the house, two doors opened and closed in quick succession and Ingleson broke off to listen to the sound of footsteps in the driveway. "Reinforcements," he said cryptically.

"The first of many," said Coghill. "You'd better let them in before they wake the whole street."

They arrived within a few minutes of each other, Kingman casually dressed and looking suntanned from the weekend he'd spent in Bournemouth, Tucker in a formal lounge suit and Franklin still in the dinner jacket and black tie he'd been wearing to attend a Sunday evening charity concert at the Festival Hall. The only absentee was Doctor Harrison, who'd telephoned to say that he could see no point in coming to the house if the police were satisfied Whitfield had committed suicide, and that being the case, he proposed to carry out the usual postmortem in the morning.

An element of farce about the whole business was compounded by the two forensic men, whose combined efforts to repair the fuse so that they could see what they were doing ended in a blowout each time the main switch was tripped. After three unsuccessful attempts to restore the lighting, Franklin finally lost his temper and told them to clear off and come back in the morning. The police photographer, uninhibited by the pitch-darkness, used up a reel of film and departed shortly before the ambulance arrived to collect the body. By that time, the press had somehow learned of the incident and several reporters had gathered outside the house. Knowing they would refuse to budge without an official statement, Franklin decided to hold an impromptu conference by candlelight in the kitchen.

"Well, now," he began, "I don't know how those people outside got to hear about Whitfield, but it certainly looks as though one of your officers must have tipped them off, Bert."

"It would seem so." Kingman leaned against the wall, arms folded across his chest. "I'll tell you one thing, though," he growled, "whoever it was is going to wish he'd never been born when I catch up with him."

"Quite. The question is, what are we going to say to the press?" Franklin gazed at the assembled officers, then said, "Unless we're completely frank with them, they may jump to the wrong conclusions. You can be sure they'll latch on to the fact that Whitfield had been questioned at some length by the police shortly before he committed suicide, and I don't have to tell you what a meal they could make of that."

"Did he leave a note?" Tucker asked.

Coghill wasn't sure whom the question had been addressed to, but everybody was looking at him. "I didn't come across one in the living room," he said slowly.

"What about the rest of the house? Did you think to look in the study upstairs?"

The others had begun to arrive a bare ten minutes after Coghill had gotten there, but that didn't stop Tucker from implying he had been negligent. "Nobody's had a chance to yet."

"Well, it's about time somebody did," Tucker said.

"Too right." Franklin jerked a thumb at Ingleson. "You'd better check all the rooms while you're at it, Sergeant," he said.

"Yes, sir." Ingleson picked up his flashlight, left the kitchen and went upstairs. Moments later, they could hear him moving about in the study above their heads.

"Suppose there isn't a note?" Kingman said abruptly. "Suppose Whitfield made another phone call after he spoke to Tom?"

"I doubt if he did," Coghill said. "For one thing, it would have taken Whitfield at least ten minutes to prepare that scaffold and for another, Ingleson didn't waste any time getting here."

"We're going round and round in circles, getting nowhere," Franklin complained. "Those reporters will want to know why he committed suicide."

"Then I suggest we simply give them the bald facts and allow them to draw their own conclusions," Tucker said nonchalantly.

"What facts, what conclusions?"

"We can make the point that Whitfield was neither a model husband nor a reliable employee. As a result of questioning the other couriers at Travelways, we know he had a regular girl in Vienna, and according to his colleagues, they'd had to cover for him on more than one occasion when he was in the sack with her. And let's face it, he had every reason to hate his wife; she treated him like dirt, never ceased to remind him that the only things he owned were the clothes he stood up in."

"Who told you that?" Coghill asked.

"Whitfield. He dictated a very full statement and signed the original and three copies in the presence of his lawyer. Rest assured, it's all down there in black and white, the love nest at Abercorn House and the name of her last boyfriend, Oliver Leese."

"What about all the others, the men she was blackmailing?"

"Whitfield was reluctant to talk about them and I decided not to press him."

"Why?"

"I'm surprised you should ask, Inspector," Tucker said acidly.

"The way the evidence was shaping up, there was a distinct possibility that we would eventually charge him with being an accessory to both murders. Naturally, in the circumstances, I didn't want to give Quainton any grounds for claiming that his statement had been obtained under duress."

Neither premise seemed likely to Coghill. Knowing Quainton and how anxious the lawyer was to come up smelling like a rose, he couldn't see him performing a sudden volte-face in court at the preliminary hearing. Nor was he entirely sure that Tucker really believed everything he'd just said.

"There are thirty-seven names in Karen Whitfield's address book," Franklin observed quietly. "And some of those men had an equally strong motive when you think of the harm she could have done to them."

"Maybe so, but I went through every entry and the figures show there wasn't a single one who'd refused to pay up. We should also remember that Whitfield had more to gain than any of her clients. At a conservative estimate, this house, the flat in Maida Vale, her jewelry and the two boutiques must be worth all of a hundred and fifty thousand, and that's not including the money she had in the bank."

Franklin was only too eager to accept the proposition; Coghill could tell that by the way the commander kept nodding his head. The Jeremy Ashforths and the Harold Egremonts could rest easy; Whitfield had been chosen as a convenient scapegoat and the police wouldn't be knocking on their doors. Any lingering doubt that he might be doing him an injustice was dispelled by Franklin's evident relief when Ingleson returned to the kitchen and informed him there was no suicide note.

12.

Coghill left the Volvo outside the cemetery gates and walked down a wide asphalt path between row upon row of weathered headstones. Although it was no longer raining, the dark cumulus clouds on the horizon looked ominous and there was an intermittent rumble of thunder in the distance. The atmosphere was oppressive and the utter stillness was yet another sign that this was merely an uneasy lull between storms.

The freshly dug grave was off to his right, four rows back from the asphalt path and directly in line with the public conveniences and the superintendent's office near the main entrance to the cemetery. Both hands shoved deep into the pockets of his raincoat, Coghill went on past the site, looking for a secluded spot where he could watch the interment without appearing obtrusive. The same idea had apparently occurred to Harry Mace, who was standing under a large yew tree a good twenty yards beyond the burial plot.

"Morning, Harry," he said, approaching the detective sergeant. "I didn't expect to see you here."

"Nor me you, Guv." Mace removed the cigarette clinging to his bottom lip and stubbed it against the trunk of the yew tree. "Were you at the church?"

Coghill nodded. "Along with a handful of Karen's neighbors. Her son, Darren, was there, a tall gangling boy in long gray trousers and a regulation blazer. Either the headmaster's wife or the prep school matron was with him to lend moral support."

"Poor little bugger." Mace shook his head. "He's had a rough old time of it. I just hope those TV people keep their distance;

the funeral's enough of an ordeal without cameras zooming in on him."

Coghill followed his gaze and saw two camera teams had ensconced themselves in front of a laurel hedge bordering the boundary railings. It was only to be expected that the media would want to cover the funeral; Whitfield's suicide made it even more newsworthy, especially as the morning papers had carried just a brief report in the stop press.

"I doubt if they'll move in close, Harry," he said.

"They'd better not," Mace growled.

A hearse drove slowly through the main gates and was followed by a large black limousine. Then a Cortina, a dark blue Jaguar and a Mini Metro pulled up outside the entrance to the cemetery and the remainder of the small congregation who'd attended the funeral service got out.

"The woman wearing a gray head scarf is Mrs. Underwood," Mace told him. "The fair-haired lad is Christopher Youens who gave us the license number of the BMW that nearly ran over her Pekinese. But I've never seen the willowy blonde in the navy two-piece costume before."

"Ah, that's June Strachey," Coghill said. "She's the manageress of the boutique in Wimbledon."

The hearse stopped a few yards beyond the graveside and four pallbearers got out, opened the double rear doors and, with practiced ease, removed the coffin and lifted it onto their shoulders. As they did so, the funeral director alighted from the limousine and adjusted his top hat, making sure the black ribbons were hanging correctly, while the chauffeur assisted Darren and the matronly lady from the Grange Prep School out of the car. Then the procession moved slowly forward along a narrow strip of lawn between the weathered headstones toward the open grave. With almost indecent haste, June Strachey and the other mourners cut across the grass to join them.

"I feel really sorry for that youngster," Mace said quietly. "He looks absolutely shattered now, but God knows how he'll feel by the time the media are through."

"I daresay the school will do their best to shield him from the worst."

"You're forgetting the other kids, Guv; they're bound to pass on the good news about his stepfather. Ingleson tells me that the statement we released to the press virtually said Whitfield hired somebody to kill his wife."

"Ingleson is exaggerating; we simply gave them the facts."

"And invited the reporters to draw their own conclusions." Mace lit another cigarette and dropped the spent match into a trash bin full of dead flowers. "Do you believe Trevor had a hand in his wife's murder?" he asked presently.

"I'm not sure of anything, Harry."

Franklin, Kingman and Tucker all appeared to think so, and who was he to say they were wrong? Nine murders out of ten were committed within the family circle and maybe he had attached too much significance to the fact that Karen Whitfield had been a high-priced call girl.

"Tucker has a reputation for being a hardnose, Guv."

And Whitfield was the sort of man he could reduce to a jelly. Trevor had had homosexual tendencies and Tucker had been astute enough to ferret that out. He had probably threatened him with the Theft Act of 1958 and a whole string of charges under Section 30 of the Sexual Offenders Act. That, and a lurid description of the sexual perversions he would be exposed to in prison, plus the biased advice offered by Stanley Quainton, would have induced Whitfield to make an incriminating statement.

"I phoned Swansea earlier this morning," Mace said abruptly. "It appears Pittis sold the BMW to a garage in Southwark."

"Did you pass the information on to the Regional Crime Squad?" Coghill asked him.

"There was no need to; the central licensing bureau had already been in touch with them. I suppose I should have told the Regional Crime Squad that I know a used car dealer in that neighborhood who's about as straight as a corkscrew, but it sort of slipped my mind."

"We're all inclined to be forgetful at times," Coghill observed in a neutral voice.

The priest was looking up at the lowering sky, hands clasped together in supplication. The matronly woman standing next to Darren gave him a gentle nudge and he bent down, picked up a handful of loose earth and dropped it into the grave.

"I was wondering if I shouldn't have a word with him, Guv? You can never tell, he might be able to put me on to the guy who sold the white Mini to Pittis."

"How well do you know this villain?"

"We go back a long way," Mace said.

The small crowd of mourners began to drift away from the graveside. Darren, his head bowed, walked on stiff legs toward the waiting limousine, the priest at his side murmuring comforting words which probably fell on deaf ears.

"What do you think, Guv?"

"I think you should renew an old acquaintance, Harry."

The hearse started moving and came on past the yew tree, the limousine close behind. The priest spared them a brief glance, his curiosity plainly aroused, but Darren looked straight ahead, tight-lipped and obviously struggling to hold back the tears.

"I'll be on my way then."

"Yes, you do that." Coghill watched the two vehicles make a double left turn to follow a parallel road back to the main gates and then set off toward the superintendent's office.

The wreaths and floral tributes had been laid out neatly in line on the path fronting the office, their attached cards prominently displayed so that he could see at a quick glance who had sent them. The Underwoods, the Youens, the headmaster and staff of the Grange Preparatory School, June Strachey and the staff of Karen's boutiques in Fulham and Wimbledon; the names of those outside the immediate family circle who'd wished to remember her were few in number and entirely predictable. It was no surprise either to find that Quainton should have sent a bunch of roses, but Coghill thought the dedication to a valued friend and client was a breathtaking piece of hypocrisy, even by the lawyer's standards.

He went on out through the main gates, got into the Volvo and sat there for some minutes staring blankly through the windshield. Away over to his left, two council workmen were busy shoveling clods of earth into the grave where Karen Whitfield was lying and somehow it seemed to him that it wasn't only her coffin they were burying from sight. Nobody is above the law; he remembered telling Kingman that the night he'd picked him up from Gatwick Airport, and even if Bert was right and he did have a lot to learn, he still happened to believe it was true. He started to reach inside his jacket for the notebook containing the names and addresses of some of the men whom Karen Whitfield had blackmailed, then realized he was only temporizing, because he already knew Ashforth's number.

The cloudburst started as Patterson approached the outskirts of Woodford. It began with a loud thunderclap and a few hesitant raindrops, then the heavens suddenly opened and released a torrent that swamped the windshield wipers and reduced visibility to a few yards. Shifting gears into second, he inched his way into the High Street and turned off into a side road to park the Mini within easy walking distance of the Central Library. In no great hurry, he sat there listening to the newscast on the car radio while waiting for the downpour to ease off. Whitfield was still grabbing the headlines and the inference that he may have known the identity of the man who'd killed his wife was particularly gratifying.

A phone-in followed the news, and some garrulous but largely incoherent man launched into a tirade about the latest unemployment figures. Bored by the sound of the man's voice and inability to express himself, Patterson switched off the radio and lit a small cheroot. Ten minutes later, the rain no longer bucketing down, he got out of the Mini, slipped on a plastic mac and walked back to the main thoroughfare.

Three elderly women, a young mother with a two-year-old boy in a stroller and a lanky teenager whose orange-colored hair was cut like a Mohican were sheltering in the entrance to the Central Library. There were even fewer people inside the building and the girl on the inquiry desk greeted Patterson with a warm smile which suggested she was genuinely pleased to see him. The way she promptly asked if she could be of any assistance also told him that she knew he was a stranger to the district.

"I've only just moved into the neighborhood," Patterson said, before the girl had a chance to ask.

"And you'd like to join the library?"

"That was my first question." He smiled. "The second one is, where do I find a copy of the electoral roll without going to the Town Hall?"

"Right here." The girl crouched down, rummaged under the counter and produced a list printed on foolscap which was almost half an inch thick.

"My word," Patterson murmured, "I hadn't realized there were that many voters in Woodford."

"Yes, it's a pretty big constituency. Of course, that doesn't mean to say this roll is a hundred percent accurate. Some people will have moved away since the return was completed, and you'd be surprised just how many householders either can't be bothered to complete the necessary form or fail to send it in on time."

"I think you've just described one of my neighbors. I was asking him last night when the roll had been made up and he said he couldn't remember filling out the form whenever it was the Town Hall had sent them out."

"Last September," the girl told him. "And he would have received a reminder two months later."

"Really? Well, let's hope he did do something about it." Patterson gently removed the electoral roll from her grasp. "Can I use the reading room to study this?" he asked.

"Yes, of course you can." The girl pointed to her right. "It's the first door on your left," she said.

Patterson thanked her, walked into the reading room, sat down at a vacant table and opened the electoral roll. The streets were arranged in alphabetical order; locating Cherry Tree Road, he ran a finger down the list and saw that the woman living at Number 154, whom he knew as Denise Rousell, was shown as Mrs. O. D. Beaumont. Although he didn't know exactly what they stood for, the capital letters after her surname indicated that she had been awarded some kind of decoration. Intrigued to know what it was, he returned to the main hall, followed the directional signs to the reference section and looked them up in *The Concise Oxford Dictionary*. From a volume entitled *British Decorations, Honours and Awards*, he learned that the Order of the British Empire was conferred upon civilians, government officials and members of the armed services in recognition of especially meritorious service. A footnote tartly added that it was the practice in some government departments to regard the order as a consolation prize to be awarded on retirement to hardworking but less able civil servants who'd been passed over for promotion. While it was difficult to guess a person's age from the sound of a voice on the telephone, Patterson had a shrewd suspicion that Mrs. O. D. Beaumont was numbered among those who'd received an OBE in lieu of a golden handshake.

He wondered just what sort of post Denise Rousell had held when she'd been working for the government. One thing seemed certain; if the KGB was relying on her to evaluate the video tapes and identify the clients, it must have been the kind of sensitive appointment in which she would have rubbed shoulders with a lot of VIPs. He scanned the bookshelves, pulled out a copy of *Whitaker's Almanack* and went through the index. Government and Public Offices looked like a good bet and, turning to page 362, he started with the Ministry of Agriculture, Fisheries and Food, and progressed as far as the Horserace Totalisator Board before he spotted the most likely answer:

> The Central Office of Information, Hercules Road; a common service department which produces information and publicity material and supplies publicity services for other government departments which require them.

Although the definition of its responsibilities ran to a full twenty-two-line paragraph, the opening sentence told him all he needed to know. Smiling to himself, Patterson returned the *Almanack* to its shelf space and dipped into his jacket pocket to consult the list of retailers he'd copied from the Yellow Pages before leaving the flat in Linsdale Gardens. The Camera and Cine Shop in

Leytonstone was the nearest and it offered a discount on a wide range of goods including the guillotine and splicer he needed to edit the tapes. There was also a Hertz rental agency in the borough, which was another plus.

Caroline Brooke signed the receipt docket, handed it to the messenger, then waited until he'd left the office before she opened the padded envelope and extracted a cassette. It was graded confidential, and there was also a caveat on the red star security label which stated:

> THE INFORMATION ON THIS TAPE IS ULTRA SENSITIVE AND IN ACCORDANCE WITH DEPARTMENTAL STANDING ORDER DI5/11 DATED 6 MAY 1976 THE RECIPIENT IS REMINDED THAT HE/SHE IS PERSONALLY RESPONSIBLE FOR ENSURING THE MATERIAL IS NOT REPRODUCED IN ANY FORM WHETHER VISUAL OR AUDIO.

There were other safeguards to be observed when handling ultrasensitive information and, mindful of these, she checked the sashcord window to make sure it was fully closed and locked the door. That done, Caroline opened the bottom drawer of her desk and took out a battery-powered Sony recorder. Adjusting the attached headphones so that they fitted snugly over her ears, she inserted the cassette and depressed the play button.

The tape ran silent for a few seconds, then a well-modulated voice with a slight north country accent said, "This is a recording. Mr. Ashforth is not at home. If you would like to leave a message and your phone number, he will contact you on his return from Birmingham this evening. Please wait for the tone signal before speaking."

There was a long bleep followed by a brief pause, then the caller said, "My name's Coghill. I'm a Detective Inspector with V District of the Metropolitan Police. I have reason to believe you were very friendly with the late Karen Whitfield and that over a number of years you gave her several large sums of money. These payments were in respect of a debt amounting to twelve thousand pounds, a little over half of which was still outstanding at the time of her death. Naturally, we want to know the full details of this business arrangement you had with Mrs. Whitfield. As this is a matter of some urgency, I expect you to phone me this evening without fail. You can reach me on 992–9015."

Coghill had sounded angry throughout and the way he'd slammed the phone down confirmed her impression. Although they had never met, she knew a great deal about him and wasn't surprised that he'd stepped out of line. Other police officers might be prepared to turn a blind eye on Ashforth, but not Coghill; the more people tried to warn him off, the more obstinate he was likely to become. That had been the opinion of the DI5 contact at Scotland Yard, and events had proved him right.

Caroline removed the headphones, buzzed Vaudrey on the office intercom and asked him if he could spare her a few minutes.

"I'm rather busy at the moment," Vaudrey told her. "Unless it's really vital, I'd like to clear my in tray first."

"How long will that take, Nicholas?"

"Do I detect a note of urgency in your voice?" he countered.

"Well, let's just say that I've received a red star package from our eavesdroppers and I'm pretty sure you won't enjoy listening to the replay."

"I see." Vaudrey sighed, then said, "Some people just can't take a hint, can they?"

"I wouldn't have bothered you if I hadn't considered it important," she said tersely.

"Dear me, we are in a tizzy. I'm afraid your Freudian slip is showing, Caroline. I was referring to Coghill."

It seemed to her that she wasn't the only one who'd made a Freudian slip. In the last six months alone, K Desk had added a further seventeen names to the list of hostile intelligence agents and IRA sympathizers whose telephones were being tapped, yet Vaudrey had immediately singled Ashforth out from all the rest. She supposed it could have been an inspired guess, but thought it more likely he'd had prior warning from the head of Surveillance.

"I'm sorry to hear he's been making a nuisance of himself,"

Vaudrey continued. "However, I don't think we need lose any sleep over this development."

"You don't want me to do anything about it then?"

"Why should we? It won't take Coghill's superiors long to discover what he's up to and they'll soon put a stop to his nonsense."

"I wonder," she mused.

"You sound doubtful."

"Well, I do have some reservations about their ability to stop him before any damage is done. Coghill is no fool and I get the strong impression he suspects there is a tacit agreement that some of the more influential people who knew Karen Whitfield will not be questioned. I'm sure that's why he gave Ashforth his private phone number."

"I take your point, Caroline."

"In that case, I really think you should hear this tape."

"All in good time," Vaudrey said. "I'll give you a buzz as soon as I'm free. Okay?"

"Yes."

There wasn't anything else she could say. If Vaudrey continued to stall her, she could threaten to go over his head and take the matter up with the director general, but that was very much a last resort. Extracting the cassette, she walked over to the security cabinet, placed the tape on the middle shelf and picked up the top secret file on Patterson. Since Thursday, when it had been opened with a loose minute to Vaudrey, the dossier had now become an inch thick. The latest addition was headed "Common Denominators" and had been an attempt on her part to find a connecting thread between the men Karen Whitfield had blackmailed. In the end, the conclusions she had drawn hardly justified the time and effort that had been spent on the analysis; some men were members of the same London club, others enjoyed similar leisure pursuits, but no overall link had emerged.

However, it was a fact that Ashforth had had several interviews with Raschid al Jalud when he was making a documentary film on the Libyan economy and she wondered if it was worth reminding Nicholas of this. His initials in the top left-hand corner of the paper finally convinced her that she would simply be wasting her breath. Vaudrey knew what was at stake, had done so ever since she'd sent the loose minute at Folio 1 warning him that Jalud would undoubtedly be recalled from London should Coghill ask to interview the Libyan diplomat. What was it she had said in the concluding sentence?—"I therefore strongly recommend that we take such preventative action as is necessary to safeguard our interests." Despite his apparent lack of urgency, she was quite certain that Vaudrey would have remembered that piece of advice and was equally convinced he had already acted on it.

13.

The barmaid was a mature woman in her early forties with a voluptuous if slightly overripe figure. She was wearing a pair of skin-tight black toreador pants and a midnight-blue silk blouse with a ruffled collar and a plunging neckline that revealed an awe-inspiring cleavage. She had dark frizzy hair, a wide generous mouth and a touch of flabbiness under the jaw which before very long would become a double chin. Mace wasn't sure whether her violet-colored pupils were natural or the result of wearing contact lenses, but they were easily her best feature. Like her other plus points, they were something he couldn't help noticing, especially as she seemed determined to give him the full benefit of her obvious charms. Only too aware he was no oil painting, he couldn't think why the barmaid had taken such a shine to him, but it was a fact that, although the pub was now filling up with the lunchtime trade, she always returned to him whenever there was a free moment between serving customers.

"You friend's a bit late, isn't he?" she observed.

"Not by his standards," Mace said. "He's never punctual."

"And it doesn't bother you?" She shook her head. "I must say you're remarkably patient."

"You need to be in my job."

"Oh? And what's that?"

"I'm a police officer—a detective sergeant with V District."

"You—a copper? You're having me on."

"Now, why would I do that?" he asked.

"I don't know." A couple of furrows appeared above the bridge of her nose as she gave the question further thought. "Maybe you thought it would impress me."

"I'd be taking a chance. To some people, we're the pigs."

"I prefer 'copper,'" she said and smiled.

"Yes? Well, that's nice to know, but this copper will find himself in deep water unless he checks in. Any idea where the nearest phone booth is?"

"I'm not sure. Hang on a moment while I have a word with the landlord."

She moved to the far end of the bar, exchanged a few brief words with a harassed-looking man in shirtsleeves, then returned to inform Mace he was welcome to use theirs. Raising the counter flap, she unlatched the half-gate and showed him into a small office in rear of the bar. In the process, she held on to his elbow and contrived to rub shoulders with him.

"It's all yours, sergeant."

Mace wondered if she was referring to herself or the room. "Thanks," he said, playing it safe. "I guess you've saved my bacon."

"Vera, my name's Vera."

"Right."

"What's yours?"

"Harry," Mace said, and gave her a weak smile.

"I'll see you later then, Harry."

He nodded dumbly, waited until she had closed the door behind her, then dialed the station, using one of the two emergency lines. The number rang for a good two minutes before Ingleson answered.

"Busy, Fred?" Mace asked him drily.

"No more than usual. What can I do for you?"

"I was just checking in."

"I see. Where are you calling from?"

"The Bricklayers' Arms in Southwark."

"You crafty old sod."

"It's not the way you think, Fred. I've got a meet on with one of my snouts. There's a fair chance he can put me on to the dealer who sold the white Mini to Pittis."

"A fair chance?" Ingleson laughed. "Knowing the lousy sort of information your snouts produce, I'd say you're being wildly optimistic, Harry."

Mace had to admit there was a grain of truth in the allegation. Although his sources were no worse than anyone else's, they'd never come up with anything really big, except on one occasion. Three years back, he'd received what had seemed a red-hot tip that a heavy mob was planning to knock over a Securicor armored van on its way to the Midland Bank in Wandsworth. The information had sounded convincing and the source had had a fairly good track record until then, two factors that had weighed heavily with Bert Kingman and persuaded him that they should act on it. The Flying Squad and just about every other gung-ho character in the Met had gotten in on the act and it had been a right bloody fiasco from beginning to end. While the police were busy tailing the Securicor armored van and watching the bank, the heavy mob had ripped off a supermarket in Richmond and got clean away with eleven thousand in cash. It was an incident Mace wanted to forget, but some of his colleagues wouldn't let him.

"You want to put your money where your mouth is, Fred?" Mace said belligerently.

"Maybe. Tell me more."

"The source is a used car dealer who's as bent as they come. He's a man with a lot of contacts in the curbside trade and he's out there now, making a few inquiries on my behalf."

"Doing you a favor, is he, Harry?"

"You could say that."

"A fiver says the answer's a lemon."

"You're on." Mace glanced at the disk on the telephone, then added, "Listen, if the guv'nor should want to get in touch, he can ring me on 703–1157."

"I'll make a note of it, Harry, but I don't think you'll be hearing from Coghill; he left for Guildford about three quarters of an hour ago."

"To see Egremont?"

"Go to the top of the class," Ingleson said. Then a phone rang in the background and he told him he was wanted on the other line.

Mace hung up, puzzled to know why Coghill had apparently changed his mind. Back at the cemetery, Coghill had given him the impression he was going to take the easy way out and let sleeping dogs lie, but now it seemed the men who'd been with Karen Whitfield were no longer off limits. In the end, the whys and wherefores didn't really matter, and although Egremont was small beer compared with the likes of Jeremy Ashforth, at least the investigation was moving in the right direction again.

Egremont was fifty-three, an inch or two under six feet and was, Coghill thought, a good stone heavier than he should have been for his age and height. He exuded an air of bonhomie and his florid complexion gave the impression of a successful businessman who had wined and dined a little too well all his working life. An hour earlier, a phone call had reduced him to a quivering jelly, but now Egremont was acting as though he didn't have a care in the world. Coghill suspected that his newfound air of confidence was entirely due to a liquid lunch hurriedly taken before Coghill had arrived at the house in Alexandra Avenue. Even though he'd obviously been sucking a peppermint to disguise it, the smell of brandy was still present on his breath as they shook hands on the doorstep.

"Do come in, Inspector." Egremont stepped to one side and waved a plump hand. "The drawing room is the second door on your left. I'm sure you'd like some coffee, wouldn't you? Edith made a pot before she departed for the golf club."

"Edith?" Coghill said.

"My wife. She would have liked to meet you, but she's in the semifinals of the ladies' foursomes and she couldn't let her partner down at the last minute."

"Well, it's you I wanted to see, Mr. Egremont."

"So you said, but Edith happens to know you by name. You see, she used to work in the police department at the Home Office before we were married." Egremont reached past him and opened the door to the drawing room. "That's why she would have welcomed the chance of meeting you face to face."

"It's a small world," Coghill said. "Who knows, maybe there'll be another opportunity."

The drawing room was spacious and looked out on to a large garden with a wide expanse of lawn leading to an ornamental pond covered with water lilies. Clumps of irises had been planted in each corner, and between the stepping stones on the far side there was a statue of a small boy astride a dolphin. Directly behind the statue and in front of the screen of silver birch trees at the bottom of the garden was a crescent-shaped flower bed crammed with floribunda rosebushes, lace-cap hydrangeas, lupines and delphiniums, the latter beaten down and looking pretty sorry for themselves after the heavy rain that morning.

"You have a very nice house and garden," Coghill observed.

"Yes, it was my mother's pride and joy before she passed away in 1978."

Egremont, it seemed, was one of those people who took refuge in euphemisms; he couldn't call a spade a spade and bring himself to say that she had died.

"White or black, Inspector?"

Coghill turned away from the French windows. "White, please," he said.

"You will join me in a glass of brandy, won't you?"

"It's a little early in the day for me." Coghill sat down in an armchair near the fireplace and helped himself to a teaspoonful of brown sugar.

"And of course you're on duty."

"Yes." He stirred the coffee and raised the cup to his lips, his eyes on Egremont. The older man didn't look quite as confident or relaxed as he had a few minutes ago and his hand trembled slightly as he poured himself a generous measure from the bottle of Courvoisier on the silver tray. "How long have you been married, Mr. Egremont?"

Egremont stared at him, obviously taken aback by a question he hadn't anticipated. "Two and a half years." His voice was a croak and he took a sip of brandy and tried again. "Edith had been married before, but there were no children to complicate things. Her first husband was fatally injured in a traffic accident in 1962. She was quite young at the time, only twenty-four, and it must have been a terrible blow for her." He gulped again at the brandy, then went on at machine-gun speed. "I had known Edith for years before I proposed to her. We were both members of the Civil Service Sports Club and keen on badminton. That's how we met. I'm a lucky man, Inspector. I have a very loving and understanding wife, my mother left me well provided for and I was eligible for premature retirement with full pension rights and generous redundancy terms when the government decided to cut down on the number of civil servants. We were doubly fortunate in that Edith was able to take advantage of the same scheme." He smiled nervously. "Naturally, a number of our friends and acquaintances are very envious and jealous that we should be so well off, but whatever we have, we've earned. Contrary to what most people think, the Civil Service isn't a nine-to-five job with endless cups of tea from Monday to Friday."

"We all have our crosses to bear." Coghill finished his coffee and set the cup and saucer down on the occasional table. "How and when did you meet Karen Whitfield?" he asked bluntly.

"That's just it, I've never laid eyes on her."

"Your phone number is in her address book."

"So you said when you rang me." Egremont paused to have another nip of brandy and then topped up his glass. "It's all very puzzling," he said, shaking his head. "And embarrassing too. Believe me, I've been racking my brains, wondering how on earth she got hold of my name."

"I bet you have," Coghill said quietly.

"The only explanation I can think of is that one of my colleagues must have been impersonating me."

"I'm afraid that won't do."

"Are you calling me a liar?" Egremont said belligerently. "Because if that's the way you're going to behave, the sooner I get in touch with my solicitor, the better it will be for both of us."

"Don't be silly, Mr. Egremont. I've seen you on film performing with Trevor Whitfield."

It was a lie, but Egremont believed him. The color drained from his face and the glass in his right hand trembled.

"Oh, my Christ." He closed his eyes and repeated the phrase over and over again. Eventually, he placed the brandy glass on the table, took out a handkerchief and blew his nose. "This is the worst thing that's ever happened to me," he mumbled. "What in God's name will Edith think?"

"Maybe you can keep it from her," Coghill suggested. "All I want is a few straight answers to a few questions. Provided you cooperate, I won't be here when your wife returns from the golf club."

"And I'll never see or hear from you again?"

"That depends on how frank you are." Coghill shrugged. "I'm not anxious to make another trip to Guildford, but I will if later on I discover you've held something back from me."

Egremont gave it a lot of thought, fortifying himself all the while with several large nips of brandy. Finally, having summoned up sufficient Dutch courage, he said, "I met Karen Whitfield one rainy evening in March 1971. I was at a bit of a loose end, because Edith had telephoned me at the office earlier to say that she would be working late and would have to cry off the date we'd made to play badminton. I'd only been introduced to Edith the week before and I had this feeling she'd had second thoughts about our date, because she sensed I wasn't like most other men. Women can, you know."

"I'll take your word for it," Coghill said.

"Yes. Well, as you might imagine, I was pretty down in the dumps, so I went to a couple of pubs in Soho and had a few drinks to cheer myself up before going home to Guildford. To cut a long story short, I had one too many, and on my way to the Underground station at Tottenham Court Road, I happened to notice this walk-up flat next to a newsagent in Duke Street. The door was open and there was a visiting card above the buzzer which said: 'Model—top floor—please come up.' So I did."

"And met Karen Whitfield?"

Egremont nodded. "I don't know what prompted me to walk

up that dimly lit staircase; perhaps it was the drink or a subconscious desire to find out what sort of man I was, or a combination of the two. Anyway, as things turned out, the experiment was a ghastly failure, but Karen was very kind and understanding and I found her easy to talk to. In fact, apart from my mother, she was the only woman I felt completely at ease with until I really got to know Edith. I suppose that's why I became one of Karen's regulars."

Egremont had continued to see her once every three or four months, first at Duke Street, then at Abercorn House after she'd moved to Maida Vale. In the beginning, he'd regarded Karen as a sort of counselor but, with the passage of time, the nature of these private therapy sessions had become much more torrid and her fees had gone up and up. With the passage of time also, she'd discovered his real name and what he did for a living, worming the information out of him bit by bit.

Coghill said, "What exactly was your job at the Ministry of Ag and Fish?"

"I rose to the dizzy heights of assistant principal," Egremont told him. "At one time, I was a member of the team that renegotiated our entry terms to the Common Market for the Wilson government."

"And as a result, you got yourself into the newspapers?"

"Yes."

"That's how Karen Whitfield got your number and was able to put a price on her silence."

"You don't have to tell me, Inspector," Egremont said bitterly. "The price became even more inflationary after Edith insisted I put the announcement of our engagement in the *Daily Telegraph.*"

The initial demand had been for a lump sum of five hundred. After his mother had died in 1978, the hush money had risen to one thousand pounds per annum, from which plateau it had leapt to forty pounds a week following the announcement of his engagement to Edith. At the same time, Egremont had been informed that once they were married, he would be faced with an additional increase which would take their joint incomes into account.

"The bitch was bleeding me white. Then the government announced their redundancy scheme for civil servants and it seemed a heaven-sent opportunity to get out from under. The way I saw it, Karen would no longer be in a position to blackmail me if I left the ministry."

"But she proved you wrong," Coghill said.

"Oh yes. I should have known Karen wouldn't give up that easily. A week after I'd retired, she wrote a letter calmly informing me that her board of directors had agreed to my request that I should be allowed to invest in Karen Boutiques Limited. The sum involved amounted to exactly one-third of the golden handshake I'd received on leaving the Civil Service. I told her to go to hell."

"And?"

"Well, since then I've had a string of letters from her accountants who keep threatening to take me to court unless I pay up. The last one arrived just over a week ago."

"Are they all from Robert Atkinson and Company?" Coghill asked.

"The name doesn't ring a bell." Egremont got to his feet and lurched round the armchair to the writing desk in the nook formed by the chimney breast. Unlocking the drop leaf with a key he took from his waistcoat pocket, he rummaged through the pigeonholes and returned with a wad of letters. "This chap calls himself Lear," he said. "Can't make head nor tail of his first name. The initial letter's an O."

The scrawl above the signature block was indecipherable, but Coghill was reasonably sure Oliver Leese had signed it. People who went in for assumed names invariably chose an alias that began with the same initial letters as their own. The legal terminology was a clear indication that Quainton had drafted the letters, but of course he couldn't prove it.

"I know I shouldn't say this," Egremont rasped, "but in my opinion the man who killed that bloodsucking whore deserves a medal. The world is a better place with her under the sod. And the same applies to that poisonous little creep who was supposed to be her husband."

"Did Karen Whitfield ever subject you to any other kind of pressure?"

"Like what?"

"The Common Market negotiations," said Coghill. "Did she ever question you about them?"

"Jesus Christ, Inspector, you surely don't think she was interested in obtaining classified information, do you?"

The thought had occurred to him. If the security services had impounded the address book, it would explain why Tucker hadn't interviewed any of her former clients.

"Money was the be-all and end-all as far as she was concerned." Egremont took a pace backward and fell into the armchair. His left foot caught the underside of the occasional table and knocked his brandy glass onto the floor, the dregs seeping into the carpet. "Damn," he said, "I do believe I'm a little tipsy."

He was all of that, Coghill thought. Egremont's speech had gradually become more and more slurred and he was finding it difficult to focus his eyes on Coghill. "Did you introduce any of your friends or acquaintances to her?" Coghill asked.

"Good God, I'm not that stupid." Egremont retrieved his glass and poured himself another large measure of brandy. "Anyway, Karen didn't need me to go pimping for her. She used to do her own advertising when she was plying for trade in Duke Street."

"What sort of advertising?"

"Contact magazines, cards in shop windows. You know the kind of thing—'Young lady gives French lessons under strict supervision.'"

According to Tucker and the Criminal Records Office, Karen Whitfield had had no previous form, yet it was inconceivable that her activities in Duke Street had escaped the notice of the Vice Squad. Coghill figured there was only one inference to be drawn from that: at least one senior officer in the squad must have been on her payroll.

"It's past three o'clock," Egremont said anxiously. "Edith will be back any minute."

"I thought your wife was playing golf?"

"No. Actually, she went to the library. I told her one of my former colleagues was up for a background check and had nominated me as a referee. I said you were an ex-police officer working for the security service. It was the only explanation I could think of."

In a panic-stricken moment, Egremont had told his wife a pack of lies to allay any suspicion. Now he was going to have an even harder time explaining why he was drunk in the middle of the afternoon.

"You'd better make yourself another pot of coffee," Coghill told him. "And while you're at it, pour a little brandy into the spare glass. You don't want your wife to think you're a solitary drinker."

"You're leaving?" There was a pathetic note of eagerness in his voice.

"I don't think I need trouble you any longer."

"Will I see you again?"

"I doubt it," Coghill said.

Egremont struggled to his feet and accompanied him to the front door. He was still standing there, swaying like a sapling in a strong breeze, when Coghill got into the Volvo and pulled away from the curbside.

The simile was not inappropriate. Egremont was a weak man who'd spent his entire life bending with the prevailing wind. Coghill thought it likely he'd always been dominated by women with strong characters, first his mother, then Karen Whitfield and now his wife, though he couldn't be sure of her. He wondered what had prompted Edith to marry him. An attraction of opposites, a desire to mother somebody or a need for companionship? As far as Egremont was concerned, it had probably been an urge to protect himself. Although a homosexual relationship between consenting adults was no longer a criminal offense, people who indulged in that kind of thing were still considered to be a security risk by government departments. Marrying Edith would have been a drastic step for him, and, in Coghill's view, he just wasn't ruthless enough to hire a professional killer to murder Karen Whitfield.

Then, suddenly, it occurred to Coghill there was possibly a much simpler and more direct method of tracing the number-one suspect. Easing his foot on the accelerator, he kept a sharp lookout for a public phone and, spotting one on the outskirts of Guildford, he pulled into the curb and stopped.

A faint hope that his source had meant what he'd said and would get back to him with some worthwhile information was the main reason Mace had stayed on at The Bricklayers' Arms long after closing time. There was also Vera; that she regarded him as some kind of hero figure was very flattering to the ego, especially as his had taken a battering. If he'd had one less drink on the house, if Ingleson hadn't reminded him that his record since joining the CID was nothing to write home about, he would never have accepted her hospitality. As it was, he had a guilty conscience. In all the years Mace had been married, he had never so much as looked at another woman, yet here he was closeted in a small back room with a bird who'd made it very clear that she wasn't averse to a bit of slap-and-tickle. So far, he'd managed to keep his distance but it was a losing battle; every time Vera fetched him a beer from the bar, she moved her chair closer to his until their knees were touching and her left hand was resting possessively on his thigh. At a loss to know how he was going to extricate himself from the situation, Mace was moved to a silent prayer of thanks when the telephone suddenly rang. Leaning forward, he snatched the receiver from the cradle and answered the call.

Coghill said, "Still waiting for your source, Harry?"

The number where he could be reached wasn't the only thing Ingleson had told Coghill. Good old Fred had obviously made a few derisive comments, hinting that Mace's unreliable informer was giving him the runaround.

"I'm expecting him to show up at any moment," Mace said, and tried to sound convincing.

"Really? Well, once you've seen him, I want you to check out all the housing agencies in the London area—Flatland, the City Bureau and so on. Have a word with the manager of each agency and ask them if they were approached by Oscar Pittis or anyone else with a Christian name and surname beginning with those same initial letters. This would be on or shortly before the first of July, the day he cleared out of the flat in Highgate."

"It's a bit of a long shot, isn't it, Guv?"

"Have you got a better idea, Harry?" Coghill asked him.

"No. I'll get cracking on it."

"You do that," Coghill said and hung up on him.

"Trouble?" Vera asked.

"There's a cold wind blowing and I'm on the receiving end." Mace smiled. "I'll have to be on my way—duty calls and all that."

Vera nodded, stood up and helped him to his feet as though he were an old man. "Will I see you again, Harry?"

"Anything's possible," he said.

She walked him through the deserted bar, unlocked one of the doors in the entrance and gave him a farewell peck on the cheek before he stepped out into the street.

His car was parked in a side road behind the pub and as he strolled toward it, Mace was aware that his legs were none too steady. How many beers had he had? Three, or was it four? It must have been a least four Heinekens, and that didn't include the whiskey chasers Vera had been plying him with betweentimes. He took several deep breaths, hoping this would clear his head, but the muzziness persisted. Although in no condition to drive, he nonetheless unlocked the door and got in behind the wheel.

The interior was like an oven and he wound down the window before inserting the ignition key to crank the engine into life. Shifting into first gear, he forgot to release the handbrake, with the inevitable result that the car stalled the instant he took his foot off the clutch. He was still attempting to get himself sorted out when a black police constable appeared by the open window and asked to see his driver's license.

"I'm a detective sergeant in the CID," Mace told him and

produced his warrant card to prove it. "And I'm on duty," he added.

"If you say so, Sergeant."

"What's the matter, sunshine? Don't you believe me?"

The constable met his uneasy smile with a blank expression. "I think you've been drinking, Sergeant," he said.

"I've had a couple," Mace admitted.

"I've also reason to believe you're unfit to drive. That's why I must ask you to accompany me to the police station."

Mace closed his eyes and silently let rip with every four-letter word he knew. They would breathalyze him, the blood test would be positive and twenty-nine year's unblemished service would count for nothing. And the bitter part, he thought savagely, was that his informer had proved to be as unreliable as Ingleson had always said he was.

14.

Patterson fitted the last cassette onto the winder, then slowly rotated the crank to examine each frame as it passed through the gate. The task of compiling a montage from the thirteen video tapes in his possession had proved to be a time-consuming and intricate job, one which demanded a marked degree of patience and the utmost concentration. In some cases, the identity of the client had become apparent early in the porno movie; in others, the exposures he wanted had appeared toward the very end. On this particular occasion, he reached the midway point before the VIP looked at his reflection in the two-way mirror and was captured by the hidden camera.

Satisfied with the quality of the pictures, Patterson reversed the crank to obtain a suitable lead-in, then, having severed the film, he wound it forward again and made a second cut some twenty-odd frames after the subject appeared in full view for the first time. That done, he placed the film clip on one side and spliced the two severed halves together.

So far, so good, he thought. One more join and the montage would be complete. As a trailer, it lacked artistic merit and the sound track would be pure gobbledegook, but he wasn't entering the clip for a prize at the Cannes Festival. All he needed was enough footage for Denise Rousell to recognize what was on offer. If she wanted time to study an individual face, he had only to operate the freeze button on the video remote control.

He checked the join to make sure the adhesive had taken, then rewound the foreshortened tape and removed the cassette. About to splice the last piece of footage to complete the montage, he was interrupted by a peremptory ring on the doorbell to his room.

Irritated by the unwelcome intrusion, he left the worktable to see who the caller was and found himself face to face with his landlady, Mrs. Drobnowski. Unless his memory was at fault, he was sure she was wearing the same brown silk dress and apron he'd seen her in the day they first met. She had, however, dispensed with the well-worn carpet slippers for a pair of high-heeled, open-toed sandals.

"Oh, Mr. Pearce." Mrs. Drobnowski gave him a fleeting smile and at the same time tucked a stray lock of hair into the bun at the nape of her neck. "I half expected to find you weren't at home. I didn't recognize the car outside the house."

"The Mini's in for repair," Patterson told her. "I hired the car from Hertz."

"Oh, that explains it."

She took a pace forward as though she expected him to invite her inside, but Patterson wasn't having any of that and refused to give way. He didn't want her to see the equipment on the worktable, or catch a glimpse of the bathroom where he'd lifted the linoleum and removed one of the floorboards in front of the pedestal washbasin to get at the cache of video tapes.

"What can I do for you, Mrs. Drobnowski?" he inquired politely.

"I just wanted to tell you the electricity would be off from nine A.M. to five P.M. tomorrow. My husband's taking a day off to rewire the flat on the ground floor."

"Well, thanks for telling me," he said.

"If there's anything perishable in your fridge, I'd be happy to keep it in mine until the power is back on." The fleeting smile made another brief appearance and she tried to move forward again.

"That's very kind of you, but right now I've only got half a pint of milk and a small pat of butter, so I think I'll be okay."

"You're sure?"

"I'm sure," Patterson said and slowly closed the door in her face.

People like Mrs. Drobnowski were dangerous; nosy, observant, inquisitive, they didn't miss a trick and were a threat to his security. One thing was crystal-clear; within the next twenty-four hours, the KGB would have to give him a definite yes or no, because the longer he stayed in Linsdale Gardens, the greater the risk would be.

Patterson glanced at his wristwatch, saw that it was seventeen minutes after four and realized he would have to get a move on. Denise Rousell had said seven-thirty for eight, but it was essential he arrive at her bungalow a good hour ahead of the stipulated time, conclude their business and get the hell out of there before any interlopers from the Soviet Embassy showed up to relieve him of the sample tape. With this in mind, he worked swiftly to complete the montage, then carted the spare cassettes into the bedroom. Before placing them in the cache near the pedestal washbasin, he first removed the .22 caliber Iver Johnson and examined the revolver to make sure there was a live round in each chamber. The weapon check completed, he stashed the cassettes between the joints, nailed the floorboard back in place and relaid the linoleum.

Half an hour later, Patterson drove out of Linsdale Gardens and headed north across the river toward Woodford. The smart executive briefcase resting on the seat beside him contained the sample tape and five assorted lengths of clothesline he'd purchased that morning. Beneath the slightly flared jacket he was wearing, the .22 caliber revolver rode comfortably on his left hip in a black leather holster.

The note Coghill found pinned to the blotting pad on his desk was brief, curt and singularly uninformative. It read: "Before you do anything else, report to me." Angry with Kingman and baffled to know why Bert should have written to him in such a vein, Coghill waited until his temper cooled, then went next door to find out. The customary friendly greeting was conspicuous by its absence; all he got from Kingman was a long cold stare.

"You wanted to see me?" he said, equally offhand.

"You bet your sweet life I do." Kingman leaned forward, elbows on the desk, shoulders hunched. "As of now, you're suspended from duty."

"I'm what?"

"You're not hard of hearing, Inspector," Kingman said icily. "You're suspended pending the outcome of an investigation into your personal affairs by officers from the Complaints Investigation Bureau."

"Do you mind telling me what I'm supposed to have done?"

"Certainly. You've been on the take."

"That's balls and you know it."

"I'm not so sure." Kingman studied him thoughtfully. "Ever come across a James Nicholls?"

"Nicholls?" Coghill frowned, then snapped his fingers. "Dandy Jim Nicholls, the self-styled crown prince of porn. He owned a chain of dirty bookshops and massage parlors off Soho and was making a packet until he drew a ten stretch for grievous bodily harm in seventy-seven."

"I thought you might remember him. Nicholls claims you were on his payroll when you were a detective constable with the Obscene Publications Squad."

"If you believe that, you've got to be out of your tiny mind."

"Don't get stroppy with me," Kingman growled. "I'm only the fucking middle man. Nicholls has made a statement and the assistant commissioner has decided the bloodhounds should follow it up. And I can't say I blame him; the Obscene Publications Squad wasn't exactly lily-white in your day."

That was putting it mildly, Coghill thought. With very few exceptions, the squad had done very nicely thank you, and he'd been put under a lot of pressure to go along with the others and take his share of the kickback. Twice he'd found an envelope containing £150 in used notes in the top drawer of his desk, and there had been a good deal of consternation when he'd immediately turned the bribe over to his superior officer. One of the detective sergeants had taken him aside and told him he'd better watch his step, and after he'd ignored that friendly piece of advice, every dirty job going had come his way. When this tactic had failed to intimidate him, a couple of muscle men had put him in the hospital for a month with a broken jaw and three cracked ribs. With the benefit of hindsight, Coghill was now inclined to believe that his promotion to detective sergeant and subsequent transfer to Serious Crimes had been their way of getting rid of him.

"My fingers were never sticky," he told Kingman.

"Yeah? Well, some people are beginning to wonder how you managed to afford a flat in South Kensington on a detective constable's pay."

"Janice had a job, too. The building society took her salary into account when they gave us a mortgage on the property."

"Good," said Kingman. "Let's hope she can produce her pay slips."

"After eight years? You've got to be joking."

"The Complaints Investigation Bureau won't think it's a joke. They'll want proof that your wife contributed toward the deposit on the flat and without it, you're in the shit."

"This whole business is beginning to stink," Coghill said angrily. "I think I'm being set up."

"You're what?"

"Muzzled, gagged, neutralized; whichever way you want to put it. Somebody in Whitehall is determined to keep the Whitfield-Leese investigation on a short leash and the word went out that the VIPs in Karen's address book are strictly off limits. Overall responsibility for the dual investigation went to the Regional Crime Squad because the high-priced help knew they could rely on Tucker to keep his nose clean. This morning I tried to get in touch with Jeremy Ashforth; that's why I've been suspended."

"That's a load of rubbish," Kingman snapped.

"Is it? How long has Nicholls been inside? Five years? So why did he wait until now to point a finger at me?"

"You're not the only officer he's named and he didn't suddenly open his mouth. Nicholls has been talking to the CIB ever since he was transferred from Parkhurst back to the Scrubs nine weeks ago."

"Four years ten months is still a long time. What persuaded him to break his vow of silence?"

"Remember Operation Countryman, when our revered commissioner decided to bring in the provincial yokels to purge the

Met of corruption? Maybe Nicholls saw how well some of his friends had done out of that little caper and figured he'd better take a leaf out of their book. Anyway, I hear his wife was fed up with traveling to the Isle of Wight on visiting days."

"That was part of the deal, was it? He'd talk to the CIB if we moved him back to London?"

"Something like that," Kingman agreed.

"I see. And when did Nicholls mention my name for the first time? Yesterday? The day before? A fortnight ago? Or right at the beginning?"

"You'll have to ask the bloodhounds from CIB," Kingman said testily.

They were like cat and dog, circling each other, spitting and snarling. Whatever the final outcome, things would never be the same again between them, but Coghill no longer cared.

"That could be a mite embarrassing," he snapped. "I mean, they may have casually asked Nicholls if he'd ever met me and he figured a nod was as good as a wink, used his imagination and told them what they wanted to hear."

"I've already said you weren't the only officer he named."

"Well, Nicholls was coached by experts, wasn't he? My guess is the others were thrown in for good measure to make it look right."

"You know something?" Kingman drawled. "I was going to suggest you have a word with the Police Federation so that they could put you in touch with a hot-shot lawyer. Now I'm beginning to think you should get them to make an appointment for you with a reputable shrink. Meantime, you'd better get off home and introduce yourself to the two officers from Complaints who are probably waiting on your doorstep."

Loyalty was supposed to work both ways, down as well as up, something Kingman conveniently appeared to have forgotten. Coghill doubted if he would get much help out of him, but there was an innocent party who deserved to be protected and it was worth a try.

"About Janice," he said tentatively. "Do we have to drag her into this?"

"I think you'll find they've already interviewed her. Franklin rang me earlier this afternoon to ask if I knew her present address and I said I thought she was still living at seventeen Brent Way in Hendon. I hope my memory wasn't at fault?"

"It wasn't," Coghill said grimly.

He wondered what Janice had said to them, wondered too if she had pulled the rug out from under his feet. There had always been a vindictive streak in her character, and there was a distinct possibility it had surfaced following the bitter row they'd had yesterday after Whitfield had phoned him.

"That's a relief." Kingman rubbed his nose as though it had an itch, then said, "All I need now is your warrant card. Naturally you'll get it back once the CIB are satisfied you're in the clear."

Coghill reached inside his jacket, took out his warrant card and tossed it on to Kingman's desk. "What makes you think I give a fuck one way or the other," he said and then walked out of the office.

Patterson turned into Cherry Tree Road and stopped opposite number 154. Grabbing the executive briefcase from the adjoining seat, he got out of the Ford Fiesta and walked up the narrow front path between two strips of grass that hadn't seen a lawn-mower for several weeks.

The woman who answered the door had iron-gray hair cut short and a squarish masculine face with the down of a moustache clearly visible on the upper lip. About his height and weight, she was wearing a checkered shirt with the sleeves rolled up and a pair of loose-fitting gray slacks covered with dog hairs. The brief flicker of recognition in her eyes confirmed his hunch that Orlov's people had photographed him when he was in Paris.

"Hi, Denise," he said, smiling. "My name's Henry Kingfisher."

"You're early," Denise said, then added, "I wasn't expecting you until seven-thirty."

"I must have misheard you." Patterson moved forward, forcing her to back off down the hall. "Still, now that I'm here we might as well get on with it."

"The kennels stay open until six P.M.."

"It won't be the end of the world if you close a few minutes early for once," Patterson told her calmly.

She hesitated, then with a slight shrug of her shoulders, Denise Rousell turned about and led him into the living room at the back. Like the slacks she was wearing, both armchairs, the sofa and the Axminster carpet needed a good brushing. There was also an unpleasant smell coming from the kitchen next door where several large saucepans of offal were gently simmering on a low gas. In the left-hand corner of the room was an old twenty-one-inch television set, its cabinet scratched, the top marked with circular rings, as though it had been pressed into service as an occasional table. By contrast, the video machine standing next to it looked brand new.

"When did you get that?" he asked.

"The rental people delivered it this morning."

"Yeah? Well, suppose you draw up a chair, make yourself comfortable and we'll see what sort of a picture we get."

"I'm afraid you'll have to wait until I've fed the animals," she said.

"Is that a fact?" Patterson walked over to the window and looked out. Away in the background, a train moved from left to right along the embankment toward the Underground station at Roding Valley, and even though the windows were closed, the rattle of its wheels was clearly audible. As far as he could tell, the noise had no effect on the dogs; in the nearest pen, a Labrador was nose to nose with a Dalmatian bitch in the adjoining cage, while beyond them, a Great Dane lay on its side apparently fast asleep.

"You know something, Denise?" he said. "I think you're trying to snow me. Those dogs out there aren't hungry, and I don't see any kennel maid."

"I expect she's in her room."

"Bullshit. You don't have anybody living with you, Mrs. O. D. Beaumont; I've seen a copy of the electoral roll at the central library."

"You're very thorough," Denise said acidly.

"It's the only way to survive in this business." Patterson opened the briefcase, took out the cassette and loaded it into the video machine. He noticed her handbag lying on the sofa next to a pile of mimeographed newsletters from various kennel clubs and, crossing the room in a few strides, he picked it up and thrust it at her. "You'll need something to write on," he said. "A diary, the back of an old envelope, anything to hand. You're going to see a lot of VIPs in the next few minutes and I want you to make a list of their names."

"I presume you'll tell me just who they are, Mr. Kingfisher?"

"Wrong," said Patterson. "You'll get them from the soundtrack. Not that you'll need any prompting to recognize these men."

"I think you're overestimating my importance in the scheme of things. I was only a humble clerical officer when I retired from the Civil Service."

"The hell you were." Patterson laid a hand on her shoulder and pushed her down into an armchair. "Point one: clerical officers don't end up collecting an OBE. Point two: I know the KGB expects you to put a price on the merchandise, and they're not in the habit of using a nobody to do that kind of job. Point three: you can't stall me forever, so let's cut out the bullshit."

He waited until Denise Rousell had found a pocket notebook in her handbag, then switched on the video machine, picked up the remote control and moved around the armchair to stand behind her. Setting the tape in motion, he brought the picture sharply into focus and held it momentarily on freeze the instant Karen Whitfield unmasked Jeremy Ashforth. He repeated the process with the subsequent clips and was amused to see that Denise Rousell was visibly nauseated by some of the more perverted acts of sexual congress she witnessed on the screen.

"That must have been quite an education for you," he said when the tape finally ended.

"Yes, one I could have done without." She twisted around in the chair to face him, her bottom lip curled. "Furthermore, I don't believe the people I represent will be interested in acquiring these films."

"Try convincing Viktor of that. After seeing Raschid al Jalud in action, he couldn't wait to get in touch with Moscow and London."

"He didn't know how you'd acquired the cassettes."

"I'll tell you this," Patterson said, "it won't bother the people in Dzerzhinsky Square. They're not squeamish like you."

He thought there might be some reluctance to use the material while the heat was on, but three or four months from now, other events would have overtaken the Whitfield affair and, with very few exceptions, nobody would connect the KGB with her murder. The exceptions were the VIPs, but they had their reputations to protect and would keep their mouths shut.

"The asking price is half a million U.S. dollars." Conscious that Denise Rousell was watching his every move, Patterson walked over to the video machine, retrieved the cassette and, collecting his briefcase, returned to his former position behind her. "I'll accept payment in any major currency," he continued. "Yen, guilders, French or Swiss francs, Deutschemarks, but pounds sterling and rubles are out." He placed the palm of his right hand against her jaw and gently forced her head around until she was looking at the screen once more. "The Bank of England has a long arm and the Soviet currency is only good for papering walls."

"You've an inflated opinion of their value, Mr. Kingfisher. I think you'll be lucky to get one-tenth of the asking price."

Her reaction didn't surprise him. He and Viktor might have shaken hands on the deal, but from previous experience, he'd known there was a distinct possibility Moscow would decline to honor their verbal agreement.

"Three hundred and fifty thousand dollars," he said. "That's the bottom line, take it or leave it."

"You're in no position to dictate terms," Denise told him curtly.

"Yeah? I can't believe you're that naive, Denise." Patterson placed the briefcase on the floor, opened both locks and placed the cassette inside. Then, removing the five assorted lengths of clothesline, he stuffed them into his pocket and straightened up. "I can sell the cassettes one at a time to other parties. Naturally, it'll take a while longer, but there won't be a shortage of buyers. The Italian, French, German and U.S. intelligence agencies will be only too anxious to acquire a slice of the material on offer. Be sure you pass the good word on to your friends."

"I think you'll find they will receive the news with equanimity," she said primly.

"I'm not interested in your opinion. Viktor's associates have until eleven o'clock tomorrow morning. When I phone you then, I want a straight yes or no. Any hedging and the deal's off." Patterson drew the revolver from the hip holster and laid the barrel against the right side of her head just forward of the temple. "I don't intend to hurt you," he said quietly, "but if you scream or try to resist, I'll hammer the butt into your skull. You get the message?"

"Yes." She swallowed nervously and repeated the assurance although her voice refused to rise above a whisper.

Patterson said, "I'm glad we understand one another. Now lean forward and clasp both hands behind you."

Second thoughts killed the question which had begun to form on her lips, and with an involuntary shudder, Denise Rousell leaned forward and crossed her hands behind. Patterson holstered the revolver, lashed her arms at the wrists and elbows, then made her lie down on the floor, where he proceeded to truss her legs around the ankles and above the knees. As a final touch, he used the remaining length of clothesline to draw her ankles up to her elbows until she was arched in a bow.

"You may suffer some discomfort," he told her, "but it won't be for long. Your friends from Kensington Gardens will release you when they arrive at seven-thirty. You see, I'm wise to you. Why should the KGB part with good money for something they can get for nothing? With their technical resources, they can get all the stills they need from this one tape. How, when or where they intend to grab it is immaterial. The important thing is that you've seen the license number of my car and I need a head start."

"You're mad."

"No," Patterson said, "just careful."

He took a handkerchief, folded it diagonally and gagged her, knotting the ends tight to force her mouth open as though she were yawning. Then, having locked the briefcase, he picked it up and walked out of the room. He opened the front door and put the catch down to prevent the lock from reengaging when he closed it behind him. Although the door now appeared to be firmly shut, he knew it would swing back on its hinges at the slightest touch.

Satisfied he hadn't overlooked anything, Patterson got into the Ford Fiesta and drove back to his flat. The route he took was not the shortest distance between two points, and throughout the hour-long journey, he kept one eye focused on the rearview mirror. Although it soon became apparent that he was not being followed, Patterson did not relax his guard until he turned into Linsdale Gardens.

15.

The footsteps in the corridor were brisk and purposeful, the heels striking the floor with the distinct military precision Caroline Brooke had come to associate with Vaudrey. The rhythm was also a rough guide to his mood. A slow, measured tread was usually a sign that he was either deep in thought or worried about something, while a normal, infantry marching pace was indicative of anger or elation. When he walked into her office moments later, the half-smile on his mouth told her it was the latter.

"Morning, Caroline," he said cheerfully. "Have you heard the news about Coghill?"

"What news?"

"He's been suspended." Vaudrey strolled over to the window and stood there gazing out into space, both hands thrust deep into the jacket pockets of his blue pinstripe. "A man called Nicholls, one of the former porn kings of Soho, has made a statement alleging that Coghill was on his payroll when he was a detective constable with the Obscene Publications Squad."

"That's a long time ago." Her voice was neutral, but the doubt showed in the way she shook her head, a gesture which was lost on Vaudrey who was still facing the window. "Was Coghill the only police officer he accused?" she asked diffidently.

"No. As a matter of fact, three of his former colleagues have also been suspended. Their names didn't mean anything to me, but I understand two of them were previously questioned by officers from the provincial forces drafted in for Operation Countryman. They were given a clean bill of health on that occasion and it's possible there's no substance to these latest allegations either."

"Where did you hear that, Nicholas? On the grapevine?"

"One has one's friends and acquaintances," Vaudrey said enigmatically.

It was a masterly understatement. Vaudrey's contacts were legion and embraced every government department in Whitehall. These contacts, which he had cultivated assiduously over the years, enabled him to keep a finger on the public pulse without going through the usual channels. Although Vaudrey maintained that he'd never abused this unofficial "old boy" network, Caroline Brooke could recall any number of instances in the past when it was obvious that a word in the right ear had ultimately produced the information he'd wanted.

"Do we have any idea how long the investigation of these police officers will take?" she inquired.

"It's difficult to say." Vaudrey shrugged, then turned about to face her. "In some cases there is circumstantial evidence to support the accusations of bribery and corruption; in others, we only have Nicholls' word for it."

"So where does Coghill stand?"

"Oh, he has a lot of very awkward questions to answer."

"I find that hard to believe."

"Really?" Vaudrey raised his eyebrows. "I didn't realize you knew him, Caroline."

"I don't."

"Then I fail to see how you can be so positive he's innocent. I trust you've not allowed yourself to be unduly impressed by the photographs you've seen of him in the newspapers. I admit he has a strong, rugged-looking face and I can appreciate that a lot of women would find him attractive, but it's irrational to judge a man's character by his appearance."

The acid reproof touched a new nerve, especially as she had to concede that there was more than a grain of truth in Vaudrey's observation. Instinct, however, was not the only reason why she was convinced the allegations were false. A highflyer, ambitious, intelligent and a potential source of trouble; that had been her assessment of Coghill, but Nicholas had repeated it word for word and with considerable vehemence. The fact that a few days later he had seemed completely indifferent when she'd told him Coghill had tried to get in touch with Jeremy Ashforth had been merely a pose. Knowing the way Vaudrey operated, she was convinced more than ever now that he had anticipated the event and had already set the wheels in motion to deal with the threat.

"His suspension is just a little too convenient, Nicholas," she said tartly. "We've gone out of our way to protect the VIPs Karen Whitfield was blackmailing; then Coghill decides to step out of line and within a matter of hours of our knowing this, he's under investigation."

"A purely fortuitous coincidence." Vaudrey smiled. "And it's not the only bit of luck we've had. If Cadbury had been really on the ball, we could have been faced with some very embarrassing publicity."

"Cadbury? Who's he?"

"The detective superintendent from S District."

"His name is Rowntree," Caroline told him.

"I knew it was some brand of chocolate." Vaudrey perched himself on the radiator, left foot firmly planted on the floor to retain his balance, the other swinging idly like a pendulum. "Leese had an answering machine connected to his telephone," he continued. "Anyone who rang the flat while he was out was advised to try 01–813–2693. Fortunately for us, Tucker got hold of the tape and decided Special Branch were the people to check it out. The phone number led them to a studio in the Edgware Road near Marble Arch. It appears Leese operated behind a legitimate business front—wedding photographs, minor fashion shows, formal portraits and the like—but the real profit came from his involvement with hardcore pornography. The contents of his filing cabinet in the office upstairs showed he had produced and directed several blue films in collaboration with a Dutch entrepreneur, which would explain what he was doing in Amsterdam last week. Special Branch also found a photocopy of an IOU made out to Karen Whitfield for eight thousand pounds and dated the third of March 1971."

"The address book." Caroline snapped her fingers. "Leese must be one of the six men I couldn't identify. There were only two symbols against the entry, a canvas mounted on an easel and a little girl. No payments had been made to reduce the original debt and I assumed the client was an up-and-coming portrait artist whom Karen Whitfield saw as a long-term investment."

"He was all of that," Vaudrey said dryly. "And I fancy he did more than photograph the little girl. That was her hold over him, the reason why he became her accomplice. Can you imagine the salacious articles the press would have run had they discovered that Karen Whitfield had been leading a double life?"

"Is it likely they would have done so?"

"You're being naive again," Vaudrey said. "There isn't a police station in the Metropolitan area that doesn't have a tipster on some reporter's expense account."

"And as you've said before, we don't want any adverse publicity."

"It wouldn't be in the public interest. But there's more to it than that."

"You amaze me, Nicholas."

"Sarcasm doesn't become you," Vaudrey told her. "You know damn well this department can't function properly if it's in the limelight. However, rest assured there'll be no coverup. Any former client of Karen Whitfield who's in a sensitive government post will be removed and sent elsewhere, but it has to be done discreetly and with the minimum of fuss."

"There are thirty-six entries in that address book, Nicholas. We've managed to put a name to thirty-one of them and of that total, you're proposing to deal with rather less than half. What happens to the others, the Jeremy Ashforths?"

"Let's wait and see. You never know, they might be useful to us one day." Vaudrey left his perch on the radiator, walked over to the door and then suddenly turned about as though he'd just remembered why he had dropped into her office. "Oh, by the way," he added, "you'd better get to work on the Libyan scenario. We may well need it any day now."

Caroline stared at him, round-eyed, her mouth half open.

"What Libyan scenario?" she asked in a small voice.

"The one we'll put to Raschid al Jalud. He doesn't know it yet, but he's about to bait a trap for Patterson. Naturally, he'll deny all knowledge of the man, but we'll hit him with a surveillance report, the one where our people observed him with Patterson in Northumberland Avenue. We'll also quote the registration number of the Datsun and then disclose everything we know about his association with Karen Whitfield." He glanced at his wristwatch and looked up smiling. "I'd like you to knock out a draft on those lines. Make it top priority and give me a buzz as soon as it's ready."

"You'll have the draft before noon."

"Good girl." Vaudrey flashed her another smile, then wheeled out of the office before she had a chance to ask him just who was going to approach Raschid al Jalud.

Mace left the Underground station at Blackfriars and walked toward Upper Thames Street, his shoulders slumped, a hangdog expression on his face. Nothing had gone right for him from the moment the black police constable had booked him for drinking and driving late yesterday afternoon, and the way things were going this morning, it looked as though his run of bad luck was destined to continue for the foreseeable future.

The Borough of Southwark was one of his former stamping grounds and the desk sergeant was an old acquaintance, but despite their long-standing friendship, there wasn't much he'd been able to do for him. The breathalyzer and blood tests had proved Mace was over the limit, and the chief inspector in charge of the local police station was a very progressive type who was determined to back his constable in the interests of race relations or some such crap.

"Sorry, Harry," the desk sergeant had told him, "but that's the way it is. My guv'nor refuses to turn a blind eye and the best I can do for you is sit on the paperwork for a couple of days."

Although it was only a brief stay of execution, Mace had immediately taken him up on the offer in the faint hope that within the next forty-eight hours he might somehow redress the balance by running Pittis to ground. Truth was, a part of him had known all along that he was being stupid, but it had taken a restless night to make him see he was only compounding the offense. Over breakfast, he'd rehearsed how he would break the news to Coghill, only for his resolution to founder ignominiously the instant he learned the younger man had been suspended. In the circumstances, he should have telephoned Kingman to inform him of the impending charge, but knowing the superintendent thought him next to useless, he lacked the courage to do that.

All he could do now was to pursue the line of inquiry Coghill had suggested yesterday and so far he'd made a real hash of it. Precious time had been wasted because he'd assumed Pittis was a creature of habit who would have moved from one expensive flat to an equally expensive address elsewhere. Consequently, Mace had begun his inquiries with the Flatlands agency in Victoria, where of course he'd drawn a complete blank. He wondered if his visit to the City Bureau would prove equally negative.

The agency was in an old Victorian building opposite a stretch of waste ground near the junction of Semple Road with Upper Thames Street. Mentally crossing his fingers, Mace climbed the wooden staircase to their office on the second floor, saw a door with the message "Inquiries—please walk in" stenciled on the frosted glass, and did just that. There were two desks inside but only one receptionist, a thin girl in a pair of faded blue jeans and a T-shirt who was standing at a small table in the window measuring instant coffee into a mug.

"Be with you in a tick," she said, her back still toward him.

"No hurry." Mace eyed the shrouded typewriter and the single wilting rose in a narrow long-stemmed vase on the desk just inside the door. "Where's your colleague then?" he asked.

"On holiday at Lake Como, the lucky devil." The girl switched off the electric kettle, poured the boiling water into the mug and added a dash of milk from a carton. Opening a small tin, she dropped two saccharin tablets into the coffee and stirred it with a plastic spoon. "You looking for somewhere to live?" she asked.

"Sort of," Mace admitted.

"Well, whatever the landlord is asking per month, we take the equivalent of a fortnight's rent on the initial payment as our commission." The girl finished stirring the coffee and returned to her desk. "It's as well to get these things straight before we go any farther. Saves a lot of heartburn later on." She gave him a fleeting smile and sat down. "Now, how much do you want to pay? Bed-sitters range between fifteen and twenty-five pounds per week, depending on the area and facilities provided. A self-contained flat with single bed, sitting room, bath and kitchenette starts at fifty-five."

"I'm not looking to pay anything," Mace said.

"That's all I need," the girl said, "a comedian."

"I'm a police officer."

"It amounts to the same thing."

"All right," Mace said evenly, "you've had your little joke, now look at the pretty badge."

The girl stared at the crest of the Metropolitan Police embossed on the front cover of the warrant card he was holding, her eyes popping, mouth agape. "Oh God, you weren't kidding." She smiled nervously, then said, "Look, I know there isn't a tax disk on my Fiat, but it's not like you think. I posted the insurance certificate and check for the road fund tax to Swansea a week ago and I'm still waiting for the license."

"That's not why I'm here," Mace told her.

"Thank the Lord for that," she said with feeling.

"I'm trying to locate a Mr. Oscar Pittis. It's possible he may have called on you last Thursday looking for accommodation."

"Pittis?" The girl wrinkled her brow. "The name doesn't strike a chord with me."

"He's about five foot eight or nine, round face, light brown hair, hazel eyes and has a Canadian accent."

"Pearce, Oliver Pearce, the insurance salesman." The girl swiveled around to face a narrow filing cabinet and pulled out a drawer labeled "L to Q." She went to the P's, flicked through the cards and extracted the one she wanted. "Yes, here it is—seventeen Linsdale Gardens, Kennington, three self-contained flats in an old Edwardian house. The property is owned by a Mrs. Drobnowski who lives at 48 Richouse Terrace."

"Drobnowski." Mace shook his head. "Nothing like a good old-fashioned English name."

"She's English. Her husband served with the Polish forces during the war and stayed on in this country. He's a cantankerous old sod at the best of times. According to our records, we made an appointment for Mr. Pearce to view the flat last Thursday."

"Did he take it?" Mace asked.

"Oh yes, he sent us a money order for our commission the same day." The girl looked up. "Do you know where Linsdale Gardens is?" she asked.

"Not exactly."

"Where's your car?"

"I left it at home," Mace said.

"Well, Kennington is the nearest station if you're going by the Underground." The girl left her desk, walked over to the large map of London displayed on the far wall and pinpointed the street. "You want to turn right outside the station and go down the Clapham Road. Richouse Terrace is the sixth turning on your right and Linsdale Gardens is only a short walk from there."

"Thanks a lot," Mace said. "You've been very helpful."

"It's my pleasure." Her face clouded. "About my tax disk?" she said anxiously.

"What tax disk?"

"The one on my Fiat."

"Oh, that," Mace said airily. "Well, I daresay the license is held up in the post somewhere."

"Yes."

"And one good turn deserves another. Right?"

"I like to think so," she murmured.

Patterson returned the Ford Fiesta to the Hertz agency in Leytonstone, then walked on down the High Road and turned into Flax Mill Lane. The Mini was where he'd left it the day before, two hundred yards from the junction and right outside the Willard-Jones Primary School on the left-hand side of the road. Unable to find a parking lot within reasonable walking distance of the rental agency, he had taken one look at Flax Mill Lane and decided the Mini was unlikely to come to much harm there. The quiet side street didn't have a rundown look about it, the school kids ranged in age from five to eight years and he'd slipped the school janitor a couple of quid to keep an eye on the car.

It seemed no one was too young to indulge in vandalism and it was evident the janitor had more of an itchy palm than an eagle eye. Both wipers were missing, the aerial for the car radio had been snapped off at the base and the offside rear tire was as flat as a pancake. Changing the wheel was no problem and took only a few minutes of his time; the naked windshield, however, was the kind of technical infringement of the Road Traffic Act which he thought was bound to attract the attention of an officious police officer. Head lowered, he walked on a few yards, spotted one of the missing blades, bent almost in two, lying in the gutter and picked it up. He straightened the blade out and jammed it on to the protruding spindle for the sake of appearances.

With the eleven o'clock deadline in mind, Patterson had allowed himself ample time to return the Ford before contacting Denise Rousell. Although irritating, the unforeseen delay was therefore scarcely crucial. This optimistic thought remained with him as he drove south toward the river, and was given a further boost when he phoned a disgruntled Denise Rousell from Shoreditch and learned that the KGB had agreed to pay the equivalent of $350,000 for the video cassettes. Not even the traffic jam near London Bridge which subsequently held him up for almost twenty-five minutes could dispel his euphoria.

16.

There were a number of Minis parked in Linsdale Gardens, but all of them were the wrong color and none had been left anywhere near number 17. There was, however, a vacant space at the curbside opposite the terraced house which Mace thought significant. On the information available, anybody else would have assumed that Oliver Pearce and Oscar Pittis were one and the same man, but with his whole future in the balance, he wanted to be absolutely sure. Mrs. Drobnowski had been out when he'd called at her house a few minutes earlier, but one of the other tenants would know if Pearce owned a white Mini and that would clinch it for him.

Mace crossed the road, tried the front door and found it was ajar. There was nothing to indicate who lived in which flat, but in a room off to the left of the hall he could hear somebody hammering nails into the baseboard of the dividing wall. He went on inside, called out a couple of times but got no answer. Avoiding a large reel of cable in the entrance to the ground floor flat, he poked his head around the door.

The electrician was on his hands and knees, his sleeves rolled up to reveal knotted biceps reminiscent of a gnarled tree trunk. Wiry hair that was mostly gray crowned a bloated face displaying a web of tiny purple veins on the cheeks, the hallmark of a man who was fond of the bottle.

"Anybody at home?" Mace asked him when he finally stopped hammering and looked up.

"I'm the landlord. What do you want?"

It wasn't the friendliest greeting Mace had ever gotten and he understood why the girl at the City Bureau had warned him that

Drobnowski was a cantankerous old sod.

"I'm looking for Mr. Pearce. We work for the same firm and he asked me to meet him here."

"He's out."

"So I gathered. Any idea when he'll be back?"

"How would I know? I'm not his keeper." Drobnowski found another staple in the container on the floor, held it between forefinger and thumb and hammered it into the baseboard to secure the cable tapped into a 13 amp power point. "He's supposed to be collecting his car from the garage."

"That old Mini of his stlll giving him trouble?"

"Seems like it," Drobnowski grunted.

Mace rubbed his mouth, hiding a triumphant smile. There was no longer any room for doubt; furthermore, the fact that Pittis was using an alias gave added weight to the circumstantial evidence which already indicated he had probably committed both murders. A call for assistance, and Pittis was as good as in the bag. Provided there was no last minute balls-up, most of the credit for the arrest would go to him and that was something Kingman would have to take into account when the drinking and driving report finally landed up on his desk.

"Can I use the phone in the hall?" Mace asked.

"It's out of order," Drobnowski told him. "We had it disconnected when we bought the place. Didn't want the tenants complaining when they got the bill."

Mace thought he remembered seeing a telephone booth near Kennington Underground station, but that was too far away; with his luck, he would find that Pittis had come and gone again in his absence. He would have to ask one of the neighbors across the street if he could use their phone and then stay on to keep a discreet watch on Number 17 until the cavalry arrived. He wondered if he should take Drobnowski into his confidence and warn him not to tell Pittis he'd been there. He was still trying to make up his mind one way or the other when a car drew up outside the house.

"That must be him now," Drobnowski said.

"You're probably right."

Mace hesitated, uncertain what to do. There were two options open to him: he could stay put in the hope that Pittis would go straight on up to his flat or else he could try to give the impression that he'd been to see the landlord as he passed him in the hallway. Either possibility depended on Drobnowski keeping his mouth shut and it was too late now to warn the Pole about that. No matter which option he chose, Mace knew that he would have to get to a telephone and summon assistance before confronting Pittis. By the time Mace made up his mind and went out into the hall, the man he knew as Pittis was already walking up the front path. For one brief moment, their eyes locked, then Mace glanced over his shoulder and called out to Drobnowski.

"Don't forget what I told you," he said in a loud voice. "The existing circuit will only take an extra two thirteen-amp power points. If you want any more, you'll have to install another main."

Patterson froze. The man standing in the doorway had dark receding hair and a middle-aged spread. His light gray suit was rumpled, the jacket unbuttoned probably because it was too tight for him. There was no telltale bulge under either arm and he could see the stranger wasn't wearing a hip holster. The advice he'd just given Drobnowski suggested he was a building inspector, except that there were beads of perspiration on his forehead and his faint smile was decidedly wary.

He didn't pretend to know how the fuzz had tracked him down, but he was quite sure the middle-aged man was a police officer. In the wake of this assumption, Patterson arrived at two separate conclusions simultaneously. First, if the police had been there in force, they would have been lying in ambush inside the house ready to jump him the instant he crossed the threshold. And secondly, it was evident that this plainclothes officer was hoping to bluff his way past him in order to get to a telephone. If he allowed him through, every man on the beat, every prowl car in the London area would know the license number of his Mini long before he made it to Heathrow Airport.

There was, Patterson decided, only one solution to the problem. His mouth creased in a warm smile, he moved toward the other man. "Well, hello there," he said affably. "I was wondering when you were going to show up."

Patterson was banking on an element of surprise and got it. A friendly greeting was the last thing his adversary had expected and it rocked him back on his heels.

"I'm Detective Sergeant Mace," he blurted out.

His voice, Patterson noted, was steady and at odds with his ashen face and the nervous tic below the right eye. "Detective Sergeant Mace," he repeated. "Well now, this is a real pleasure. Like most American tourists, I've a great admiration for you people."

"Don't do anything foolish," Mace warned him.

"Believe me, I'm not about to."

They were within touching distance of one another now, the open doorway a few feet behind. Still smiling, Patterson reached out as though to clap Mace on the shoulder, then seized his forearm and jerked him forward. At the same time, he drove the rigid, outstretched fingers of his right hand into the sergeant's throat to shatter the trachea and esophagus. Mace sagged at the knees and instinctively clawed at his shirt collar, trying to rip it open in a futile attempt to breathe. Lifting the dying man in a bear hug, Patterson carried him into the hall and laid him on his back. As he turned away from him to close the front door, Mace started to thrash about, grunting like a stricken animal while his heels drummed an erratic tattoo on the floor.

Farther down the hall, Drobnowski paused in the act of hammering another staple into the baseboard and called out to ask what the hell was going on.

"It's my friend," Patterson said loudly. "Come and give me a hand, he seems to be having some kind of a fit. I think it could be a heart attack."

He knelt down on the left side of Mace and thumped his chest repeatedly so that when Drobnowski ran out into the hall, it looked as though he was attempting to stimulate a heartbeat.

"Run and phone for an ambulance," Patterson snapped. "He's going to die if we don't get him to a hospital."

Drobnowski hesitated, then nodded his head and moved toward the door. As he did so, Patterson stuck out a leg to send him sprawling onto the floor. In one fluid motion, Patterson came up into a crouch, swung around and threw himself on top of the Pole, both knees slamming into the small of his back. Virtually paralyzed from the waist down by the savage impact on his kidneys, Drobnowski moaned in agony and tried to reach behind him to relieve the pain. Still pinning him down with both knees, Patterson swiveled around until he was sideways to the Pole, then, using the outside edge of his right hand like an axe, he chopped down, delivering one rabbit punch after another until he finally succeeded in breaking Drobnowski's neck. A few feet away, Mace lay motionless on his back, mouth open, tongue protruding, eyes glazed and sightless.

Patterson sank back on his heels. Out of necessity he had killed two men in a little over a minute, but if one threat had been eradicated, another was just around the corner. Sooner or later, Mrs. Drobnowski would undoubtedly drop in to see how her husband was getting on with the rewiring. Exactly when this might happen depended on whether or not she was expecting him to come home for lunch and at what time. Twelve-thirty? One o'clock? What the hell did it matter? Neither possibility afforded him enough time to make a clean getaway; his only hope was to make her think her no-good husband had sneaked off to have a drink somewhere.

Patterson straightened up, grabbed Drobnowski by the heels and hauled him into the ground-floor flat. That done, he returned to the hall, dragged Mace into the same room and then searched through Drobnowski's pockets. One yielded a handful of loose change, a pack of John Player filter tips and a box of Swan Vesta matches, while in the other, he found a bunch of Yale keys. There was also a small imitation-leather wallet in the hip pocket containing twelve pounds, a dog license and a selection of creased snapshots. He took the money, ripped up the license, scattered the snapshots around the body and tossed the wallet onto the floor. He did the same with Mace, except that in his case, he turned all his pockets inside out and kept the warrant card. For good measure, he also stamped on the Parker fountain pen, reducing it to fragments.

The scene he'd arranged was intended to give the impression that robbery had been the prime motive and, with any luck, it would buy him a little more time. Unless Mace was known to the local CID, there was also reason to believe he would not be immediately identified. Locking the two men inside the room, he opened the street door again and then went on up to his apartment on the first floor.

Patterson could not recall a previous occasion when he had been in such a tight corner. He had arrived in Britain with two Canadian passports, one made out to Oscar Pittis, the other in the name of Oliver Pearce. Both were now useless, because Mace had succeeded in tracing him to Linsdale Gardens. Just how and why the police had linked the two names was beyond his understanding and wholly irrelevant at the moment. Right now, his number-one priority was to disappear without trace, and that presented certain difficulties. His only fallback was a West German passport and the open-ended return half of an airline ticket from Munich to London. Herr Otto Prole wore spectacles with thick lenses, had a facial blemish, blue eyes, bushy eyebrows and fair hair the color of pepper and salt. The spectacles and contact lenses were still in his possession along with the partly used cachets of hair dye, but he'd ditched the rest of his disguise at Heathrow on Saturday, flushing it down the toilet. An adhesive bandage in the right place would take care of the facial blemish and with a certain amount of improvisation, he was sure he could do something to his eyebrows to make them appear thicker than they were.

Aware that every minute counted, he lifted his suitcase down from on top of the wardrobe, dumped it on the bed and then cleared everything out of the closet, the chest of drawers and the laundry basket. He packed hurriedly: spare suit, clean shirts, underpants and socks at the bottom, shoes and dirty linen on top, the video cassettes in between and around the edges. Any nosy customs officer at Munich who wanted to examine his baggage would now have to sift through a pile of dirty laundry before he reached the tapes and the sight of all that soiled linen might deter him from going any farther. Although nobody would arrest him for bringing a collection of porno movies into the Federal Republic, cops were the same the world over; whatever their nationality, they were just naturally inquisitive and he wasn't anxious to get into a hassle with them.

Patterson glanced around the room to make sure he hadn't overlooked anything. The movie equipment he'd purchased yesterday was a dead giveaway and would have to be abandoned together with the Mini on the way to Heathrow. Although the car was bound to come to their notice in the end, he saw no point in making things easy for the police, and anything that helped to snarl up the manhunt was a bonus. Leaving the suitcase open on the bed, Patterson collected the adhesive he'd used to compile the montage of film clips, went into the bathroom and stripped to the waist.

He tore a strip from the lavatory roll and placed the toilet paper on the glass shelf above the pedestal washbasin. With a pair of nail scissors, he then took several clippings of hair from around his ears and carefully placed them on the toilet paper. Next, he smeared both eyebrows with a thin coating of adhesive, moistened his fingertips under the tap and painstakingly transferred the minute hairs to both eyebrows, thickening them up until he achieved the effect he wanted. While the adhesive was setting, he worked on his hair, diluting the blond tint in the washbasin before applying it with a nylon brush. Then, he emptied the concentrated tint into a tooth mug, dipped a comb into the dye and ran it through his hair, paying special attention to the back and sides, where the pepperish coloring would be more noticeable. Finally and very gingerly, he colored his eyebrows, using a toothbrush to press the tint right down to the roots.

There remained only the facial blemish, described in the passport as a reddish-brown birthmark on the right cheekbone. Pinching the flesh between forefinger and thumb to bruise it, Patterson nicked a V in the cheek with a razor blade, gritted his teeth and deliberately shaved off the top layer of skin. The blood welled, coursed down his face and dripped into the washbasin. A facecloth pressed over the wound stemmed the flow long enough for him to fish the Ronson lighter out of his pocket and cauterize it with the naked flame. The pain was agonizing and he could feel the bile rising in his throat as he staggered into the room and returned with a tin of brown shoe polish. Hand shaking, he rubbed a smear of polish into the seared flesh, staining it a reddish brown, then covered the greater part of the mutilation with an adhesive bandage. Later on, when the wound had cauterized, he would remove the sticking plaster. In the meanwhile, it would look as if he'd nicked his face when shaving.

He stepped back a pace, looked down and saw that he'd forgotten to replace the floorboard and linoleum after he'd removed the video cassettes from their hiding place. He knelt down, reached inside the cavity and brought out the Iver Johnson .22 caliber revolver in its leather hip holster. A feeling that he would be naked without it was counterbalanced by the knowledge that the chances of getting the revolver through the security check at Heathrow detected were virtually nil. Patterson weighed the revolver in his hand, finally decided to leave the handgun behind and shoved it between the joists. He replaced the floorboard, stamped on it to drive the nails home and quickly relaid the linoleum.

A glance at his wristwatch showed that it was past one o'clock and the cool head which had carried him thus far began to desert him. Fear took over and everything he did from there on became a frantic race against time. Mind in a whirl, he crammed the shaving tackle and used cachets into the washbag, emptied the tooth mug and rinsed the basin. Grabbing the shirt, he went next door and dressed hurriedly, his fingers all thumbs as he struggled to button the shirt collar and knot the tie. Stay loose, he told himself, sound advice that went unheeded when he discovered the goddamned contact lenses weren't in the jacket pockets. Close to despair, he searched the chest of drawers again and eventually found them under the paper lining of the bottom drawer.

Passport, spectacles, airline ticket, folding money? He ran his hands over his body, checking to make sure he had them, jammed the trilby on his head, then grabbed hold of the suitcase and emptied half the contents on to the bed as he lifted it up. "Shit!" He screamed the word aloud, stuffed the clothes back inside any old way and snapped the locks. The executive briefcase? He whirled around, delved under the wardrobe and pulled it out. Remembering to open the door first, he picked up both pieces of luggage, ran down the staircase and stowed them in the back of the Mini, then returned to collect the movie equipment.

Calmer now, Patterson got into the car, switched on the ignition and cranked the engine. Shifting into gear, he pulled away from the curbside, went on up to the junction and turned left into Richouse Terrace. Instinct prompted him to look in the rearview mirror as he neared the Clapham Road and his newly found air of confidence immediately evaporated at the sight of Mrs. Drobnowski striding purposefully toward Linsdale Gardens. He realized then that when her husband failed to answer the door, she would undoubtedly look through the window and see the two bodies lying on the floor inside the flat.

Just how much leeway he would have before she called the police was problematical, but it was essential he ditch the Mini and fast. With that thought in mind, he abandoned the car in Elm Lane and walked the rest of the way to Kennington Underground station. The Northern Line to Leicester Square, then out to Heathrow on the Piccadilly. It was the only solution, but the journey would take well over an hour and he had a nasty premonition that time was running out for him.

17.

Caroline Brooke added a period to the sentence she had just typed, realigned the carriage to begin the next paragraph and found she had reached the bottom of the page. Thanks to Vaudrey, who'd hacked the original to pieces with his corrections, the second draft of the so-called Libyan scenario was taking her much longer to complete than she had anticipated, and there was still some way to go. Operating the shift lever, she released the typescript from the carriage, extracted the carbon and placed the original and top copy in her pending tray. She slipped the carbon between another two sheets of A4 size paper, fed them into the Olivetti and typed the figure 4 at the top of the page, more or less in the center. Then she leaned back in the chair and took a bite out of the ham sandwich one of the clerks had brought in for her. Her mouth was still half full when the telephone rang.

The contact at Scotland Yard was a Lowlander from Motherwell whose Scottish accent after living in London for the past eighteen years had been subdued to a mere rolling of the *r*'s. It was, however, apt to surface and become very noticeable whenever he became excited or angry. The brogue was so evident on this occasion that she surmised he was both angry and excited.

"Oliver Pearce," he snapped. "Does the name mean anything to you?"

"Not in the least," Caroline told him, but the alarm bells were ringing and it wasn't too difficult to guess what was coming next.

"It will. We believe he's also known as Oscar Pittis and he's the number-one suspect for the Whitfield/Leese killings. As of now, we're crediting him with another two, Leopold Drobnowski and Detective Sergeant Mace. The bastard tried to make it seem as though robbery were the motive, stole all their cash and lifted the sergeant's warrant card, but overlooked the snapshots in his wallet. Among them was a photograph of a celebration dinner held by the CID officers of V District. That's how we identified him so quickly."

"I see."

"Do you, Miss Brooke?" His voice was sharp, the tone cutting as a claymore.

"Not really," she lied. "I'm afraid it was an automatic response."

"You're fencing with me, lassie, and it won't do you any bloody good. You've been tapping me for information ever since the Whitfield case broke, for reasons you've never fully disclosed. Now the boot's on the other foot and I'm coming to you for information. My superiors are saying that you people have a shrewd idea who this Oliver Pearce really is."

"That's nonsense," Caroline told him firmly.

"Don't give me that."

"I'm sorry, but it happens to be true. If you don't believe me, I suggest you get in touch with Nicholas Vaudrey."

"I don't know Mr. Vaudrey from Adam and I've no intention of making his acquaintance right now, Miss Brooke. You're the one I'm used to dealing with and you've got exactly one hour from now to come up with his name. If I haven't heard from you by three-fifteen, someone's head is going to roll."

There was a loud clunk as he hung up on her. Replacing the receiver, she buzzed Vaudrey on the office intercom, then remembered he'd gone out to lunch. He was a creature of habit, so she assumed Vaudrey was lunching at his club and dialed 930–9721, only to discover that he wasn't lunching at the Army and Navy. She rang the flat in Cheney Walk, got a long continuous burr which indicated the number was out of order and wondered if Nicholas was at home or whether his housekeeper had simply unplugged the phone, as she was apt to do when she didn't want to be disturbed. Getting nowhere fast, she tried every section head in DI5 and those contacts of Vaudrey's in other government departments that she knew of, but to no avail. Finally, Caroline rang the flat again and found the line was still allegedly out of order.

It had been a really excellent lunch, mainly because the duck pâté, fresh salmon, strawberries and cream had been ordered from Fortnum and Mason, and they had therefore been spared the culinary efforts of Vaudrey's housekeeper. Two large gin and tonics, a bottle of Muscadet and a very agreeable liqueur brandy with their coffee and cigars had contributed to Walter J. Zellick's affable mood and sense of well-being. If the American was intrigued to know why Vaudrey had phoned him the previous evening to invite him to lunch, he had succeeded in concealing it up to now. A small furrow and the way he was contemplating his cigar told Vaudrey that he would be unable to contain his curiosity much longer.

"That was a great lunch, Nick," Zellick said, breaking a lengthy silence. "And I've enjoyed talking about old times."

Vaudrey smiled. They had become acquainted in April 1967, when the CIA had quizzed him about counterinsurgency operations in Malaya and he had spent a fortnight at Langley as the guest of Walter Zellick, who had been detailed to look after him. Between then and August 1979, when Walter had been posted to Grosvenor Square as the resident CIA officer, they had met on only two subsequent occasions, once in Cyprus quite by chance and again in Paris during a symposium held by the Direction de la Surveillance Territoire on antiterrorist measures. In the last three years however, they had seen a great deal more of each other and if they weren't the closest of friends, they were at least congenial acquaintances.

"About Patterson," Vaudrey said idly. "You'll be pleased to hear the situation is developing nicely."

"That's kind of a vague statement, Nick." Zellick leaned across the table and tapped his cigar over the ashtray. "What exactly do you mean by nicely?"

"I mean I've found the right man to lean on Raschid al Jalud.

His name is Coghill, a Detective Inspector with V District who at one time was in charge of the Whitfield investigation. You may have seen his photograph in the newspapers?"

Zellick nodded. "Why the past tense?" he asked casually.

"Because the case has been transferred to the Regional Crime Squad and Coghill is currently under suspension, pending the outcome of an inquiry by the Complaints Investigation Bureau into allegations of bribery and corruption." Vaudrey topped up the American's glass, then helped himself to another brandy. "It's all very fortuitous. I mean, we could easily have arranged for one of our own people to pass himself off as a police officer, but you can't beat the genuine article."

"Especially if he's been on the take."

"We don't know that," Vaudrey said evenly. "Neither does Jalud, though it may be politic to lead him to think so. Take it from me, by the time we've finished with him, Jalud will be only too eager to set Patterson up."

"Yeah? What makes you so sure Coghill will agree to act as the go-between?"

"It's a matter of psychology, Walter. Coghill is a great believer in crime and punishment and he has this simple conviction that nobody should be above the law. Now he's discovered there are exceptions to the rule and he's angry because certain people appear to enjoy a special kind of immunity. As a direct result of this, the investigation is being hamstrung and a killer is still at large, free as a bird on the wing. Offer him a chance to put this right and he'll grab it."

"I think you're being wildly optimistic, Nick."

Vaudrey shook his head. The American might have his doubts, but he fancied he knew his man. Coghill was the living male embodiment of the statue on top of the Old Bailey, sword upraised in one hand, scales weighed in the balance in the other and a blindfold around the eyes.

"Well, okay," Zellick said, "let's suppose you're right about him. How do we smuggle Patterson out of England, assuming you can lift him?"

"I don't see any difficulty. After all, there are quite a number of American bases in the UK and your planes are flying in and out every day."

There was, Vaudrey thought, no need for him to elaborate. They could put Patterson on a Military Air Transport cargo flight to the USAF base at Frankfurt am Main, then transfer him to the States. They could show what they liked on the flight manifest; spares, official mail and returned stores weren't subject to scrutiny by Her Majesty's Customs and Excise.

"I don't know," Zellick said thoughtfully. "All hell would break loose if this got out."

"I won't say anything if you don't," Vaudrey said.

"I was thinking of Coghill."

"The Official Secrets Acts will keep him quiet." He did not add that Coghill would never know whom he was working for, nor did Vaudrey mention the prefabricated evidence which would lead Coghill's superiors to question his mental stability if he did try to bring the affair out into the open.

"You've got to persuade him to sign the declaration first," Zellick pointed out.

"He already has, way back in 1974 when he was put on the list of CID officers who were to see all the Intelligence reports concerning the organization of the Provisional IRA active service units in England. Special Branch and the Antiterrorist Squad were adamant that every officer to be briefed by them had to sign the Official Secrets Acts first."

"Great. I guess everything's buttoned up, Nick."

"Not quite. There is the little matter regarding your side of the bargain."

"Don't give it another thought," Zellick said airily. "We'll take care of Noraid."

"Oh, come on, Walter, you know very well that's just a story we cooked up for the benefit of Caroline Brooke." Vaudrey allowed the statement to hang in the air for the time it took him to leisurely finish his brandy. Then he said, "What I really want is complete and unfettered access to the CIA computer at Langley. There is to be a formal agreement in writing, signed by the present director and witnessed by his deputy."

"You're out of your tiny mind."

"The memorandum consists of two copies," Vaudrey continued, unperturbed.

"You mean you've already drawn it up?"

"I thought it would save a lot of time if I did."

"Jesus H. Christ," Zellick said, awed by the other man's brazen audacity.

"Actually, he had nothing to do with it." Vaudrey left the table, went out into the hall and returned moments later carrying a black official-looking briefcase embossed with a crown and the initials EIIR in gilt. Unlocking it, he produced both copies of the memorandum and handed the carbon to the American. "It's brief and to the point," he said cheerfully. "Shouldn't take you more than a few minutes to read it."

It would, however, take Zellick considerably longer to appreciate the full import of the document and marshal his objections. Security of information was bound to be near the top of the list and, knowing how the CIA distrusted British Intelligence, Vaudrey had taken steps to preempt any argument on that score. A computer terminal with spare capacity was already *in situ* at the British Embassy in Washington, and he had stipulated that all printouts obtained from Langley would be dispatched to London by courier at irregular intervals. Although it would have been quicker to transmit the information by satellite, there were too many links in the chain, and the code that could not be cracked by a hostile intelligence service had yet to be invented. The service provided by the Queen's Messengers might be slow, but it was a lot safer, especially if there was no set pattern to their movements.

"Let's see if I've got this straight." Zellick looked up from the document, eyes gray as slate. "You want to be plugged into every major department—Europe, Asia and Latin America?"

"Until such time as you change the recognition code."

Vaudrey was under no illusions; no matter what the agreement said, the CIA would unilaterally terminate the facility. Exactly when they would do this was pure conjecture; at worst, the blocks would go on the moment the plane taking Patterson to Frankfurt was airborne, at best, the CIA might stay their hand until they were satisfied the British were unlikely to apply for his extradition. Neither possibility disturbed him. The USAF were obliged to clear their flight plans with Air Traffic Control at West Drayton and with their assistance, the estimated time of departure could easily be delayed for anything up to six hours. And if you asked the right questions, it was amazing how much information you could retrieve from a computer in that time.

"There's nothing like shooting for the moon, Nick." Eyes downcast, Zellick reached across the table and, as though guided by radar, unerringly found the ashtray and stubbed out his cigar. "If you could put this deal together, there's no limit as to how far you'd go."

The American wasn't telling him anything he didn't already know. In his own mind, Vaudrey was absolutely sure he would be the leading contender for the post of director general when the present incumbent retired. Alternatively, the Cabinet Office might well decide he was just the man to run the SIS, and a transfer to Century House as deputy control would be seen as a preliminary step in this direction. It wouldn't be the first time an outsider had been placed in charge of the Secret Intelligence Service, and he wouldn't be arriving empty-handed either. Nine-tenths of the information extracted from Langley would be of direct interest to the SIS and the Foreign and Commonwealth Office.

"How long have you been kicking this idea around?" Zellick asked out of curiosity.

"Less than a week. Since Thursday morning, to be precise."

The idea had been germinated by the loose minute Caroline Brooke had sent him about a possible connection between Raschid al Jalud, Orville Patterson and Karen Whitfield. Had she not been quite so meticulous, had the surveillance team assigned to Jalud been a little less observant, the operation would never have been conceived. It had therefore been triggered off by a stroke of pure luck, but of all the really big intelligence coups he knew of, Vaudrey could not recall a single one that had been planned in advance. However, to initiate a covert operation on the spur of the moment was one thing; carrying it through to a successful conclusion was quite a different proposition. Security was all-important and, in this connection, a breach of security usually occurred because too many people were in the know. It was for this reason that he had deliberately misled Caroline Brooke from the outset.

"I've got to hand it to you," Zellick said eventually. "This projected operation of yours is one of the boldest and most original I've ever come across. Trouble is, it will never get off the ground."

"You think your director will refuse to cooperate?"

"Why should he? Sure, we'd like to lay our hands on Patterson, but he's not worth the price you're asking."

"That's where you're mistaken," Vaudrey said mildly. "It's on record that Patterson was involved in the biggest drug smuggling racket of the whole Vietnam war. I know he was a brilliant combat soldier and I'm also aware that he became a damn good field agent, but he didn't have the brains, the necessary connections or the ability to organize an operation of that magnitude. Common sense tells me the knowhow was supplied by influential friends within the CIA and it was they who set up the numbered accounts in Switzerland on his behalf after he'd killed those two FBI agents in Galveston."

"You should pack your bags and go to Hollywood," Zellick growled. "The movie industry is always on the lookout for a good scriptwriter."

"There was a much simpler way of dealing with the problem," Vaudrey continued unabashed. "To quote a CIA euphemism, they could have arranged for Patterson to be 'terminated with extreme prejudice,' but they didn't. Instead, they provided him with a number of false passports and got him out of the States. One wonders why they went to so much trouble over this man and there can only be one answer to that question. At some stage, Patterson must have warned them he had taken out an insurance policy, and that if anything unpleasant should happen to him, the FBI or the attorney general would receive a very interesting dossier."

"It gets better all the time."

"How right you are," Vaudrey said affably. "You're anxious to question Patterson because the CIA has good reason to believe some of these men are still with the agency."

"You couldn't be more wrong, Nick." Zellick was good-humored, a little condescending and very, very patient, as though conversing with a mentally retarded child. "Read our telex again, the one we sent you in October 1980. There was no CIA involvement in drug smuggling, and Patterson had resigned from the agency eighteen months before the shoot-out occurred in Galveston. We circulated his description and background information to British Intelligence when we learned he was working for the Libyan government because we have a common interest in maintaining stability in the Middle East. There are no, repeat no, sinister implications."

"Really?" Vaudrey pursed his lips, then said, "Tell me something, Walter. Why didn't the FBI get in touch with Interpol?"

"You checked?"

"The moment I received your telex. A friend of mine from Scotland Yard happened to be seconded to Interpol Headquarters at St. Cloud at the time and I rang him out of sheer curiosity."

"I don't know." Zellick shrugged. "I guess the FBI must have slipped up."

"Or else they'd been led to believe Patterson was dead."

"I'm getting awfully tired of this game, Nick. I think it's time I was on my way."

"Yes, of course. What airline will you be using? Pan Am or TWA?"

"Jesus." Zellick sighed and shook his head. "You never give up, do you?"

"I've no reason to, because I can't lose. We'll catch this dissident agent of yours and when we do, we'll make him an offer he can't resist and he'll tell us where to look for his insurance policy." Vaudrey picked up the carbon copy of the memorandum that Zellick had discarded, slipped it into the manila envelope together with the original and handed it to the American. "However, on the whole, I think it's infinitely preferable that we enter Langley via the front door rather than the back, don't you?"

"You may have a point," Zellick conceded reluctantly.

"I'm glad we understand one another." Vaudrey took Zellick by the arm, gently steered him into the hall and opened the front door. "About your flight," he added as they shook hands, "may I suggest you travel on British Airways Concorde? We can't afford to waste time and it would be helpful if you completed the round trip to Washington in a day."

"I'll think about it."

"You do that, Walter."

Vaudrey closed the door behind the American and thought he had earned himself another brandy. Then, remembering that the telephone in the hall had been disconnected, he decided he'd better plug it in again before returning to the dining room. It started to ring as he backed out from under the table and got to his feet. Lifting the receiver, he heard Caroline Brooke say, "Thank God I've got you at last."

From a few staccato sentences, it rapidly became evident that her problems were over while his were only just beginning. All of a sudden, for reasons nobody could have foreseen, his sleight-of-hand had become impaired and the juggling act was about to come tumbling down. He felt vulnerable, the whole rosy future he had so recently visualized now in jeopardy.

"We've no choice," Caroline said, winding up. "Like it or not, we've got to release all the information we have on Patterson. The police are certain the real identity of the killer is known to us and there will be hell to pay if we continue to deny them access."

"No." Vaudrey was conscious his voice sounded hoarse and instinctively cleared his throat. "No, that's quite the wrong way to handle this situation. Our information is top secret and it won't help them one bit to know the man they're after is called Patterson."

"It's all very well for you to take such a lofty attitude, Nicholas," she told him vehemently, "but I'm the one who's on the firing line."

"And if you kindly give me a chance to get a word in edgewise, I'll provide you with some overhead cover." He paused long enough to weigh the conflicting factors and decide on a course of action, then said, "I don't want the CIA or Raschid al Jalud dragged into this. Instead, you may tell them we think Pittis could be Oswald Pemberton, a former intelligence officer in the United States Army who served with the Green Berets in Vietnam and was given an honorable discharge in 1971. You can also say he first came to our notice when the SIS told us they'd heard he was working for the Libyan government and was believed to have passed through the United Kingdom on several occasions. If pressed, you can let it be known that Century House wanted us to keep an eye out for him without involving Special Branch. You get the idea?"

"Yes, but I don't think my angry Scotsman is going to be very impressed, Nicholas."

"I haven't finished yet," Vaudrey snapped. "I want you to stress the fact that this man has at least four different aliases to our knowledge, but that they all have one common denominator, the Christian name beginning with an *O*, the surname with a *P*. Then go on to suggest in your usual tactful fashion that perhaps Special Branch should carry out a simultaneous check at Heathrow, Gatwick, Luton and Stansted airports to see if any airline has a passenger booked on one of their flights with the same initial letters."

"I'll be told I'm teaching my grandmother to suck eggs."

"Sometimes one has to."

"Yes, but—"

"No buts, Caroline. Just get on with it."

Vaudrey put the phone down, went into the dining room and helped himself to another brandy. As he saw it, there were three possibilities: Patterson might already be on his way out of the country, the police might pick him up at one of the airports or he might evade arrest and go to ground until the hunt lost momentum.

Although somewhat thin on the ground, the surveillance section had been covering the principal airports ever since Caroline Brooke had tentatively identified Patterson, and there was reason to believe they wouldn't allow him to slip through their fingers.

The fact that Patterson was still in England a week after Karen Whitfield had been murdered was a good sign. Or was it? There was a blank period unaccounted for between the time he'd moved out of the flat in Highgate on Thursday morning and the discovery of the two dead men in Linsdale Gardens early this afternoon, and it was conceivable Patterson had been out of the country for all or part of the intervening four days. Vaudrey told himself that kind of speculation was unproductive, put the disturbing thought out of his mind and concentrated on the other two possibilities.

If the American was alarmed by any unusual activity at the airport and took off, the game plan would still be more or less viable, though it would be much more difficult to execute. It would be damn near impossible to execute should Patterson end up in police custody. Somehow, he would have to persuade the director of public prosecutions to make the American an offer he couldn't refuse, the location of his insurance policy in exchange for a rigged trial. Plead diminished responsibility, spend five, perhaps six years in Broadmoor with the criminally insane until the affair was forgotten by the public, then walk out a free man. Vaudrey supposed Patterson might find that infinitely preferable to a life sentence of thirty years.

It was a practical solution, but although his contacts throughout Whitehall were legion, none of them had sufficient clout to make it happen. He wondered if he should involve the director general, then rejected the idea out of hand; he was unlikely to get any support from that quarter, and could well find himself in the shit instead. His only hope was an assistant principal in the Foreign and Commonwealth Office who claimed he was on first-name terms with the secretary to the prime minister. However, that particular avenue would have to wait until Zellick returned from Washington with the memorandum signed by the director of the CIA. Meantime, there was nothing more he could do except keep his ear close to the ground.

Two hours seven minutes to go. Patterson stared at the naked redhead occupying the center pages of *Playboy* magazine and contrived to appear relaxed and unconcerned, even though there were butterflies in his stomach and his mouth was tinder-dry. It wasn't his fault that he'd picked a lousy day to travel, but he certainly hadn't made things any easier for himself by presenting the return half of the airline ticket to the girl at the Lufthansa desk. With an apologetic smile, she'd told him the 1503 flight to Munich was fully booked, and so was the shuttle via Frankfurt which left fifteen minutes later, but then little miss efficiency had said she'd heard British Airways had spare capacity on their flight to Munich departing at 1740 hours and he'd been maneuvered into a position where he'd had to say, "Okay, get me a seat with them."

The whole goddamned business had been a mental aberration on his part. Not counting the money in his billfold, he still had close to four hundred pounds in Deutschemark traveler's checks and could have flown to Cairo and back, but no, he'd had to be too clever by half. By the time the girl from Lufthansa had confirmed the reservation with British Airways, it had been too late for second thoughts. Copenhagen, Rotterdam, Brussels, Paris, Geneva, were all feasible escape routes, but there was no way he could have approached either the Scandinavian Airways, KLM, Sabena, Air France or Swissair desks without her seeing him, and it was essential he keep a low profile. In the circumstances, it was also vital he not allow himself to get boxed in, and it was for this reason that he'd decided to stay in the main concourse and give the departure lounge a miss until the very last moment.

Some instinct prompted Patterson to look up from his magazine at the same moment that a man in a dark blue pinstripe approached one of the clerks on the British Airways desk. He watched their heads come together, saw the clerk turn to her companion, exchange a few words and reach for the clipboard on the counter. It wasn't necessary to possess a Mensa IQ to guess she had asked for the passenger list for the 1740 flight to Munich. A faint hope that he was allowing his imagination to run riot was dispelled when she pointed to the Lufthansa desk.

Patterson laid the magazine aside, picked up his luggage and strolled toward Heathrow Underground station as casually as he knew how. He had no plan in mind, only a notion to get clean away and find a place where he could merge into the background, somewhere where his American accent would be accepted without comment. As he neared the exit, it occurred to him that there were a number of USAF bases in the Cambridge area.

The news had come like a bolt out of the blue, a brief announcement at 4:27 on Capitol Radio, and even now, hours after the first terse report, Coghill found it hard to believe that Harry Mace was dead. He supposed his reluctance to accept it had a lot to do with the fact that he was largely responsible for what had happened. No need to ask himself what Harry had been doing in Linsdale Gardens; the poor old sod had gone there looking for Oscar Pittis because he'd told him to check out the rental agencies and one of them had come up with an address.

Coghill reached for the bottle of Chivas Regal on the table and poured himself another large double. There was, he thought, a lot to be said for a good old-fashioned wake. As far as he knew, there wasn't a drop of Irish blood in his veins and the whiskey had been malted in the Highlands, but that was only a minor quibble. He raised the glass to his lips in a silent toast, then put it down again to answer the phone. It was a bad mistake and he regretted lifting the receiver the moment he found he had Janice on the line. Nothing she said about police harassment made a great deal of sense, but he gathered the CIB officers had been to see her again.

"What did they want this time?" he asked.

"Nothing much." She laughed mirthlessly. "It seems the Inland Revenue plans to prosecute me and Eric for tax evasion. They say they can prove that some of the names on our deduction cards were fictitious."

"And were they?"

"How would I know? I wasn't the wages clerk." Her voice was a shade too defensive and he suspected the worst.

"I think you should talk to a solicitor, Jan."

"Do you know one who doesn't expect to be paid for his services?"

"No, but you needn't worry about that. I'll foot the bill."

"That's big of you, Tom," she said. "Really big, considering the trouble you've got me into. You and your sticky fingers—I wish to God I'd left you before you joined the Obscene Publications Squad."

"You don't know what you're saying."

"That's just where you're wrong," she snapped.

The phone went dead as Janice hung up on him. A split second later, Coghill heard a faint click and knew there were eavesdroppers on the line.

18.

Patterson rolled out of bed, walked over to the window and opened the curtains. The dawn chorus had woken him at some ungodly hour, and from then on the festering sore on his cheek had kept him wide awake. He sidestepped to the vanity unit, peered into the mirror above the washbasin and grimaced at the yellow matter seeping from under the adhesive bandage. Gritting his teeth, he raised one corner of the sticking plaster and ripped it off to expose an ugly raw patch encrusted with pus. He soaked a facecloth under the cold water tap, then cleaned the infected wound as best he could before covering it up with a fresh and larger-sized bandage. After that, he washed, shaved, brushed his teeth and changed into a pair of khaki linen slacks, a plaid shirt and a pair of stout walking shoes he'd purchased from a sports outfitters off the Charing Cross Road.

The Bergen rucksack had come from the same store and was an essential stage prop for an elderly American serviceman who was allegedly spending his furlough hiking through the British countryside. It was the only plan Patterson had been able to devise on the spur of the moment late yesterday afternoon when, from Heathrow, he had doubled back into London on the Underground and deposited his briefcase and traveling bag in a luggage locker at St. Pancras station. Returning to St. Pancras after making the necessary purchases, he'd collected his luggage and found a vacant cubicle in the men's washroom, where he'd changed and then packed the video cassettes into the rucksack, together with a clean change of underwear, a couple of spare shirts and his shaving tackle. That done, he'd dumped the unwanted luggage in another locker, made his way to the bus terminal at Victoria and booked himself a seat on a coach going to Newmarket. From there, he'd walked to Southwold Priory and stayed the night at The Red Lion, the only hotel in the village.

Little more than a country pub, The Red Lion had ten bedrooms, a small dining room and an even smaller lounge for the residents. The hotel didn't rate a single star in the AA handbook and its cuisine was understandably ignored by the *Michelin Guide*. It did, however, suit Patterson for two very practical reasons. In the first place, the large USAF base at Lakenheath was not too far away and the presence of American servicemen in that part of Suffolk was an everyday occurrence. And secondly, the villagers who frequented The Red Lion were the sort of people who kept themselves to themselves. The proprietor was even less inquisitive; if a senior American noncom wanted to spend his furlough visiting all the local churches to take brass rubbings, that was his business and no one else's.

Patterson flopped into a chair and lit a cigarette. Including the loose change in his pockets, he had just over thirty-eight pounds. He also had the equivalent of another four hundred in uncashed Deutschemark traveler's checks, but they were made out to Otto Prole and consequently no longer of any use to him after what had happened at Heathrow Airport yesterday. Pittis, Pearce, Prole; he had already run out of names and passports, now it seemed he was about to run out of folding money. Thirty-eight pounds would pay his bill at The Red Lion and keep him going for a day or two, but it wasn't enough to get him out of the country. Money wasn't the only problem there; with the British watching every air and seaport, he couldn't make it on his own.

The Russians or the Libyans? Patterson was certain both parties would be interested in acquiring the video cassettes for free and it was therefore merely a question of deciding who would serve his interests best. Although the KGB were easily the more efficient, the local resident officer wouldn't lift a finger until he had a green light from Moscow Center. Furthermore, he would make sure the First Chief Directorate knew all the latest facts before its members made a decision, and that meant there was a very good chance Moscow Center would give him a wide berth. But even if they did agree to extend a helping hand, Patterson could never be sure they weren't planning to double-cross him somewhere along the way. Thirty years in a British jail or the Gulag Archipelago after the KGB had sucked him dry? One was as bad as the other.

The Libyans? Well, they would be less inhibited by political considerations than the Russians, but Jalud was a treacherous little bastard and there was the added danger that he had a personal score to settle with him. As far as Jalud was concerned, though, he still believed Patterson had the incriminating video tape and that gave Patterson a certain amount of leverage.

Somebody rapped on the door, then a key turned in the lock and a buxom young woman walked into his room carrying a tray. "Your morning tea and newspaper," she told him. "It was the *Daily Mail* you ordered, wasn't it, Mr. Orville?"

Patterson stared at her blankly. Up to now he'd always chosen an alias with the same initial letters as his own and for a moment the name didn't click. "Yeah, that's right," he said finally.

The girl nodded, cleared a space on the bedside table and put the tray down. "Breakfast is served from seven-thirty onward, sir."

"Thanks."

Patterson wondered if he ought to tip her, but by the time he'd dug some loose change out of his pocket, the maid had already left the room and closed the door behind her. Still preoccupied, he got to his feet, went over to the bedside table and unfolded the newspaper.

He'd always understood the British police rarely gave the press details of a suspect they wanted to interview, lest the subsequent trial be prejudiced in some way, but that unwritten law had apparently gone by the board in this instance. There he was in the middle of the front page, a Photofit that made his bowels sink, with a caption in heavy type directly above. The Photofit was a good likeness, and he immediately began to worry that the girl who'd brought the early morning tea had seen it and made the connection. As far as he could recall, she hadn't seemed nervous or tense, nor had there been a glimmer of recognition in her eyes when she'd looked at him, though, truth to tell, he hadn't really paid much attention to her.

His every instinct was to cut and run, but somehow Patterson managed to put the thought out of his mind, knowing that he'd only draw attention to himself if he gave way to panic. Breakfast first, then check out of the hotel and make tracks; that was the sensible thing to do, provided he had the balls to see it through.

He stubbed out the cigarette, poured himself a cup of tea and started packing his kit. When that was done, he took time out to study the ordnance survey maps he'd purchased in Newmarket.

"Slima Avenue is a five-minute walk from Acton Town Underground station. Go down Gunnersbury Lane toward Uxbridge Road and then take the first turning on the left beyond the school playing fields. Monument House, where Coghill lives, is a small block of flats on the right-hand side of the road approximately one hundred yards from the junction. His apartment is on the second floor and facing the staircase."

The briefing from Surveillance had been very thorough, though Caroline Brooke could have wished otherwise. Had their directions been less precise, she would have had a good excuse to phone Vaudrey and make one final attempt at persuading him to cancel the operation. As it was, she had long since exhausted every conceivable argument, and without being able to bring some additional pressure to bear on him, there was no earthly reason why he should change his mind now. If the Photofit likeness of Patterson which had appeared in all the newspapers had failed to deter him, he certainly wouldn't pay the slightest scrap of attention to what she had to say. As she pressed the bell to his apartment, she wondered if the same would go for Coghill.

Some photographs flatter to deceive and in his case it seemed as though the camera had lied. Coghill looked much older than she'd expected, his face pale and drawn and the pouches under his eyes more in keeping with a middle-aged man whose dissipated youth had finally caught up with him. He was, she decided, suffering from the mother and father of a hangover.

"Detective Inspector Coghill?"

"Yes." A faint smile competed with and finally lost out to a puzzled frown. "Have we met somewhere before?" he asked. "Your face seems vaguely familiar."

"I don't think so. My name's Patricia Wentworth," she said, using her mother's maiden name. "I'm a civil servant."

"Really? Which department?"

"The Ministry of Defense, Intelligence and Security Co-ord."

"That's a new one on me." He glanced at the identity card she had produced from her handbag, then said, "It doesn't do you justice."

It wasn't intended as a compliment, just a plain statement of fact. The Administrative Support Section had worked overtime to process the fake ID and the flashlight had caught her unawares, so that her eyes looked as if they were popping out of their sockets.

"I don't take a good photograph," she said.

"Few of us do, Miss Wentworth."

"Still, as long as the War Department constables can recognize me." Caroline returned the ID card to her handbag and closed the fastener. "I know it's a bit of an imposition," she said politely, "but do you think you could spare me a few minutes of your time? It's rather important."

"Yes, of course." Coghill stepped to one side and opened the door wider. "The sitting room is in a bit of a mess," he said. "I haven't got around to cleaning it up yet."

She could see at a glance that he wasn't exaggerating. Although the curtains had been drawn back and both fanlight windows opened, the room was still polluted with the aroma of stale tobacco smoke. From the number of butts in the ashtray on the low coffee table, Caroline figured he must have got through almost two packs of cigarettes. The lone tumbler and the empty bottle of Chivas Regal beside it also suggested it must have been quite a wake he'd held for Detective Sergeant Mace, even if it had been a solitary one.

"Tell me something, Miss Wentworth," Coghill said thoughtfully. "How did you get hold of my address?"

"When you work for a department like Security Co-ord, there isn't a door you can't unlock. As a matter of fact, I know a great deal about you, Detective Inspector."

She started with his parents, where and when they'd been born, then moved on to his own date and place of birth, the schools he'd attended before studying law at Nottingham University and his career in the Metropolitan Police Force.

"Did they also tell you that I'm under suspension?" he said angrily.

"They did, but it's irrelevant."

"Not to me it isn't."

"It will be if you ring 888–9000 with a request for authentication."

"Of what?"

"Of me," Caroline told him. "Who I am, who I represent."

"You mean some clown is actually going to admit there is such a department as Intelligence and Security Co-ord?"

"No, but if you check the dialing codes, you won't find a treble eight exchange listed anywhere, and that should tell you something."

"I'll take your word for it, Miss Wentworth." Coghill hesitated, then with a slight shrug, he walked over to the phone and lifted the receiver. "What did you say the number was?" he asked.

"Treble eight, nine thousand."

The exchange and extension number would cease to exist the moment Coghill hung up. Although it had taken the Administrative Support Section half the night to tie the bogus number into the GPO network, the connection with the automatic switching station could be severed in a matter of minutes. No such department as Intelligence and Security Co-ord existed within the Ministry of Defense, and if he had a mind to, Coghill could spend the rest of his life looking for a Miss Patricia Wentworth and never find her.

"Blonde and quite attractive, five seven and a half, weight one twenty-six, wearing a pink skirt and flowered blouse." Coghill put the phone down and eyed her from head to toe. "Your friend's not exactly forthcoming with his compliments, is he?"

"I daresay Karen Whitfield didn't receive too many from Raschid al Jalud either, but then she was only interested in the size of his wallet."

"Now I know what happened to the address book."

"You sound as though that's a sore point."

"You're absolutely right, Miss Wentworth, it is." Coghill pointed an accusing finger at her. "Whitfield, Drobnowski and Harry Mace; one suicide and two murders and they're all down to your department. If you people hadn't interfered, they would still be alive today."

"The fact is, we didn't interfere," Caroline said in a level voice. "On the contrary, Scotland Yard sought our assistance from the moment we informed them there was reason to believe Karen Whitfield had been associating with a Libyan diplomat whom we had been keeping under surveillance because of his involvement with the IRA and other terrorist groups. At the request of your superiors, our cipher experts examined her address book and broke the code. Just what the Regional Crime Squad did with the information we provided is far from clear to me, but it's quite evident they failed to capitalize on it. Furthermore, even if your people had worked on that book from now until doomsday, they would never have found the name of Orville Patterson between the covers."

"Patterson? Who's he?"

"You know him better as Oscar Pittis."

Caroline paused. The difficult part was over, and from now on she would be on firmer ground. It was always easier to brainwash a person when fiction was replaced by facts, when the lying stopped and the truth began. Adhering to the scenario that Vaudrey had rewritten a third time yesterday evening, she started with Patterson and gave Coghill a résumé of his military service and CIA background, then rapidly moved on to his subsequent involvement with Qadhafi's regime. How, when and where he'd first met Jalud was of no consequence; the fact that the Libyan had sent for Patterson when Karen Whitfield had threatened to expose him suggested they had known one another for some considerable time.

"Jalud had every reason to want her dead. Qadhafi is a distant kinsman on his wife's side and Jalud knew he would be finished if the colonel learned about his perverted sexual exploits with

Karen Whitfield. In fact, this is the very point you should make to Jalud if he refuses to cooperate."

"That would make two of us then," Coghill growled. "You may be a very bright and persuasive young woman, Miss Wentworth, but you're up against someone here who's sales-resistant. I'm in enough trouble as it is, without you people adding blackmail to bribery and corruption whenever it suits your purpose."

"You want to catch the man who killed Harry Mace, don't you?"

"You know I do, but I don't see what that has to do with this Raschid al Jalud."

"The answer's very simple," Caroline told him quietly. "Every exit has been sealed off and there's no one else Patterson can turn to for help. He may think the KGB will agree to smuggle him out of the country in exchange for the video cassettes he stole from Leese, but after what happened in Linsdale Gardens yesterday, the Soviets won't touch him with a barge pole."

"And of course you're monitoring all incoming calls to the Soviet Embassy?"

"I expect DI5 is," she said evasively. "I'd certainly be surprised if they weren't."

"So how come the Libyans are immune?"

"They aren't, but you can't bug every phone booth in London and we're pretty sure this is how Patterson has kept in touch with Jalud until now. That's why we're aiming to turn Jalud around before he decides to get in touch with him again."

"Is he pliable, this diplomat of yours?"

He was nibbling at the bait just as Vaudrey had prophesied. A few more jerks on the line and Coghill would be hooked.

"He's the original India-rubber man; twist his arm and he'll jump through a hoop."

"Something tells me I'm the man who's been elected to make him do it."

Caroline nodded. "Well, you're the obvious choice," she said. "After all, your picture has been in all the newspapers, which means Jalud will make the connection the moment he sees you."

"That should unnerve him," Coghill said drily.

"He'll be even more nervous when you get around to his sex life."

"You're taking an awful lot for granted, Miss Wentworth. Before you go overboard, I'd like to know whether or not this is a joint operation. To be even more specific, just who is going to have jurisdiction over Patterson—the Security Services or the Met?"

"We're only interested in recovering the video cassettes."

"You're ducking the question and very smoothly too." Coghill smiled. "Ever thought of going into politics, Miss Wentworth?"

"Patterson will stand trial for murder," she said firmly. "You have my word on it."

It was a spontaneous decision, the culmination of a nagging presentiment that what they were doing in the interests of the state was morally indefensible. It was also a fact that she no longer had any faith in Vaudrey's judgment. A born intriguer, he had first led her to believe that their aim was to destroy Noraid's ability to keep the IRA supplied with arms and ammunition. Then yesterday evening, in a last-ditch attempt to stifle her mounting objections, he'd told her the real objective was to gain access to the CIA computer at Langley. Whatever the crock of gold at the end of the rainbow, Caroline believed the price they were paying was already far too high and the time had come to call a halt.

Coghill said, "I assume this is a covert op? I mean, Jalud would claim diplomatic immunity if we tried to interview him officially, so everything has to be off the record. Right?"

"Yes." There wasn't much else she could say.

"Maybe you're off the record too, Miss Wentworth? Maybe when this is over, you'll cease to exist?"

"I promise you it won't be like that."

"Doesn't matter anyway." Coghill jerked a thumb over his shoulder. "The Complaints Investigation Bureau has put a wiretap on my phone. That's why I repeated your name and description."

"Oh God, that's bloody marvelous," she spluttered, then shook with laughter.

"You mind sharing the joke?"

"Nicholas Vaudrey, my boss . . ." Caroline took a deep breath and almost choked, trying to contain her laughter. "The man who got you suspended," she gasped. "It looks as though he has dug a pit for himself."

A broad smile slowly appeared on Coghill's face. "Yes, well, I could have told him the CIB were apt to let their enthusiasm run riot, Miss Wentworth."

"Brooke," she said. "My real name is Caroline Brooke."

"It has a nice ring to it."

"So has the truth."

"What's this, a new beginning?"

"I'd like to think so."

"Good," said Coghill. "Now suppose you tell me when, where and how we're going to screw Jalud."

There was a time when he could hack thirty miles a day over rough country with a sixty-pound pack on his back, an M16 slung over one shoulder and 200 rounds of 5.56mm ammunition in bandoliers across his shoulders, but not any more. The passing years had exacted their toll so that now, a mere four hours after leaving The Red Lion hotel, Patterson felt bushed and about ready to quit. There were blisters on both soles, the back of one heel was chafed and his legs were lumps of iron. The sore feet could be attributed to a new pair of shoes which hadn't been broken in yet, but the other aches and pains were symptomatic of a man who was over the hill.

Patterson hooked both thumbs under the web straps of the rucksack to ease the weight on his back. Thirteen cassettes including the trailer he'd made for Denise Rousell, a couple of shirts, a clean change of underwear, shaving tackle, a pair of pajamas, and the rucksack felt as though it weighed a ton. Head bowed, shoulders slumped, he trudged on around a bend in the narrow lane.

The hamlet was on him before he knew it; a few houses grouped around a stagnant duck pond in the middle of the village green, a general store, a Saxon church and a pub called The Grape and Vine. The bright red telephone kiosk near the Y-junction at the far end of the green looked decidedly out of place, as did the stark bus shelter opposite the signpost. Mildenhall to the left, Chippenhurst to the right; he pulled the map out of his hip pocket, opened it out and studied it carefully. Little Fordham, he decided, then glanced across the green and saw he needn't have bothered. The village name was there in faded letters on a weather-beaten signboard above the entrance to the general store and post office.

He had covered just over nine miles since leaving Southwold Priory and was now due north of Newmarket. Nine miles in four hours. It was just as well that nobody at The Red Lion had recognized him from the Photofit; had they done so, the police would have grabbed him long ago, but as it was, he hadn't seen a single prowl car. He glanced at the pub across the village green from him, saw that it was open and made toward it. Leaving the rucksack by a table near the entrance, he went inside, ordered a beer and two ham sandwiches, then returned to the rustic bench on the forecourt.

The beer was cool, the ham lean and fresh, but he was too busy thinking to notice it. Patterson remembered one of his former colleagues in the CIA who'd served with the Eighth Air Force during World War II once telling him that the whole of East Anglia had been one gigantic airfield, and he could well believe it. An hour or so back, he'd passed a disused base, the runway choked with weeds, cattle grazing by the derelict control tower. He'd also seen a dozen other possible sites where a light aircraft could land and take off again without any difficulty. The pilot would have to fly in and out at treetop level to avoid being detected on the radar and he would need some kind of homing beacon, but that wasn't an insuperable problem. On the other hand, he couldn't afford to divulge the location of the pickup point until the last possible moment, and that meant he would have to acquire a two-way radio. And when you were dealing with a man like Jalud, it was also advisable to have an ace up your sleeve. The Libyans or the Russians? The old doubts returned, raising questions he couldn't answer.

Patterson finished his beer and sandwiches, hoisted the rucksack onto his back and limped across the village green toward the bright red telephone kiosk. On the flip of a coin he decided to try his luck with Denise Rousell and dialed her number. A voice he didn't recognize answered the call and said, "Cherry Tree Kennels. Can I help you?"

"My name's Henry Kingfisher," Patterson told her. "I'd like to have a word with Mrs. Beaumont?"

"One moment please."

He heard the girl put the receiver down and listened to her footsteps fading into the distance. A minute later, the silence was broken by a rapid bleeping and he fed another coin into the box. By the time she returned, it had cost him a further twenty pence to keep the line open.

"I'm afraid Mrs. Beaumont isn't available." The girl paused, then said, "Would you care to leave a message?"

"No, it's not important."

Patterson hung up and backed out of the kiosk. No two ways about it, the word had gone out that he was *persona non grata* and, like it or not, he was stuck with Jalud. Hooking his thumbs under the webbing straps, he walked up to the Y-junction and turned right for Chippenhurst.

19.

The temperature was in the high nineties, with a humidity rate to match. The lawn in front of the main building was a checkerboard of brown and green patches with deep fissures that the sprinklers had been unable to contain in the long summer drought. In the far distance, the shimmering heat waves made the thick belt of trees that screened the CIA complex from State Highway 193 seem like a desert mirage.

"It stinks, Walter. Like bad fish."

Zellick dragged his eyes away from the window and faced the assistant director. It was the third or fourth time Ensor had made the same observation and, even with the newly added simile, he was becoming a mite repetitive.

"I think we should tell this limey creep what he can do with his memorandum."

"Is that what you're going to advise the director, Frank?" Zellick drawled.

"Maybe." Ensor picked up the typewritten agreement and skimmed through it again. "If Patterson is wanted on four counts of murder one, I don't see how the hell Vaudrey can deliver him to us."

Neither did Zellick. When he'd arrived at Heathrow earlier that morning and picked up a copy of the *Guardian* from the newsstand, the banner headlines above the Photofit had nearly persuaded him to cancel his reservation on the Concorde flight to Washington. The fact that Patterson's real name had not been disclosed by the press was the main reason he'd finally boarded the plane. The other consideration was the possibility that Vaudrey might persuade the director of public prosecutions to do a deal with Patterson. Although he'd already drawn Ensor's attention to this option, he thought it advisable to mention it again.

"There's always the Broadmoor angle, Frank. A few years in a mental hospital is a whole lot better than a life sentence, and I think Patterson could buy it."

"Vaudrey's just guessing," Ensor growled. "Our man doesn't have anything to trade. Patterson knew a lot of people in the Mideast, here and in 'Nam. We drew up a list of nineteen possible suspects who are still with the Company and checked them out. Every man came through smelling like a rose. We found absolutely no evidence to indicate that a single one of them was living above his income."

"So you think there are no rotten apples in the barrel?"

"I wouldn't take any bets on that," Ensor said.

Zellick didn't blame him. No screening system was a hundred percent foolproof and the wheeler-dealers who'd made a fortune out of narcotics were professionals, people who were used to covering their tracks. All the same, Ensor was going around in circles, avoiding the real issue, and time was running out.

"I'm supposed to check in at the airport in a little over two hours from now," Zellick said tentatively. "Maybe your secretary should book me on a later flight?"

"Don't push me into making a snap decision, Walter. This whole business needs thinking about very carefully." Ensor waved the memorandum at him. "Right now, I don't see how the director can sign this document and live with it afterwards. Okay, we can pull the plug the moment we get Patterson out of England, but Vaudrey will still have a copy of the agreement and I'd like to know what he'll do with it."

The inference was very clear to Zellick. He knew Vaudrey better than anyone else in the Company and was expected to provide the answer.

"Well, I guess he might be tempted to lean on the director, threaten to blow the whistle on him if he didn't restore the computer facility, but Vaudrey must know that would never work."

"So?" Ensor said impatiently.

"So I think he's trying to lull us into a sense of false security.

According to paragraph 6 of the agreement, we're not required to disclose the recognition code until Patterson arrives at a mutually agreed RV near the departure airfield. Of course, he won't be formally handed over to us until Vaudrey hears from his people in Washington that their computer is locked into our data bank and the system is functioning properly. But that's fair enough, isn't it? I mean, it's not unreasonable for the British to want some kind of safeguard."

"Right."

"And the price seems negligible from our point of view since we'll be airborne half an hour later and the facility can be terminated the moment we're clear of their air space."

"That thought had occurred to me."

"But what if we're held on the ground for a couple of hours? Vaudrey can milk an awful lot of information in that time and the beauty of it is, he knows we won't be able to do a damn thing about it."

"Yeah." Ensor nodded sagely. "If we cut the link, Vaudrey informs the police he has reason to believe we're trying to smuggle a fugitive out of the country and the end result is a major diplomatic row and the director gets fired in the process."

"And you," Zellick said.

"There'd be a whole lot of other casualties, too. You could wind up looking for another job, Walter."

In Roman times, the messenger arriving with bad news had invariably been one of the first victims of the subsequent purge. Some traditions refused to die and it seemed this custom was about to be revived.

"Maybe we should fire those nineteen suspects?" Zellick suggested drily. "Then Vaudrey wouldn't have a trump card up his sleeve and we'd be off the hook."

Although it was meant as a joke, Ensor took it seriously and considered the possibility, his lips pursed, his dark eyes glinting in the few seconds he needed to assess the pertinent factors and reach a decision.

"Unfortunately, it's not a fail-safe solution to the problem, Walter. The trouble with relying on the list is that we can never be sure we haven't overlooked somebody." Ensor smiled fleetingly. "What we need is a large slice of luck, like Patterson succumbing to a fatal heart attack."

"Before Vaudrey has a chance to interrogate him," Zellick added.

"You catch on fast, Walter."

"I do?"

"Don't go coy on me. You know very well the director will only agree to sign this memorandum if he's satisfied it will never come into effect."

"I think," Zellick said slowly, "I think you'd better spell out in words of one syllable exactly what it is you expect me to do."

Ensor did exactly that, in sufficient detail to leave no room for doubt. One hour and twenty minutes later, Zellick was cooling his heels in the departure lounge at Dulles International Airport. In his briefcase, the top copy of the agreement was signed, witnessed and date-stamped just the way Vaudrey had specified.

Raschid al Jalud lived within a short walking distance of Regent's Park at number 26 Nash Walk, a street named after the nineteenth-century architect who'd designed the terraced houses. As the official residence of the cultural attaché, the building itself was definitely at odds with the proletarian image Qadhafi liked to project, though, once inside, Coghill got the impression that Jalud and his household staff had done their best to rectify the situation. The interior hadn't been decorated for years and was suitably drab. The wallpaper in the entrance hall had faded from cream to a streaky yellow, while the baseboards and doorframes were a dull shade of chocolate brown.

The study at the front of the house, where Coghill had been told to wait for the diplomat, was in no better shape. A lot of feet had scuffed the Persian carpet and its intricate weaving had suffered in the process, becoming threadbare in places. The desk was utilitarian, so were the two armchairs, but they were undoubtedly in line with the austere tastes of Colonel Qadhafi, whose stern image gazed down from a picture frame above crossed daggers on the far wall.

Coghill glanced at his wristwatch, saw that it was just after six-forty and wondered how much longer he'd have to wait before Jalud deigned to put in an appearance. The Libyan had left the Embassy in Prince's Gate more than two hours ago and had visited the mosque in Regent's Park on his way home, where he'd finally arrived shortly after six. Kept informed of his movements by the surveillance detail, Coghill had gotten there ten minutes ahead of him and had been twiddling his thumbs ever since.

A murmured conversation reached him from the hall and he thought he recognized the surly voice of the Baluchi manservant who'd grudgingly admitted him to the house. Then the study door opened and Jalud walked into the room. He was about five six, slim with a narrow waist, and his sharp features reminded Coghill of a weasel, just as Caroline Brooke had said they would.

"Detective Inspector Coghill?" The voice was small like its owner.

"Yes, sir." Coghill made to shake his hand, but the Libyan ignored the gesture and promptly sat down behind the desk.

"You're with the Diplomatic Protection Group, I believe?"

"That's what I told your manservant." Coghill added another "sir" for good measure. Politeness was said to cost nothing, but in this instance it hurt.

"I can't understand why you should approach me directly, Inspector, when there are recognized channels of communication. If this is a matter affecting the protection of the Embassy and its staff, you should have contacted our security officer, Mr. Mahmood Omani. Surely you're aware of that?"

"This isn't some vague threat, it concerns you directly."

Coghill moved up to the desk. Jalud had tried to intimidate him, but his angry tone of voice had been marred by a curious lisp as though he had a loose denture plate in his mouth. Close enough now to smell his breath, Coghill realized he was sucking a peppermint in a futile attempt to conceal the fact that he'd been at the bottle. Another of the disciplines of the Islamic faith had been abandoned in the need to fortify himself before they met face to face.

"What exactly do you mean? Am I in some sort of danger?"

"Yes, sir. From the man who murdered Karen Whitfield."

"You can't be serious." Jalud tried to look incredulous, but it didn't come off. His face was stiff, his eyes furtive.

"Oh, but I am."

Coghill reached inside his jacket for the snapshots Caroline Brooke had given him. Then slowly and very deliberately he laid them down, face up and one at a time, like a banker in a pontoon school dealing to a gambler who was trying to make twenty-one the hard way. Abercorn House, Karen Whitfield striding across the forecourt and Jalud leaving the apartment building with the blurred figure of Nolan, the Irish hall porter, framed in the entrance. Three separate photographs that supported the circumstantial evidence they already had.

"I've never met that woman." Jalud looked up, wild-eyed, a trembling finger still pointing at her picture. "Never."

"How about Orville Patterson?" Coghill tossed a head-and-shoulders mug shot onto the desk. "Maybe his face is more familiar?"

"No." The denial was accompanied by a long, drawn-out hiss.

"We can prove he murdered Karen Whitfield."

"Why should that interest me, Inspector?"

"Because you were seen with Patterson in Northumberland Avenue last Wednesday evening. He met you outside the Playhouse Theatre and you drove off together in the direction of Trafalgar Square in a Datsun, license number CVA 231Y. The vehicle had been hired from Rent-A-Car Limited of 285 Kilburn High Road and was later found abandoned less than a mile from this house."

"It's a lie."

"We have two witnesses, Mr. Jalud."

"That's impossible, I was at home on Wednesday evening. They must have mistaken me for somebody else."

"I don't think so," Coghill said evenly. "I'm afraid you're the one who made a mistake, the day you met Karen Whitfield. You want me to describe what she did to you in her apartment in Abercorn House?"

He bored in on Jalud and spelled out the sordid details of their fun and games, adding a little flesh to the erotic symbols Karen Whitfield had entered in her address book. He told him about the camera behind the two-way mirror and the microphone in the base of the table lamp and how Leese had captured every perverted sexual moment on film.

"You know something, Mr. Jalud?" Coghill said, winding up. "Somehow I don't think that's quite what Colonel Qadhafi had in mind when he appointed you to be his cultural attaché in London. As a matter of fact, I'm absolutely sure you wouldn't last five minutes if he knew what you'd been up to."

There was a long silence, broken only by the swish of tires on the smooth pavement of the road as a car drove past the house. Upstairs, somebody with heavy footsteps crossed the room directly above their heads.

Finally Jalud said, "What is it you want from me?"

"Now that's more like it." Coghill pointed to the phone on the desk. "Sooner or later, Patterson will call you because there's no one else he can turn to for help. When he does, we want you to play along with him and agree to do whatever he asks, but don't sound too enthusiastic or eager to please, otherwise he'll smell a rat and back off."

"I'm not sure I care for that allusion," Jalud said and stretched his mouth in a thin smile.

The way Coghill saw it, the only thing wrong with the allusion was that it cast a slur on the whole rodent family. Aloud, he said, "If Patterson sticks to his usual procedure, he'll establish contact first, then direct you to a public phone box. That's when he'll get down to business, but don't worry, I'll be there to hold your hand."

"Do you mean you're going to stay with me the whole time?"

Jalud sounded anxious and with some reason. His wife and family would be curious to know why a British police officer was sitting on his tail, something which would take a bit of explaining.

"Only after Patterson has established contact."

"I see."

Jalud looked relieved. There was also a calculating expression in his eyes which flashed a warning to Coghill.

"Don't try and get smart, Mr. Jalud," he told him. "We'll be listening to every word you say."

"You speak Arabic perhaps?"

"No."

"Patterson does."

"Yes, but your English is so much better than his Arabic. In any event, the people who will be monitoring the conversation were trained at the Middle East School of Languages in Beirut."

Coghill left him to mull it over and walked out into the hall. There was no sign of the surly Baluchi manservant, but the Arab bodyguard dressed in flowing robes who'd arrived with Jalud was sitting on a ladder-back chair opposite the study. A cheery smile drew no response, and he continued to sit there lifeless as a statue, hawk face immobile and black eyes unblinking while Coghill let himself out of the house.

The Volvo was parked around the corner in Braemore Avenue, approximately 200 yards' walking distance from the Libyan's residence. Caroline Brooke had opened the sun roof, wound down both side windows and was reclining in the passenger seat, her eyes half closed, drowsing in the warm evening sun.

"How did you get on with Jalud?" she asked him as he got in beside her.

"We didn't part the best of friends, but he'll jump through the hoop, just as you said he would."

"Good." Caroline reached between the seats and picked up a Pye two-way battery-powered radio. Depressing the transmit button, she said, "Bulldog, this is Whippet. Our rabbit is nibbling, over."

Somebody breathed into the mike and produced a rushing noise; then a voice with a lilting Welsh accent said, "Roger. Stay on listening watch. Out."

Caroline turned the volume up slightly, placed the radio on top of the dashboard and leaned back in the seat again. "Better make yourself comfortable, Tom," she said. "We could be in for a long wait."

Her forecast proved wildly inaccurate. A few minutes later, Bulldog broke wireless silence to inform them that Jalud had reluctantly agreed to wait for a further call on 580–4444 from 8:00 P.M. onward.

"Any idea where that number is?" Coghill asked.

"Tottenham Court Road, opposite the Dominion Theatre," Caroline told him. "Patterson has used that particular phone booth before."

"When?"

The question went unanswered. Before she had a chance to reply, the surveillance detail in Nash Walk came on the air to report that their rabbit had left his hutch and was scampering toward Regent's Park Underground station.

Patterson wiped his mouth, left the paper napkin on the greasy plate, then picked up his rucksack and walked out of the snack bar on St. Stephen's Road. Despite the castle museum and cathedral, Norwich was off the beaten track for most American tourists, but it was the only town of any consequence in that part of East Anglia where he could be sure of obtaining the equipment he needed. To get there from Chippenhurst, he'd first hitched a lift into the small market town of Thetford, then caught a local bus, which had taken the best part of two hours to cover the remaining twenty-nine miles. It had been past four-thirty by the time the bus had dropped him off in the city center, and he'd then scoured the main shopping precinct looking for a store which sold the kind of specialized equipment a radio ham would consider essential, only to draw a complete blank. There was no shortage of citizen's band and ship-to-shore, but he needed a set in the ultrahigh-frequency range in order to talk to a plane, and that was an item the retailers didn't stock.

There had been no problem, however, with the rest of the equipment: from a stationer's he'd purchased a protractor, set square, plastic ruler and a pair of dividers, while the flash lamps which incorporated an orange winking light had been acquired from the main Ford dealer as well as from a corner shop that sold car accessories. The remaining items on the list, consisting of a pair of collapsible hazard warning signs with red illuminating reflectors and a roll of fluorescent masking tape, he'd obtained from a store that specialized in camping equipment.

Patterson turned right into Ber Street, went on past the church and entered the phone booth, one of several he'd selected beforehand in different parts of the city. Dumping the rucksack on the floor, he dug out a handful of loose change and arranged the coins in a neat pile on top of the box. Then he glanced at his watch, saw that it was two minutes past eight and lifted the receiver.

The man was in his early twenties and obviously fancied himself. He had dark curly hair and the sort of excessively handsome face Coghill always associated with commercials for aftershave and male deodorants. He was wearing a snug-fitting pair of Daks which drew attention to his genitals, and the blue silk shirt had been left unbuttoned to the waist to reveal a heavy silver crucifix partially buried in a forest of black hair. He smiled a lot into the phone and the way his free hand kept gesticulating led Coghill to assume he was chatting up a bird. The fact that he'd been on the phone for over a quarter of an hour without ever once feeding a coin into the box, also suggested that either he'd reversed the charges or else he'd discovered a method of swindling the Post Office. With the minutes ticking away, Coghill was on the point of physically removing him, when he suddenly hung up and backed out of the phone booth. Grabbing hold of Jalud, Coghill shoved him inside and closed the door behind them.

"We don't have much time," he said, "so just listen carefully and don't interrupt until I've finished. When you answer the phone, I want you to hold the receiver away from your ear so that I can hear every word. Let Patterson do most of the talking, but like I said before, don't be too eager to please. And just remember this, if you bitch it up, a very blue movie with you in the starring role is likely to find its way to Colonel Qadhafi. Got it?"

Jalud nodded, then flinched as the phone rang. Taking a deep breath, he answered the call and croaked a hello into the mouthpiece.

Patterson said, "I'm going to make this short and sweet. You've read the newspapers and know the state of the market. Everything's gone to pot, but the stock I'm holding is worth a fortune in anybody's money. And there's no need to remind you that part of the material on offer can either make or break you, is there?"

"No." Jalud moistened his lips. "No, I'm only too aware you're in a strong bargaining position."

"Right on." Patterson chuckled, then the time-up signal cut in and Coghill heard him feed another coin into the box. "Okay," he continued, "the deal is this. You get in touch with ECAS Limited and arrange a trip to the Continent on my behalf and the entire stock is yours for free."

"What you're asking for is out of the question," Jalud protested.

"I want confirmation that a Piper Cherokee is on standby by 1130 hours tomorrow," Patterson said, shouting him down.

"I'm not sure ECAS will be able to do that; they may have other commitments."

"Don't give me that shit; you've only to snap your fingers and that fucking bush pilot will drop everything. . . ." The blips started up again, another coin went down in the box and Patterson came back at him, taking up from where he'd left off. "No buts, no arguments, just get on the goddamn phone and fix it the moment I hang up. You read me?"

Jalud glanced at Coghill, seeking guidance, and got an affirmative nod. "All right," he snapped, "all right, I'll do it."

"Now you're being sensible, Raschid. I like that."

"You would," Jalud said bitterly.

"One more thing. I think you need a rest and a change of scene. Take the day off tomorrow and go down to Southend. I want to hear the sound of a Cherokee running up when I call you at 1130 hours."

The time-up signal cut in yet again, then the bleeping note changed to a continuous burr and the line went dead.

"End of conversation," Coghill said. "You can hang up."

Jalud replaced the receiver. "What happens now?" he asked in a surly voice.

Coghill glanced over his shoulder. Caroline Brooke and two men from the surveillance detail had closed in on the phone booth while Jalud had been talking to Patterson, and they were now standing outside the door to discourage anyone else from using the pay phone.

"You can tell me about ECAS Limited," he said. "Who they are, where they hang out and what they do."

ECAS, it transpired, stood for Express Customized Air Service, an airline that had one Piper Cherokee and two short takeoff/landing obsolete Pioneers, one of which had been cannibalized to provide spare parts. The chairman of the board, major stockholder with controlling interest, operations officer and chief pilot was a former Australian citizen called Bernie Urquhart. ECAS operated from a grass strip on the outskirts of Southend and boasted they were prepared to fly anybody, anything, anywhere, any time. In the circumstances, Coghill could readily understand why such a firm would suit Jalud down to the ground.

"Anywhere, any time," he mused. "In my book that means you know how to contact this Bernie Urquhart during out-of-office hours."

"Yes." There wasn't much else Jalud could say.

"Right, just hold on a minute." Coghill opened the door, told Caroline Brooke what he had in mind, then instructed Jalud to contact Urquhart and warn him to have a Cherokee on standby from 1130 hours.

"Who'll pay for the charter?" he asked.

"I'll give you one guess," Coghill said.

Vaudrey fixed himself another whiskey and soda, walked over to the window and stood there gazing at the lights in Battersea Park across the river. It had been a long, tiring, but thoroughly satisfactory day. Coghill, Jalud and Patterson; each man had responded in exactly the way he had predicted. And Zellick was back too, suffering from jet lag, the memorandum signed and sealed though not yet delivered. A minor disappointment there, but nothing to worry about. Good old Walter was merely exercising a little native caution. What was it he'd said? "You know the old saying, Nick, seeing is believing. So I'm holding on to the agreement until I'm sure you've got our dissident spook."

Then Zellick had asked how the manhunt was going and had sounded completely flat when Vaudrey had told him Patterson had been sighted as far afield as Bristol, Liverpool, Hull, Plymouth and Southampton.

Releasing the Photofit had been the biggest mistake the police had made so far and it had proved an unexpected bonus for him. The response from the public had been quite astounding and the provincial forces had been inundated with information, all of it misleading. Vaudrey smiled; had he planned it himself, he could not have asked for a better or more confusing diversion.

20.

The house was called Deane Cottage, which Patterson thought a typical British understatement, considering the residence had four or five bedrooms upstairs and at least three reception rooms on the ground floor. It was situated in the middle of nowhere, eleven miles southwest of Norwich and midway between Old Buckenham and Tacolneston, whose combined population probably numbered less than two hundred. The property sat well back from the minor road to Tacolneston and was largely hidden from the south and west by a kidney-shaped wood. Immediately behind the house was a large field of pasture which he thought would make a passable landing strip, and the sole access to the cottage was a narrow lane that meandered through the wood and came to a dead end at the front door. The only other residence in the vicinity was an equally isolated farmhouse, and that was a good half-mile away.

It had been his intention to use the derelict World War II airfield near Thetford that he'd passed yesterday afternoon, but in the light of subsequent events, he'd changed his mind. "Never retrace your steps, make sure the route back is different from the route out." That was a lesson he'd learned the hard way in 'Nam and the habit acquired in combat had become second nature. Yesterday evening after the second phone call to Jalud, he'd caught a bus going to Diss, gotten off at Long Stratton and headed cross-country toward Old Buckenham. Then, half an hour before last light, he'd come across a small signpost planted in the grass verge by the roadside which pointed toward Deane Cottage. The surrounding countryside and a brief glance at the map had convinced him it was worth making a detour to see if the place had possibilities. The moment he saw the isolated house from a vantage point on the forward edge of the kidney-shaped wood, Patterson had decided to forget the derelict airfield.

Soon after dark, he'd worked his way forward to take a closer look at the cottage and the cars parked in the driveway. The dinner party which he'd surmised the occupants were giving had finally broken up around eleven-thirty. As the guests drove off in their respective cars, he'd seen the host and hostess silhouetted in the headlights. Both husband and wife were fairly plump and in their late fifties or early sixties. The man was a couple of inches taller than himself but nowhere near as muscular, and when they'd turned about to go back inside the house, Patterson had noticed he dragged his left leg. That, plus an obvious impediment in his speech when he'd called goodnight to the departing guests, suggested he'd had a stroke which in turn could have led to a premature retirement. From close observation, Patterson had also discovered they lived alone in the cottage, with only an old black Labrador for company.

If the location had looked good then, there was even less reason for him to change his opinion of the place in the cold gray light of daybreak. He was hungry, bone weary, chilled to the marrow from sleeping rough and almost flat broke; the cottage offered a refuge, a safe hideout where he could rest until Urquhart arrived to collect him. Patterson lifted the rucksack, slung it over one shoulder and moved out of the wood, stealthy as a hunter closing in on its prey. When he reached the narrow lane, he picked his way across the gravel, walking on tiptoe like a ballet dancer, and made his way around to the back of the house.

Some householders barricaded themselves in at night; others, who lived in areas where there was very little crime, were apt to be more complacent. The couple who lived in Deane Cottage obviously belonged to the latter category; before retiring to bed, they had drawn the curtains back in the lounge and deliberately left one of the fanlight windows open to ventilate the room. Patterson set the rucksack down, removed his shoes, climbed up onto the sill and raised the fanlight to its fullest extent. Boosting himself up until his head and shoulders were inside the room, he reached for the catch and unlatched the side window. It swung open on oiled hinges and, stepping down from the sill, he passed his shoes and rucksack into the lounge, then climbed in after them.

The debris from the night before was still in evidence: the remnants of salted peanuts and potato chips in silver dishes, ashtrays brimming with cigar and cigarette stubs, dregs of coffee in small cups and empty glasses on the mantelpiece, in the hearth and on the occasional tables beside the armchairs and settee. The dining room across the hall from the lounge was in a similar state: placemats for ten on the table, crumpled napkins, wineglasses, some bearing traces of lipstick and containing a few drops of Beaujolais, and a decanter of port.

Patterson backed out of the room, raised a squeak from a loose floorboard and froze. A minute passed, then another, the silence broken only by the Labrador snoring peacefully in the kitchen and the ticking of the grandfather clock at the far end of the hall. Eventually satisfied that no one had heard him above the other sounds in the house, he padded toward the front door in his stockinged feet and checked out the study opposite the downstairs cloakroom.

From the photographs on the wall and the assorted trophies, it was evident that the man had spent a lifetime abroad with the regular army both in peace and war. He'd been everywhere—India, Malaya, Africa, Italy, France and Germany—and along the way, he'd shot everything that had moved, from big game to man. There were two signed photographs in silver frames on the desk, one of Field Marshal Montgomery, the other of Dwight D. Eisenhower, inscribed "To my very good friend, Brigadier Rupert Deane." To the left of the door, two 9mm Berettas, a Luger automatic, a .30 caliber Winchester carbine and a Schmeisser submachine gun were exhibited in a display cabinet fitted with steel bars and wired to a burglar alarm.

Brigadier Deane also possessed an expensive fishing rod and an even more expensive-looking 12-bore shotgun which, in contrast to the firearms, he merely kept in a leather gun case on top of the display cabinet. Patterson eyed the desk, decided Deane had probably locked the cartridges away in one of the drawers and picked up the paperknife that was lying on the blotting pad. There were five drawers in all, but the one above the kneehole was too shallow for anything other than stationery. Right side or left? He plumped for the former on the grounds that since most people were right-handed, a normal person would find it easier to open and close the drawers on that side. Inserting the blade in the crevice, he pried it upward and forced the drawer open.

The cartridges were in an unsealed box right at the back between a spare fishing reel and a pair of pruning shears. According to the label, the nylon line had a breaking strain of twenty pounds and he could tell the shears were razor-sharp. He tucked both items inside his shirt, broke the shotgun open, loaded it and then went upstairs.

The Deanes occupied the room above the porch, a fact that Patterson had discovered the night before from watching the lights go out one by one. Turning left at the top of the staircase, he crept along the landing and quietly opened their door. As he stepped inside, the grandfather clock down in the hall started to chime the hour and Deane suddenly reared up in bed. For a moment he seemed unsure where he was, then he saw the 12-bore shotgun leveled at his head and his eyes mirrored disbelief.

"No heroics," Patterson told him softly. "It's loaded." Deane nodded. His wife beside him stirred and murmured his name in a sleep-laden voice. "Wake her up, but do it quietly. I don't want any hysterics."

Deane turned over onto his left side and gently shook his wife. "It's all right, Anthea," he said, trying to reassure her in a halting voice. "Don't be frightened, I'm here."

Her throat worked overtime swallowing air and there was an expression of pure terror in her eyes, until Deane took her hand, squeezed it tenderly and gradually managed to calm her down.

"That's more like it," Patterson said.

"What do you want with us?" It was a struggle for Deane to get the words out and his impediment was more noticeable than before.

"I want you to keep your mouth shut, turn over on to your stomach and cross both hands behind your back." Patterson reached inside his shirt and tossed the fishing line onto the bed within reach of Anthea Deane. "Tie him up," he snapped, "ankles, knees, wrists, elbows." The pair of shears followed, landing an inch from the reel. "And no half measures. As long as he can breathe, that's all that matters."

"My husband has a bad heart," Anthea said, with a flash of defiance.

"And it could get a lot worse if you don't get on with it." Patterson backed away from the bed and sat down on a chair. After watching her carefully for a while, he said, "You got anything special planned for today, Anthea?"

"What?" She looked up, startled.

"Are you expecting any visitors? Or going anywhere?"

"No." She shook her head, cut another length of nylon line from the reel and tied her husband's ankles together. "No, we were going to have a quiet day at home and do some gardening."

"There'll be a lot of phone calls though, won't there? Your friends ringing up to thank you for the dinner party?"

"Perhaps."

"You've left the lounge and dining room in a mess," he continued. "You got somebody coming in to clean it up?"

"Yes, the daughter of one of our local farmers. She lives about half a mile away."

"You'd better phone and put her off." Patterson got up again, walked over to the chest of drawers and found a silk scarf. "I don't care what excuse you give her, just make sure it's something she'll believe."

"I'll try."

"You certainly should, your life could depend on it."

"I won't give you any trouble," she whispered.

She wouldn't, either. In her anxiety to placate him, she had tied the line so tightly round Deane's wrists that his fingers were already beginning to swell. "You've done a good job," Patterson said, handing her the scarf. "Now gag him."

Tears welled in her eyes and began to run down her cheeks as she fumbled with the scarf and knotted it at the back of her husband's head.

"Save your tears," Patterson said roughly. "Get dressed and then you can cook me some breakfast. I'm going to be around until nightfall, and whether the day seems long or short is entirely up to you."

Kingman just knew it was going to be one of those days when he didn't get a moment to himself. The phone had been ringing nonstop from the time he'd arrived at the office and now, less than a minute after the last caller had hung up, the damned thing was trilling again like a demented canary. Answering it with a gruff "Yes," he discovered he had Franklin on the line.

"Tom Coghill?" Franklin said casually. "You any idea where he's got to, Bert?"

"No." Kingman frowned. Something in Franklin's tone of voice sounded a warning note and he had a nasty feeling that he would find himself in the shit if he wasn't careful. "No, why should I? The CIB's got him under its wing."

"That's just the trouble, it hasn't." Franklin paused, hummed and hawed as though collecting his thoughts, then said, "They tried to get in touch with Coghill last night, but he didn't answer the phone. Same thing happened this morning."

"Perhaps it's out of order, Charlie."

"I don't think so. They've been around to his flat and he isn't at home." Franklin paused again, this time to clear his throat. "You did withdraw his passport, didn't you, Bert?"

"His passport?" Kingman gripped the phone tighter. "I took the warrant card off him. Nobody said anything about his passport."

"It's standard procedure, you know that."

"Are you implying he's skipped the country?"

"He may have," Franklin said. "I'm sure I would in his shoes. His ex-wife has been shouting her mouth off. Seems her boyfriend was diddling the Inland Revenue with her reluctant help. She claims she told Coghill about it and he encouraged her to go along with the fraud. Said if she asked for a bigger cut, the extra money would help with the housekeeping."

Kingman closed his eyes and swore under his breath. Someone had decided that Coghill had to be muzzled and now Franklin seemed to be implying it was entirely his fault that the bloody situation had gone sour.

"I don't like it, Charlie," he said fiercely. "Why should you and I end up carrying the can?"

"I'm not the one who forgot to withdraw his passport," Franklin reminded him.

"You owe me."

"What?"

"A favor," Kingman said. "Remember that little talk we had on Saturday when you said there were a number of people in the Home Office who would like to see Coghill taken off the Whitfield case? Well, now I'm presenting you with the marker."

"I'm not sure I like your attitude."

"I'm not wild about it either, but that doesn't alter the fact that you're going to tell the CIB that if Coghill really is missing, it's their fault and nobody else's."

"But..."

"No buts, Charlie, just do it." Kingman put the phone down. Not for the first time in the last few days, he found himself wishing he'd stayed in Majorca.

The airfield used by ECAS had been built for the RAF Transport Command during the latter stages of World War II. Following the cessation of hostilities, the base had been deactivated by the Air Ministry and the land returned to its former owners, with the exception of a few acres taken up by the one-time headquarters, living accommodation and maintenance area which were no longer suitable for agricultural purposes. Most of the buildings still standing had been leased by a light engineering firm that specialized in reconditioning air engines. The rest, a semiderelict control tower and part of the old dispersal apron, belonged to ECAS.

Bernie Urquhart, the chairman and principal stockholder of ECAS, was six foot three and thin as a beanpole. He had a long, angular face, drooping eyelids that looked as though they were about to close at any moment, and a black mustache that was equally lethargic. Despite a sleepy appearance and a slow, deliberate way of talking, he was far from being indolent. When money was in the offing, he had a mind like a cash register.

"Let's see if I've got this straight," he drawled. "I've been hired to fly somebody to an unknown destination on the Continent from an unknown point of departure."

"What are you complaining about?" Coghill said. "You've done business with Mr. Jalud before and he's agreed to pay you five hundred pounds for the job."

"Yeah, but he forgot to mention the plane would have to sit on the ground all day. Now I shall have to cancel an important charter flight to Newcastle-upon-Tyne and lose a very good customer who'll never come to me again. I figure I'm entitled to some compensation."

"How much?"

"Two hundred and sixty pounds for the round trip, plus another four hundred for loss of future earnings."

"You should have taken that into account when you quoted a price," Coghill told him.

"I agree," Jalud said, then glared at the Australian. "You've already had all the money you'll get out of me."

It was another way of saying there would be no more lucrative contracts if Urquhart insisted on pushing his luck. Judging by his ironic smile, Coghill figured the Australian had already concluded that the special delivery service he'd been running for Jalud was a thing of the past. Clandestine flights in and out of the UK depended on absolute secrecy, and that no longer pertained. Jalud had showed up with a police officer and that was all the evidence Urquhart needed to know his cover had been blown.

"Okay, let's forget the compensation." Urquhart smiled, as if to show it was all the same to him. "Let's talk about my passenger instead. Something tells me he's a real hard case. I mean, you don't have to be a genius to guess that you people wouldn't go to all this trouble unless you wanted him pretty badly. Putting two and two together, I'd say this passenger is the same man who's been grabbing all the headlines lately."

"And?" Coghill said quietly.

"A little danger money would come in handy."

"Perhaps that's something we can discuss after the 11:30 call."

"Why not? Anything to please you, Miss Brooke." Urquhart turned in her direction and looked her over from head to toe, first appraising her bare, shapely legs, then moving slowly upward. "Anything," he repeated with special emphasis.

"Try pleasing me instead," Coghill said.

"Something eating you, old sport?"

"Yes. I just don't think you're in a position to drive a bargain."

There was another and more personal reason for his anger. The truth was, he'd taken exception to the way Urquhart had eyed Caroline, obviously visualizing the body underneath the navy blue skirt and white silk blouse. It occurred to him that his attitude was wholly irrational, especially since he scarcely knew her, and he wondered in passing why it was he should feel compelled to leap to her defense.

"That's where we differ," Urquhart said. "I know when I'm being asked to do somebody a favor."

"Then you're more stupid than I thought." Coghill jerked a thumb at Jalud. "The kind of charter work you've been doing for Raschid could put you behind bars for years."

"You want to check the records before you start accusing people, old sport. Every flight plan was cleared with Air Traffic Control."

"I don't give a damn what you've filed. By the time I've finished with your staff, you can use those flight plans for lavatory paper. I'll question them one at a time and I guarantee there'll be discrepancies in their stories."

Coghill wasn't sure how the two ground-staff men would react, and the ex-Army Air Corps pilot who was licensed to fly the single-engined Pioneer could be a tough nut to crack, but the secretary in the office next door was vulnerable.

"What are you suggesting then?" Urquhart grumbled. "That we leave things as they are?"

"It might be a good idea."

The telephone rang in the adjoining office, then the extension on the folding table Urquhart used as a desk started trilling—11:30 on the dot, not a minute before, not a minute after. Coghill thought that was one thing to be said for Patterson, the man was punctual.

"Remember what I said," he told Jalud. "Don't be in too much of a hurry to come to the phone, and spin the conversation out as much as you can."

Coghill leaned forward, picked up the eavesdropper that the plumbers had attached to the receiver with an umbilical cord and held it to his right ear, then signaled Urquhart to take the call. The Australian did so, giving his name and extension.

Patterson said, "My name's Kingfisher. I understand Mr. Jalud is with you?"

"He's around somewhere," Urquhart drawled. "Do you want to have a word with him?"

"That's the general idea."

"Okay. Hold on while I give him a shout."

"Where the hell is he?"

"Having a crap." Urquhart put the phone down, clumped over to the adjoining office in the control tower and jerked the door open. "Raschid?" he bellowed in a voice that made his secretary jump. "There's a guy called Kingfisher on the line asking for you."

Coghill checked the time by his wristwatch. Tracing an incoming call through the standard dialing network was never an easy task and, so far, the telephone engineers had been working on the problem for exactly one minute fifty. They needed longer much longer, but he could hear Patterson muttering to himself and there was a real danger he'd hang up and call back again later. He looked up, caught Jalud's eye and gave him the nod. The Libyan picked up the phone, licked his lips and said hello in a voice that sounded breathless.

"Jesus H. Christ," Patterson exploded. "You picked a fine time to go to the men's room."

"It was necessary," Jalud said woodenly. "I have an upset stomach."

"Fuck your stomach. Have you fixed that flight to the Continent yet?"

"Yes. It cost me..."

"I don't hear the Cherokee," Patterson snapped, cutting him off in midsentence.

"What?"

"The plane, goddamn it. I told you I wanted to hear it running up."

"Ah, yes. Well, Mr. Urquhart said..."

"I don't give a shit what your fucking bush pilot said. I'll call back in five minutes and when I do, that Cherokee had better be purring like a cat."

Jalud opened his mouth to say something, realized the connection had been terminated and slowly replaced the receiver.

"Four minutes twelve seconds." Coghill frowned. "I didn't hear him feed any coins into the box."

Neither had Urquhart, nor his secretary who'd answered the incoming call and spoken to Patterson before switching him through to the extension. As a result, Caroline Brooke suggested there was only one way to make absolutely sure, and that was for her to monitor the phone in the outer office. It was also evident to Coghill that any further delaying tactics were likely to prove counterproductive, and although Urquhart complained it would be a waste of good fuel, he didn't press the point and the Cherokee was running sweetly when the second call came through at 11:40.

This time around, Patterson spoke to Urquhart. The conversation was brief, entirely one-sided and was terminated at 11:42. In the intervening two minutes, Urquhart was given details of their proposed flight, departing Southend at 2115 hours for Bordeaux, and instructed to obtain the appropriate clearance from the British and French civil aviation authorities. He was also warned to stand by for a final telephone call fifteen minutes before the estimated time of departure.

"Kingfisher's a real sly bastard," Urquhart said. "He knows the

Cherokee has a maximum range of 385 miles, so he picks an airfield near the limit which just happens to be equipped with a radar ground control approach. And the phone call at 2100? That's when he tells me where we're really going."

"What did you expect?" Coghill said. "The man's a professional."

And he was a rank amateur in comparison. Patterson was fourteen years older and fourteen years more experienced. He'd beaten the Viet Cong at their own game and was a born survivor. He had Caroline's word for that.

"Can you spare me a minute, Tom?"

"Yes, of course." Coghill turned around, saw Caroline jerk her head toward the door and followed her out of the control tower. She walked on past the two Pioneers and the Piper Cherokee on the dispersal apron and didn't stop until they were well out of earshot. "What's the matter?" he asked.

"I'm not sure, Tom." A thumb crept toward her mouth and she nibbled at the nail. "Patterson didn't use a phone booth."

"Is that official?"

"The engineers say they aren't sure, but I didn't hear any coins go down in the box."

If Caroline was right, it meant Patterson had made both calls from a private number, but the worry lines on her forehead told him there was more to it than that. "You're upset about something," he said quietly. "You want to tell me what it is?"

"They also said they'd had no luck with the first telephone call. They couldn't even give me an approximate location."

"They only had four minutes, Caroline. I'm no expert, but I think it's asking a lot to expect them to get a fix in that time."

"I think they were lying, Tom. Oh, I went through the proper channels, completed the necessary forms to obtain the home secretary's approval for the operation and submitted the request to Vaudrey in accordance with our standing instructions, but he may not have sent the application on. With his connections, Nicholas could have set the whole thing up on a completely unofficial basis. If he did, then the results of the phone tap would go directly to him and we'd be left out in the cold."

"That's a cheering thought," Coghill said.

"What are we going to do, Tom?"

"There's nothing we can do, except wait and hope for the best. If Patterson contacts us at 2100 hours, we'll know they couldn't trace the number. If he doesn't, it's reasonable to assume that your boss has grabbed him."

"We've got a conflict of interests," she mused. "You both want Patterson for different reasons, Nicholas because he wants access to the CIA computer and you because Patterson has murdered four people and it's a question of simple justice."

"And you?" he asked. "What do you want, Caroline?"

"The same as you," she said with total commitment.

21.

Vaudrey folded the map and tossed it on to the shelf behind the rear seat of the Cortina. They were clear of Woodford now, heading northeast toward Newmarket on the A11, and while his sense of direction wasn't infallible, it was unlikely the driver could lose his way on a dead-straight road. Beside him, Walter Zellick stretched out his left leg and planted it on the other side of the transmission hump in an effort to make himself more comfortable.

"Where did you say we were making for, Nick?" he asked, his voice plaintive.

"Thetford," Vaudrey said. "It's a small town in Norfolk roughly eighty miles from London."

"It's going to seem more like eight hundred." Zellick smiled ruefully. "I guess I'm the wrong build for these compact models."

Serves you right, Vaudrey thought. Friend Walter had been a thorn in his side, badgering him every hour on the hour, wanting to know how the trace was going. He'd also insisted he should be present when Patterson was finally apprehended, otherwise there would be no deal. That being the case, Vaudrey had insured he sat directly behind the driver who, being well over six feet tall, had moved his seat back, thereby restricting the amount of leg room. Petty or not, revenge was sweet.

"I hope this isn't going to be a wild-goose chase, Nick."

Vaudrey was under the impression that he'd already explained why it was necessary to base themselves at Thetford, but clearly he'd failed to convince Zellick and would have to go over the same ground again. The telephone engineers, he reminded him, were convinced both calls had been made from a private number and had traced the initial one as far as the Thetford exchange. It was therefore reasonable to assume Patterson was somewhere in the vicinity and was unlikely to move from his present hideout before 2100 hours, when he was due to contact ECAS again. When he did so, Vaudrey anticipated that his final instructions to Urquhart would help to pinpoint his location.

"Urquhart will need to know from which direction the final approach is to be made and how he'll recognize the landing strip."

"Patterson could talk him down," Zellick said thoughtfully.

"He could, but ground-to-air sets in the appropriate megahertz waveband are practically unobtainable on the open market in this country. And anyway," Vaudrey continued, "even if he had managed to lay his hands on one, the pilot would still require some form of lighting to line himself up with the runway. Urquhart won't be the only one looking for those lights."

"But have we got the manpower to do it? That's the jackpot question, Nick."

Vaudrey liked the royal "we"; to his way of thinking, it showed Zellick had identified himself and the CIA with the operation.

"Manpower isn't a problem, Walter." He jerked a thumb over his shoulder to indicate the other Cortina three car-lengths behind them. "And we can pick the sort of place we'll be looking for off the map—an isolated house somewhere in the Thetford area with a suitable landing strip nearby which is obstacle free. At the moment, I figure there are about a dozen potential sites, but we should be able to eliminate a number of these before 2100 hours. Thereafter, we'll have roughly forty minutes to find the exact location."

The calculations were simple enough. Thetford was sixty miles from Southend and the Piper Cherokee had a cruising speed of 140. The plane would therefore arrive in the area twenty-five minutes after takeoff, but the final telephone call was a quarter of an hour before the estimated time of departure. There was also a chance that the pilot might be able to steal a few extra minutes, though Vaudrey wasn't banking on it.

"Naturally I'm not relying entirely on dead reckoning. Urquhart will have company—three men from our field support unit."

"Armed?"

"They'll have more than a couple of truncheons between them," Vaudrey said.

The field support unit was composed of ex-servicemen, most of whom had been senior NCOs. The team he'd handpicked consisted of two former SAS men and a royal marine commando who'd served with the Special Boat Section.

"Can you keep the law out of it?" Zellick asked.

"They've got more leads than they can handle. That's the beauty of good public relations, Walter."

"And that good-looking assistant of yours, Caroline Brooke? She's not making any waves, is she, Nick?"

"No. Why should she?"

"I don't know. I just got the impression she wasn't a hundred percent enthusiastic when I met her on Sunday."

"You're imagining it," Vaudrey told him.

"Yeah? Well, you know her better than I do, Nick."

Vaudrey was beginning to wonder if he did. From a very early stage, Caroline had shown something less than a wholehearted commitment to the project. There was the fuss she'd made about the address book and her increasingly voluble opposition to anything that smacked of a cover-up. However, until a few hours ago, he'd believed that whatever her misgivings, she would remain loyal. Now he wasn't quite so sure. Shortly after lunch, Caroline had rung him up at the office and had sounded very skeptical when he'd assured her the phone tap had indeed been authorized by the Home Secretary. He suspected she had allowed herself to become emotionally involved with Coghill, to the point where his interests were now her interests. If this were so, then despite what he'd said to Zellick, it might be extremely difficult to keep the police out of it. In the circumstances, he decided it would be prudent to head off a potentially dangerous situation by releasing all the information he had on Patterson. There was, however, a proviso; he would only do that when he was quite sure it would be too late for Scotland Yard to act on it.

"I think we're in for a storm, Nick."

Vaudrey reared back, felt his stomach lurch. It wasn't until he glanced out of the window and saw the lowering sky that he realized Zellick had been referring to the weather.

There were times when it seemed there was nothing Anthea Deane wouldn't do for him. She had bathed his feet, lanced the blisters and dressed the festering sore on his cheek. She had prepared his meals, breakfast, lunch and dinner, and had produced a cup of coffee whenever he wanted. She had even shown him how to disconnect the burglar alarm on the display cabinet after he'd been through her husband's desk and found four live rounds. They were resting in the Luger now, three in the magazine, one in the breech, 1942 issue 9mm, their brass cases turning green with age. She hadn't raised too many objections either when he'd cut eighteen inches off the shotgun with a hacksaw.

But there had been other times when he'd suspected her passive attitude was a sham. There had been two occasions when he was sure she had tried to put one over on him; once, earlier, when she'd phoned the girl who cleaned house for her, and again, much later in the day, when one of her friends had rung to say how much she had enjoyed the dinner party. Anthea had been subtle about it, spinning the conversation out and making some very odd remarks along the way, but luckily for him, neither party had been smart enough to realize that something was wrong. Afterward, he'd frightened the wits out of her, but she was far too resilient and tough underneath for his liking and had soon bounced back again. Looking at her now across the kitchen table, Patterson decided it was time he reminded her again just who was calling the tune.

"Your husband ever kill anybody?" he asked abruptly.

The question took her by surprise and it was some moments before she answered him. "I suppose he must have," she said slowly. "Rupert was posted to Egypt in 1938, two years after he was commissioned from Sandhurst at the age of nineteen. He was with the 7th Armored Division from El Alamein to the Baltic."

That made him at least sixty-seven and much older than he looked. Recalling the signed photograph in the study, Patterson also figured he must have had a very good war to make brigadier by the time he was thirty.

"Yeah?" he grunted. "Doing what?"

"He spent part of the time on the staff, but mostly he was with his regiment, the 3rd Hussars."

"A cavalryman?"

"Yes."

"You've got to be a dogfoot infantryman to know what war is really all about," Patterson said dreamily. "I mean, you take those four VC that the 16th AVRN took prisoner at Hoc Tran in the Mekong Delta. Three men and a young woman; they came out of the jungle an hour or so before first light and walked straight into the village we'd occupied during the night. It was questionable which bunch of gooks were the more surprised, the AVRN or the VC. Anyway, our gooks were all for deep sixing them, but the U.S. adviser managed to persuade their company commander to send them back to the I-and-R platoon at battalion headquarters for interrogation. See, he figured they just hadn't appeared out of the blue and he could tell they hadn't been on the move all that long. You follow me?"

"I think so."

"Yeah. Well, I was running the intelligence and recon outfit and the battalion commander ordered me to get the location of their base and no holds barred. Furthermore he wanted the information fast, before the VC realized the patrol was missing and cleared out of the area. Trouble was, those VC weren't in a talkative mood, so after a while, we put them into a whirlybird and dropped the first one off at two thousand. We gave the others a few minutes to think about it, then we drew lots to see who would go next. He was only a little guy, ninety pounds and five foot nothing, but he put up one hell of a struggle, bracing his legs and leaning into us as we shoved him toward the door. And hollering? You never heard such a noise when he went out. Still, after that two-act drama, we didn't have any trouble getting the information we wanted. Both remaining gooks, the man and the girl, started chattering like magpies."

Patterson lapsed into silence and waited for the inevitable question. It wasn't long in coming.

"I suppose there's some moral to be drawn from that ghastly story?" Anthea said in a low voice.

"There surely is. From there on, we had this rapport going between us. Matter of fact, those two survivors became the best damned scouts I ever had. And you know why? Because they knew their lives depended on my every whim."

"Like me and Rupert?"

"You're sharp, Anthea, real sharp." Patterson looked up at the clock on the kitchen wall. "Eight thirty-four," he said. "Not much longer now."

"No."

"You want to make me another cup of coffee?"

Anthea got up from the table, walked over to the sink, filled the electric kettle under the tap and plugged it in. When she turned about, the sawed-off shotgun was leveled at her stomach.

"Relax," Patterson told her, smiling. "I'm only practicing."

Coghill walked over to the window and looked out into the gathering dusk. The trio from the field support unit hadn't moved from their previous position and were still lying on the grass within ten feet of the Piper Cherokee. Despite their casual attitude and the occasional ripple of laughter, he knew they were guarding the plane and was equally certain they'd been ordered to make sure he wasn't aboard when Urquhart took off.

They'd arrived on the dot of 2000 hours, barely ten minutes after the duty officer at Leconfield House had rung Caroline Brooke to inform her they were on the way. That had been surprise number one; surprise number two had occurred when Caroline had decided to phone the DI5 contact at Scotland Yard and give him all the information she had on Patterson, only to discover that Vaudrey had beaten her to the punch. Exactly what Vaudrey had in mind was far from clear to Coghill, but the timing of his move suggested that, despite appearances to the contrary, he was still pursuing his original goal.

"I know what you're thinking, old sport," Urquhart said. "And believe me, you've got problems."

"Have I?" Coghill turned about to face him.

"Ah, come on, don't try to bullshit me. The Cherokee's a four-seater and there are seven of us."

"Six," Jalud said tersely. "I'm going home the moment you've heard from Patterson."

"Okay, six then." Urquhart shrugged. "What's the difference? We're still over the top."

Coghill wondered how the trio from the field support unit would react when it came to the crunch. Vaudrey must have foreseen the situation and might have intimated that if necessary, one of them should stand down to make room for him. No doubt Vaudrey was confident the other two would be able to deal with him if he stepped out of line, and of course he was plumb right. Nobody ever got the better of two powerful adversaries, except in the movies.

"What are they doing now, Tom?" Caroline asked him, as though he'd spoken his thoughts aloud.

Coghill turned and looked out of the open window again. The light had deteriorated in the last few minutes and he could barely see them. A cigarette end curled through the dusk like a firefly and he caught the low murmur of their voices in the still, oppressive air. Then somebody grunted and he heard them get up and move toward the control tower.

"They're coming this way," he said in a flat voice.

"Well they would, wouldn't they? They know Patterson will phone us at any moment."

He watched them draw nearer, three look-alikes, same height and build, same hard faces, as though they'd been cast in a mold. And they were armed; their leader, Stanton, had made no attempt to conceal the fact that he was carrying a Browning 9mm automatic in a shoulder holster.

They were still some distance from the control tower when the phone rang in the outer office, but they heard it and froze instinctively. Turning his back on them, Coghill walked over to the table and picked up the eavesdropper a split second before Urquhart answered the incoming call on the extension.

Patterson said, "Take this down. You fly a dogleg to Newmarket, then change course to zero three nine degrees and descend to four hundred feet. Eleven minutes later, you'll see two orange-colored winking lights spaced a hundred yards apart. Immediately beyond them, the runway will be marked with white tracing tape. If you haven't touched down by the time you see a couple of hazard warning signs, you'll know you're in danger of overshooting the landing strip."

"Thanks for the tip," Urquhart said drily.

"You're allowed one pass, that's all. You go round and round like a spinning top and the deal's off; Qadhafi gets the porno movie and Jalud will put his frighteners on you if it's the last thing he does."

"I'm not looking for trouble," Urquhart told him. "I'll go around once and then come straight in."

"You'd better," Patterson said. "Now put Raschid on the line."

"What about our final destination?"

"That comes later. Right now, I want to talk to Raschid."

Urquhart said, "Well, okay," and passed the phone to Jalud. For a moment it looked as though the Libyan would refuse to speak to Patterson, but finally he capitulated and grunted a terse hello into the mouthpiece.

"It's good to hear you again," Patterson said.

"Is it?"

"I'll be even more happy to see your face."

"What?"

"You're coming part of the way," Patterson said coldly. "When the plane stops, you get out and walk forward until you meet up with me. I'll give you my rucksack containing the down payment and then we'll split. Of course, if you don't trust Urquhart to deliver the rest of the material, you'll have to get right back in again."

"You're mad."

"No, just cautious," Patterson said, and hung up.

Coghill placed the eavesdropper on the table. They had reached the crunch point and he still wasn't sure how to play it. As though to pressure him, Stanton leaned through the window to ask if there had been a last-minute change of plan.

"Not really," Coghill said. "But we do have a problem."

"Oh yes?" Stanton eyed him thoughtfully. "Like what?"

"Like who's going to stay behind."

"I don't see any problem there. Patterson's dangerous; we're armed, you aren't."

"It's not that simple," Caroline said firmly. "In the first place, one of you will have to make room for me, because I'm the case officer."

"Don't tell me you're pulling rank," Stanton said, mocking her.

"If I have to." She paused, then said, "I'm quite sure the director general will back me up."

Stanton gave it a lot of thought, rubbing his jaw continually. Finally, he shrugged his shoulders and said he'd take her word for it.

"Good. Now, in the second place, this is a joint operation with the police."

"Nobody's told me," Stanton said, interrupting her. "And I'm not about to believe it on your say-so."

"You don't have to. Any moment now, this phone will ring and you'll have all the proof you need."

"You're having me on." Stanton rubbed his jaw again. "Aren't you?"

"Why don't you wait and see?" Caroline invited him sweetly.

The phone rang at eight minutes past nine. Answering it, she listened intently, then requested the caller to repeat everything he'd just said and walked the phone over to Stanton. By the time he'd finished talking to the DI5 contact at Scotland Yard, Coghill knew he was home and dry.

"Newmarket, then zero three nine degrees; eleven minutes later you'll see two orange-colored winking lights." Vaudrey repeated the essential instructions Urquhart had received, slammed the phone down and backed out of the booth in the lobby of The Bell Hotel. He had picked a dozen potential sites off the map and had dispatched the backup team to check out the seven located south and west of Thetford while he and Zellick tackled the remainder. At 2015, both parties had rendezvoused at The Bell to compare notes and, as a result, had discovered that every damned one could be used as a landing strip in an emergency. He just hoped this latest information would give him a better steer.

Vaudrey crossed the lobby in a few strides and entered the residents' lounge where Zellick was occupying the only writing desk in the room, a pile of neatly folded one-inch-to-one-mile ordance survey maps in front of him. Leaning across him, Vaudrey found the one he wanted, located Newmarket, and converting the bearing from magnetic to grid, plotted it on the map. Eleven minutes' flying time was roughly the equivalent of twenty-six miles on the ground and, subtending the angle, he drew a line which stretched most of the way to the top right-hand corner.

"What does that leave us with?" Zellick asked.

"Moorfields Farm, Deane Cottage and Linton House."

"They're all in the group we looked at."

Vaudrey nodded. "From a distance and without any precise information to go on." He paused to draw two large lozenges on the map, one embracing Moorfields Farm and Deane Cottage, the other, Linton House. "This time around we'll be looking for a couple of flashing beacons."

"So which is our lozenge, Nick?"

"The nearest one, starting with Moorfields Farm."

Vaudrey glanced at his wristwatch, realized that, on his instructions, the duty officer would have already passed the details of the flight plan on to Scotland Yard, and hurriedly stuffed the maps into his briefcase. Then he left the lounge to brief the backup team who were waiting for him in the parking lot behind the hotel.

Patterson measured the bearing with his protractor, converted it from grid to magnetic and compared the answer with the figure he'd previously written on a scrap of paper. It was a pointless exercise, considering the Piper Cherokee had been airborne for the past fifteen minutes, but it was indicative of the tension he was under that he felt compelled to check his calculations for the umpteenth time.

"How much longer do I have to stay like this?"

Patterson looked up and swiveled around to face Anthea Deane. She was sitting cross-legged on the floor of the study, ankles tucked under her rump, hands clasped together on top of her head. The uncomfortable position had a twofold purpose; it was psychologically intimidating and it was impossible for her to make the slightest movement without him noticing it. As a result, he'd been able to plot a course for the Piper Cherokee and brief Urquhart without having to keep an eye on her all the time.

"What's the problem?" he asked.

"I'm getting a cramp in my legs."

"You'd better get up then."

"Thank God," she murmured.

"You can thank him after I've gone," Patterson told her. "Right now, it's a little premature."

He reached for the Luger automatic lying on the desk and tucked the barrel into the waistband of his slacks, the butt facing to the right. Then he picked up the sawed-off shotgun and motioned Anthea to move ahead of him.

"Why the hurry all of a sudden?" she demanded.

"We've got to set things up," he said vaguely.

The plane was still a good ten minutes' flying time from Newmarket, but the thought of sitting around the house doing nothing was slowly driving him nuts. The shotgun pressed into her neck, he steered Anthea down the hall into the kitchen and told her to pick up and carry the rucksack. Then he led her through the back garden into the field beyond to mark the axis of the landing strip with two orange-colored winking lights. Away to the northeast in the direction of Norwich, a flash of sheet lightning lit the dark sky; a few moments later there was a rumble of thunder, a sign that the storm which had been threatening since midafternoon was about to break.

* * *

Vaudrey pressed the transmit button on his Pye radio and blew into the mike in a vain attempt to coax it into life. In his haste to get out of the car, he'd dropped the set on the road and now the damned thing had gone all temperamental on him and refused to work. Unable to communicate with anybody, he was in something of a cleft stick. Before proceeding to Deane Cottage, he'd called the backup team at Linton House to inform them there were no signs of unusual activity in the area of Moorfields Farm. If they also drew a blank at their location, they were required to rendezvous with him; their continued absence therefore suggested they'd found something. Should he double back to Linton House or stay where he was? The question was straightforward enough, but for the life of him, Vaudrey couldn't decide which was the right answer.

"Why don't we move through the wood and take a look at Deane Cottage?" Zellick said in a low voice. "We're not achieving anything standing around here."

Vaudrey thought it over, then said, "We'll give them another five minutes."

"Well, okay, it's your show, Nick."

"There's no need to remind me."

Vaudrey moved away and cocked his head on one side, hoping to catch the sound of an approaching vehicle above the continuous rumble of thunder. Finding he couldn't, he started walking toward the bend in the road a hundred yards away. Within a few paces, the twin beams of an oncoming car briefly illuminated the hedgerow ahead, then a Ford Cortina swept around the curve and drew up alongside him.

Responding to a series of frantic hand signals, the driver waited until the rest of the backup team had alighted before he drove forward onto the grass verge and switched off the ignition. By the time he'd gotten out and closed the door quietly behind him, Vaudrey and the others were already deep in the wood and running hard. The steady note of an airplane engine prompted him to follow their example.

* * *

Patterson smiled. No doubt about it, that was a plane he could hear above the thunder and it was low and coming their way. Three, maybe four minutes from now and he would be airborne on the way to France. So okay, he was flat broke and didn't have a cent to his name, but what did that matter? There was a man he knew in Alençon who would grubstake him, an old acquaintance from Saigon days when they'd cornered the market in narcotics.

"You hear it?" he asked Anthea.

"Yes." Her voice was low, but there was no mistaking the note of relief.

"Good." Patterson grabbed hold of her elbow with his left hand. "Soon after the Cherokee rolls to a stop, a friend of mine will get out and come toward us. When he does, you and I will go forward to meet him."

"Why do you need me?" she asked.

"As a shield," he told her. "I don't take chances."

"There they are," Urquhart shouted above the roar of the aero engine. "Two orange-colored winking lights."

Coghill leaned forward, saw the flashing beacons and beyond them, the white tracing tape that arrowed the runway. As the Cherokee dropped lower and skimmed the treetops, he instinctively reached into his pocket for the 9mm Browning automatic Stanton had given him. Then, just as he thought they were going straight in, Urquhart opened the throttle and hauled back on the stick. Banking hard to port, he made a tight 180-degree turn that left Coghill's stomach somewhere on the floor and came in on the second approach, throttling back as he did so.

The ground rose swiftly to meet them, the Cherokee touched down, lifted off again, then came down to earth with a solid bump. Engine blipping, they taxied past the hazard warning signs and gradually rolled to a halt.

"I guess we've arrived, old sport," Urquhart said unnecessarily.

Coghill eased the safety catch forward on the automatic, reached for the door and in that same instant, felt a restraining hand on his shoulder.

"For God's sake, be careful, Tom," Caroline said in an anxious voice. "Don't take any risks."

"You can say that again," Stanton growled. "The last thing we need is a dead copper."

"That's what I like about you," Coghill told him drily. "You're a real little ray of sunshine."

Coghill pushed the door open, stepped down and, skirting the wingtip, slowly began to move forward, his right arm close to his side, the wrist crooked behind him to conceal the Browning. Six, seven, eight, nine, ten; he counted the paces silently, eyes probing the darkness. Thirteen, fourteen, fifteen; another clap of thunder and the first raindrops. Seventeen, eighteen, nineteen . . .

"Over here, Raschid."

Although the Cherokee was still ticking over, its engine beat was low enough for Coghill to hear the voice and veer toward it. A few yards farther on, he spotted two blurred figures, one a good head taller than the other. Drawing nearer, he saw that the smaller figure was a woman and realized that Patterson was using her as a shield. They were just twenty feet apart when another and much louder voice with a nasal accent called out to Patterson and said, "This is the police, Orville. Stay right where you are."

Both Coghill and Patterson stopped dead, but the woman had the presence of mind to hurl herself forward. As she hugged the ground, Coghill saw a stab of flame a split second before he heard the boom of a shotgun; then something very solid thumped into his chest. Legs buckling under him, he sank down onto his knees and toppled over on his left side, the blood rapidly spreading across his shirt front. Somehow he managed to hold on to the Browning and when the shotgun boomed again, he raised the automatic, aimed it at Patterson and squeezed the trigger. He went on squeezing it until the darkness closed in on him and he was no longer conscious of anything.

The darkness had closed in on Patterson too, except that in his case it happened to be permanent. Caught in the crossfire from the backup team, he lay face down in the grass, four bullet wounds in his stomach, the back of his skull blown away.

* * *

The thunder was still around, a low continuous drumbeat, which Coghill thought was very odd, because he was almost sure he could see the round yellow orb of the moon through a break in the clouds above his head. It also felt as if he were floating up to meet it, his body weightless in space, his mind befuddled from lack of oxygen. Then a stab of pain lanced his chest and brought him back to reality.

"Where the hell am I?" The words came out in a harsh whisper and in a voice he hardly recognized.

"It's all right, Tom, we're nearly there."

A soft hand squeezed his and presently the mist cleared long enough for him to see a face smiling down at him.

"Caroline?"

"Yes, it's me." She squeezed his hand again as if to give him the strength to hang on.

"Don't leave me," he croaked.

"I won't," she promised.

He'd wanted to know where they were taking him in the ambulance, but that no longer seemed important. She was there; that was all that mattered to him.

Four-thirty. Vaudrey stretched his arms above his head and yawned. Outside, the first gray light of dawn would be creeping over the rooftops of London, the air fresh from the overnight rain, unlike the cigar-laden atmosphere in the basement of Leconfield House. The acrid smoke made his eyes smart and his head was throbbing, but there were still another four video cassettes awaiting his attention and he was determined to go on to the bitter end.

Vaudrey supposed he ought to congratulate himself on having had the foresight to pass the results of the phone tap to the DI5 contact at Scotland Yard. That, plus a full and not entirely accurate account of Jalud's involvement, had preempted any possibility of an official Home Office inquiry regarding his role in the whole affair. But it wasn't enough; somehow he had to find a means of restoring his tarnished reputation before word of the fiasco at Deane Cottage reached the ears of the director general.

If ever it did, he would have Zellick to thank for that. He couldn't prove anything, of course, but he was damned sure Walter had known exactly what he was doing when he'd called out to Patterson, and was banking on his intervention to precipitate a fire fight.

Vaudrey left his chair, walked over to the video, inserted a fresh cassette and depressed the play button. By the time he returned to his chair, Karen Whitfield was back on the screen in a pair of ultrahigh-heeled shoes, black nylon stockings and a red lace garter belt. She was also wearing a mortarboard and gown and looked suitably stern as she flexed a cane in both hands.

Thirteen tapes, thirteen names; surely he could put them to use? "Where there's a will, there's a way"—that had been his wife's advice whenever the going was rough, even during her last illness. Those men in the porno films were important figures, vulnerable to pressure from a hostile intelligence service. So what if he insured that the cassettes ended up in the hands of the KGB? It wouldn't be easy and the dividends would be small, but if he played it right and bided his time, there was a good chance DI5 would pull in a few sleepers. And when all was said and done, that was a whole lot better than nothing.

He looked up at the screen again and saw that Karen Whitfield had laid the cane aside and was about to remove the pillowcase from the head of the naked man who knelt in front of her, his wrists handcuffed behind his back, his ankles chained together.

"Where there's a will, there's a way." Vaudrey smiled to himself, knowing that his wife had always been right.

CLIVE EGLETON *was a colonel in the British army until five years ago, when he retired to write full time. He is the author of ten novels besides* A CONFLICT OF INTERESTS, *including* THE RUSSIAN ENIGMA, THE EISENHOWER DECEPTION, BACKFIRE, THE MILLS BOMB, SKIRMISH, THE BORMANN BRIEF, SEVEN DAYS TO A KILLING *(made into the movie* THE BLACK WINDMILL, *with Michael Caine)*, THE JUDAS MANDATE, LAST POST FOR A PARTISAN, *and* A PIECE OF RESISTANCE. *He lives with his family in England.*